The Viking Stone

Nick Hawkes

16pt

Read How You Want

LARGE PRINT BOOKS, BRAILLE & DAISY

Copyright Page from the Original Book

The Viking Stone

Published by Rhiza Press
www.rhizapress.com.au
PO Box 1519, Capalaba Qld 4157

© Nick Hawkes, 2015

Cover Design by Production Works
Photos used by Permission.
      Viking helmet photo: Mararie
      Moody sea at night: Michael Micheletti
      Sailing boat: Den Phillips, Maldon UK
Layout by Rhiza Press

National Library of Australia Cataloguing-in-Publication entry
Creator: Hawkes, Nicholas, 1953- author
Title: The Viking Stone / Nick Hawkes.

Dewey Number: A823.4

TABLE OF CONTENTS

Prologue

Halfdan watched the flames throw dancing light across the Arab's face. The light made him look demonic.

Leif the Navigator writhed beneath him, twisting his head sideways in agony as the Arab's fingers probed the open wound in his chest.

Halfdan was no stranger to ugly wounds. He had sustained several himself. But to see one so savage in the chest of his friend and mentor—the one who the whole crew had come to rely on, brought him deep sorrow. He watched grimly as the Arab eased a bodkin arrowhead from the bloody wound. Leif was now unconscious. The Arab pressed down to staunch the flow of blood and pointed to the fire burning on the cooking slab in the centre of the longboat. The blade of a dagger rested on the hot coals.

Halfdan handed the dagger to the Arab. A moment later, he heard Leif 's flesh hiss as the hot metal was pressed against the wound to cauterise it.

He was a strange man, the Arab: strange in dress, strange in tongue and stranger still in his unorthodox medical ways. Halfdan remembered his arrival at the end of the previous summer. He'd joined the crew of a longboat trading at the edge of the Vikings' southern maritime reach. No one knew why he'd chosen to leave the magnificent cities of the Moslems for the land of the Northmen. It was a secret he kept to himself. All Halfdan knew was that he'd proved his medical skills time and time again.

The hawk-like beak of the Arab's nose accentuated his severity as he spoke. 'He is dying.'

The verdict flickered with the light along the wooden gunwales of the boat towards the soaring stem of the bow. The dragon head at its crown stared into the darkness—into the unknown.

Halfdan squatted down and reached for his friend's hand. He recognised the waxy pallor on Leif 's face as the harbinger of death. *The Valkyries had ridden tonight and chosen who would die.* He was careful to show no emotion as he watched that mysterious thing called 'life' trickle away.

A moment later, there was no pulse.

Halfdan let go of Leif 's hand and stood up.

Baldr, his second-in-command, stepped away from the knot of men gathered at the curving stern post. He walked over to the body of the navigator and raised an inquiring eyebrow.

'He is dead,' Halfdan said.

Baldr nodded.

Halfdan stared past the curving sternpost towards the shore at the glimmering lights of the Angles. They were growing in number as they massed on the high ground above the marshes. He could feel the longboat, nestled in the mud channel, pull at her mooring lines, as if it was nervous of the night.

'Sew him up in his cloak and bury him over the side. Use a ballast stone to weigh him down. We'll feast in his memory when we return—but now we must ready to sail.' As Baldr turned away, Halfdan added, 'And bury him with his sunstone. Let it stay with him.'

Baldr immediately voiced his concern. 'Halfdan, we have lost our navigator. Now you tell us to lose his sunstone as well?'

Halfdan lifted his gaze to the night sky and wondered which star was now that of his old mentor,. 'The sunstone will not be lost. It will sail another sea.' He put a hand on Baldr's shoulder. 'Don't worry, Leif has given me my own sunstone and schooled me in its use. I will get you home.'

Chapter 1

Adam waited with resignation for what would come.

'Death Row Pinnacle! You free-soloed Death Row Pinnacle at Mt Arapiles? Are you mad?'

His mother, who had hitherto exhibited her usual Sydney North Shore poise, quivered with emotion. 'Isn't that a, a, a ... what? A grade 16 climb, or something horrendous?' She glared at him across the table.

'Grade 22.'

'You climbed a grade 22 without ropes—where one slip would be fatal?'

Adam toyed with the salt cellar, rocking it round and round on its base. 'Um ... it wasn't that hard.'

'It is the action of someone who feels they have little to live for.'

An uncomfortable silence followed.

Adam risked meeting his mother's eye—then wished he hadn't. Tears streaked her cheeks. It shocked him. In all the years he had lived with his widowed mother as her only child, he'd never seen her cry. She'd always been indomitable, poised and dignified.

'I didn't believe any of the reports about you climbing dangerously until tonight.' She let the comment hang in the air where it prickled accusingly. 'Both of us, I think, appreciate that the reason for this is bound up in your grief at losing Amanda.'

Losing Amanda. Is that what it's called? Losing Amanda ... like you'd lose your car keys or TV remote. No. He didn't lose Amanda. She'd been ripped from him, along with his heart, in the cruellest way imaginable.

His mind went back two years when he'd been studying biology and education at The University of Sydney. He was at an end-of-year party, feeling he didn't quite belong, when he'd stepped forward to protect the back of a woman from the flailing arms of a fellow student. The man owning the arms had just done something rather odd with his nipple and some lemon juice.

The woman had turned in surprise and nodded her thanks. Adam had the momentary impression of deep brown eyes and full rich lips. Dark hair tumbled about her shoulders. Apologising for startling her, he'd offered to buy her a drink.

She'd stiffened slightly. 'There's no need.'

'I'd like to,' he'd stammered.

'Oh.' Her tone was guarded. 'Why?'

'It was a tip I got from an autumn spider. He offers a gift to a lady in the hope of getting to know her.'

'Doesn't she eat him?'

'Sometimes. Great care needs to be taken with the manner and timing of his approach.'

'I'm not sure I'm flattered by that. Why pick an autumn spider?

'Well, some male spiders stroke the female's web until it hums. Others wave their pedipalps in the air. The *Tibellus* species engage in ritualistic bondage. I didn't think those approaches were as appropriate.'

A twinkle of amusement had played across her face. 'But what if she isn't impressed?'

'Then he lets her eat him.'

She'd laughed.

A year later they were engaged and had tumbled out of university into Adam's four-wheel drive, full of wedding plans and hope. They'd threaded their way across the Great Dividing Range and driven due west across the vast open spaces of inland Australia to Adelaide where Amanda's parents lived. There, he'd undergone polite inspection by likeable people who seemed pleased with what they saw.

Adelaide, in late November, had charmed him with its pavement cafés, dignified stone buildings and the purple extravagance of its jacaranda trees. They'd walked arm-in-arm over the university footbridge and strolled through the city parks along the River Torrens.

Two weeks later, they'd left to drive the fourteen hours back to Sydney.

Then it had ended.

The driver of a truck carting sixteen tonnes of gravel to Murray Bridge had fallen asleep at the wheel. The massive bull-bar of his truck smashed into Adam's car at one hundred kilometres an hour on an unremarkable corner of the narrow highway winding its way through the dry mallee scrub. The last thing Adam heard before Amanda died was her scream.

It had taken a week for his body to decide whether to live or die.

Swayed by his peak physical condition, Adam had lived ... but he could never erase the memory of Amanda's last scream.

It was one month before he was able to go in a wheelchair to her grave, a sterile concrete pad with a brass plaque, surrounded by scores of other concrete pads and brass plaques. He'd been three weeks late for her funeral. *I couldn't even say goodbye.*

In hospital, plastic tubes eventually gave way to teaspoons, wheelchairs to crutches and immobility to physiotherapy. In his heart, denial gave way to reality, confusion to anger, rage to apathy and fatigue to reckless energy.

He'd driven himself through convalescence and occupational therapy with a fanaticism designed to divert attention from a grief and guilt he didn't understand. After wearing out a pair of running shoes and alarming the instructors of a local gymnasium, he had returned to the mountains. Chased by the demons of grief, he'd started to climb again.

Although some of his old friends had volunteered their company, Adam never sought it. One by one, his friends dropped away, frightened at the ferocity with which he approached every climb. With a pang of guilt, he remembered the risks he'd taken, and acknowledged it wasn't surprising reports of his climbing escapades had eventually reached his mother.

She had summoned him to meet with her at a restaurant overlooking a Sydney beach.

He faced her now across the table. Resentment rose up within him. It was his life, his hurt. How could she understand when he, himself, didn't understand? He closed his eyes and rubbed his forehead.

His mother placed her hand over his arm.

He pulled away, irritated.

His action was enough to break her normally impeccable reserve. Careless of North Shore dignity and propriety, she burst into tears. With one hand over her face and the other clutching her stomach, she bent over racked by deep, shuddering sobs.

Adam was appalled. She'd never done anything like this before, far less in public.

A waiter had hurried across to inquire if all was well. Adam waved him away but was at a loss what to do. Feeling guilty, he got up from his seat, squatted down beside his mother and laid what he hoped was a reassuring hand on her shoulder. She twisted away from him.

For some moments, he was forced to observe the rawness of pain that screamed as loud as his own. The awful difference was, he realised, her pain had been caused by his actions.

He wrapped his arms around her shoulders and pressed his face into the side of her hair. 'Mum, I'm so sorry.'

For several minutes she remained inconsolable. Desperate to make amends, he fought to find the words he knew he needed to say. 'Mum, I promise I'll be careful. Really, I will. Please don't worry.'

He only knew the sincerity of his assurances had registered when she reached up to crush him fiercely to herself. Between breaths, she sobbed, 'I, I ... I thought, by coming here, I ... I wouldn't cry.'

Eventually, she managed to bring her emotions under control. She let go of him and went off to the rest room to repair her face and her dignity.

Adam sat alone, bewildered and chastened.

When she returned, he didn't trust himself to speak and simply reached out and took her hand. Unsure of the new place he'd come to, he gazed out the window and listened to the curling surf pound the beach in the twilight ... *sh sh sh sh sh sh, WHUMP hsssssssssss ... sh sh sh sh sh sh, WHUMP hsssssssssss.*

His mother interrupted his reverie. 'Adam...' Her voice was hesitant and he waited for her to continue. '...you may remember me speaking of my friendship with James Fairclough. I've known him since my schooldays, ever since he came out from England with his parents as a child. His father was a director of some sort of engineering company.'

Adam nodded.

With growing confidence, she continued, 'James was a brilliant student who won all sorts of scholarships. What you may not know is that he has been back in England for the last eleven years and is now the Principal of a boys' boarding school somewhere in Essex, not far from London.'

She lowered her eyes. 'As your teaching plans were thrown into ruins this year, I took the liberty of writing to him to make general enquiries about whether there were any short-term teaching posts available, which might help you to get started on your teaching.' Her voice took on a hint of defiance. 'I took the liberty of including a copy of your *curriculum vitae.*'

Adam opened his mouth to protest but she rushed on, 'Only so he could better understand what might be suitable for you.' She looked up at him. 'I wouldn't have told you anything about this, except for the fact that he has replied saying that he does have a position available for one year. One of his teachers has taken a year off to complete a thesis.' She shrugged. 'Anyway, he's looked at your profile, likes it and is prepared to offer you the position if you can meet his deadline.' She removed her hand from his. 'You would need to start at the school in September, ready to teach in the Michaelmas term. The English still use some delightfully quaint names...'

Adam was stunned. He didn't know what to think. His accident had obliged him to notify the State Education Department that his convalescence would make him unavailable for fulltime work. They'd been sympathetic and had invited him to apply again when he felt able. However, they'd warned him that few full-time positions would be available until next year. As he couldn't conceive of the possibility of teaching in his current state, this had suited him well. He hadn't managed to bring himself to think about what he might do for the rest of the year.

He was amazed at the audacity of his mother. She had never meddled in his adult life. Her actions now forced him to wrestle with the possibility of a future he didn't feel ready to embrace.

He brooded in silence.

...sh sh sh sh sh sh, WHUMP hsssssssssss ... sh sh sh sh sh sh, WHUMP hssssssssssss.

Adam looked up and saw the anguish in his mother's eyes. He reached out and took her hand, as much to seek her strength as to reassure her. 'Mum, I'm not sure I can. I'm not sure I have it in me to teach anymore. I'm not sure I even want to.' He paused. 'But if I stay in the mountains...' He didn't complete the sentence. He sighed. 'When does Mr Fairclough need an answer?'

'This week.'

That shocked him.

***

Two months later, he arrived at Heathrow Airport.

Chapter 2

A curlew trilled plaintively as it winged its way through the early twilight to the mudflats. The village rooftops, huddled around the church spire, gradually lost their colour and became silhouettes against the dying light of a heavy, western sky. Edward Bryson stood outside in the evening chill, watching the mist steal gently across the saltings, closing the curtains on another autumn day. Night would come early and it would soon be dark. *A smugglers' night.*

He reflected fondly on the stories of this place. Smuggling had been woven into the fabric of this Essex coastland. The land was good and fertile. Patterned fields, edged with hedgerows, sloped gently towards the estuary. But the land was isolated, and rural isolation breeds a certain flexibility regarding laws passed in larger cities.

Adding to this attitude was the independence engendered by the harsh demands of a life eked out from the sea. For decades, local men had taken their gaff-rigged smacks out into the estuaries. There, in freezing fog amidst the shipping, they would net for shrimp and sprats. The skippers would navigate by watching and tasting the water. Sometimes they would heave a bottle-shaped piece of lead overboard on a line so they could navigate by the depth of water. If the concave end of the lead weight was armed with tallow, it would bring up a sample of the sea bottom to further help determine their position. Smack skippers knew the bottom of the estuary as well as the faces of their wives. Their understanding of the subtleties of currents, winds and tides determined the survival of their close-knit coastal communities.

It was a hard and precarious life, so if, occasionally, a fishing barrel smelled of brandy, or booms and spars had hollows where none were needed, no one enquired too diligently. Life was hard enough.

Much had changed. The lore of the sea and the skills that skippers had handed down from one generation to the next had gone. People now boated for pleasure. Their boats didn't need to contain the terrifyingly dangerous coppers of boiling water into which the freshly-caught shrimp were tossed. Nor did many stay out for three days—the length of time shrimp would keep—and a crew could work without sleep before they sailed back to their markets. Fibreglass, polyester and Terylene had brought its own culture.

With typical pragmatism, the estuary community had shrugged and adapted. If they were shocked at the prices city people were prepared to pay for houses in their village, they were at least grateful for the prosperity the newcomers brought.

The saltings, however, remained unchanged. These were large areas of mudflats on which scrubby, salt-tolerant vegetation grew. It was only ever covered by the highest of tides. These mudflats were dissected by a myriad of gullies and creeks, which afforded excellent protection for boats hiding from the excesses of the bitter east wind.

Edward loved this place with its secrets and its stories. Here were the ghosts of Vikings and Danes. Here were the villages Victorian and Edwardian aristocracy had looked to in summer to find men skilled enough to crew their outrageously oversized racing yachts. Here were tears, terror, boats and community.

A gentle, chill wind caused Edward's spare frame to shiver. It reminded him that the Brent geese would soon be flying in from Russia to escape the Siberian winter and nest within the reed beds. He too, he reflected, had discovered a sanctuary in the saltings and found some solace living in this in-between place, where neither sea nor land ever held permanent sway.

He pulled his ancient army trench coat about him, gripped the handles of his rusted wheelbarrow and began trundling it along the top of the sea wall out onto the rickety duckboards that formed the path into the muddy maze of the saltings.

The tide was out and most boats had settled deep into their mud hollows. The tops of their masts were all that could be seen projecting above the mudflats.

The wheelbarrow squeaked and rumbled along the path, past old hulls and old adventures. Edward turned onto a narrow line of wooden planks leading to a rickety pontoon.

Below him, *Sanderling* was waiting. He never tired of seeing his boat from this vantage point. *Sanderling* was a thirty-five foot, gaff-rigged smack, one of the few that had been restored and was still sailing. There was something entrancing about her wide beam and uncompromising strength; something timeless about her straight stem and solid baulks of timber. Yet there was a delicacy about her. Was it her graceful sheer or the elegance of her gull-like counter stern? Whatever it was, the chemistry was there. She was beautiful.

Edward secured the wheelbarrow to a bollard as a precaution against a rising wind, and hefted a heavy coil of rope from it. Easing the rope over his shoulders, he climbed down the ladder at the end of the pontoon and stepped onto his boat.

The deck was clean and uncluttered. Unlike a modern yacht, it had no cockpit, simply a curving bench that crossed the width of the hull. It enabled the helmsman to sit comfortably in command of the long, curving tiller. A deckhouse had been built over what was once the hold.

Sanderling's single mast thrust into the darkening sky. It was well braced with shrouds, tensioned by traditional deadeyes fixed to the iron chainplates.

This was his boat, his world.

Edward eased the coil of rope onto the deck, unlocked the hatch on top of the deckhouse and climbed down into the cabin. With practised ease, he lit a gimballed oil lamp and looked around him. The warm light danced on the varnished roof beams and caused the white painted roof planks to glow like honey. Even though some ingenious cabinetmaking had transformed the hold into a comfortable cabin, nothing could hide its utilitarian origins. The soft light highlighted the massive ribs that seemed to hold him like protective fingers.

The cabin boasted a chart table, wall cupboards and two bench seats that could convert to bunks. A tiny galley area had a single primus stove for cooking and a bucket set into a benchtop for a sink. A net had been strung from the roof, at the side of the hatchway, to hold binoculars and a foghorn—those things a helmsman required to be instantly on-hand.

An open toolbox and several partly-used pots of paint were scattered over the bench seats. The rich aromas of canvas, linseed oil and diesel, mingled with the odours of pitch and oakum, combined to form the distinctive smell of an old wooden boat.

Edward smiled. Sitting on the chart table was half a block of chocolate. His niece had obviously been there sometime during the day. The chocolate lay on top of a piece of paper. He tugged it out and read the scribbled note.

Bloody men!

Finally gave him the boot.

I needed this bolt-hole to hide in and cry. Wanted your wisdom too, but you weren't here. So I ate half the chocolate on my own. Enjoy the rest.

Give me a hug when I see you next and don't ask too many questions.

Claire.

Edward sighed. It wasn't her first note like this.

He broke off a piece of chocolate and ate it as he set about lighting the chip-burning heater against the forward bulkhead.

Once the heat had begun to drive away the chill, he sat down at the chart table. As he did, the gnawing unease and loneliness that had begun to trouble him in recent months began to manifest again. It had begun as a minor pall of depression. At first, he'd managed to mask it by being active. However, it had become increasingly persistent of late.

Was he still grieving leaving his teaching position three years ago? When he had retired, the prospect of spending more than ten weeks a year sailing had filled him with eager anticipation. Was this still the case, or did he miss the challenges of his old profession?

He pondered this for some time. No, he concluded, he had retired at the right time. And he still loved sailing.

Although *Sanderling* made heavy demands on anyone who took her to sea, he was still able to, sometimes even on his own. However, he usually had a team of willing volunteers to help him. His love of sailing remained as real as ever, but was it enough? Why was he feeling unsettled?

His wife had died after only eight years of marriage. For most of those years she had been sick, too sick to bear children. He remembered her with fondness. It had taken a long time for him to work through the black despair of grief and arrive at a point where he could embrace new beginnings. Now, after thirty-five years, he had arrived at a place of grateful memories. Yet something was crying out.

He shook his head in confusion and sought to distract himself with a book. He ran his eyes over the titles in the bookshelf above the chart table. Nestled beside *Reed's Almanac* was a battered book containing an ancient Norse saga. He took it down, flicked through the pages and began to read:

Then Halfdan made enquiries as to who best understood the lore of the sea and the ways of men. The knowing ones in the village pointed him towards the shore where Leif the Navigator was supervising the repair of a longboat.

'You have come home, Halfdan,' said Leif.

'It is so. But the Council has decreed that I must leave until I learn the ways of command and am ready to be king. Until then, I cannot call this place home. Will you take charge of the great oar and travel to the land of the Angles with me that I might learn from you?

'Do you yet have a wife who depends on you?'

'I do not.'

Leif the Navigator smiled. 'Then we must find a sailor, a king, a wife ... and a home.

Home. Edward began to reflect on his home, a home that had seen no children. As he did so, he realised that what he was missing, what he was aching for, was an opportunity to invest his heart—to give himself in some significant way to someone.

What did it mean?

From deep within, he recognised a familiar ache: the calling of his heart to come to a place that was beyond him. He bowed his head, held out his heart so it could be seen, and waited.

Outside, the tide turned and the sea stole its way back up the estuary into the creeks and channels. Eventually, it trickled into the mud berth and eased *Sanderling* afloat. Water eddied around her sternpost, causing the rudder to creak softly as she tugged at her tiller lashings.

Edward lifted his head and knew he'd been heard.

***

The young man knew that a piece of lead would shortly smash into his skull and end his life. He caught a glimpse of the silencer on the end of the snub-nosed pistol. It was being ground into his temple as a hand pushed him face down into the pillow. The strength and savagery of the attack was appalling.

Bewildered and shocked, he tried to remember what had happened. He'd climbed the steps to his dingy one-room apartment and flicked on the light switch, only to find that the light didn't work. He'd been midway through a curse, when he'd been hurled face forward onto his bed.

An electronically-synthesised voice cut into his consciousness. 'You've made a fatal mistake, boy. That mistake was to piss me off.' The hand that had pushed his face into the pillow grabbed his hair and yanked his head up before slamming it back down. 'You've been selling your gear on my patch and that's not good for my bottom-line.' The hand again jerked his head up and pushed it back into the pillow. 'People either work for me, or I get rid of them. You savvy?'

The pillow muffled his terrified whimper. 'Don't hurt me. Don't hurt me. I'll work for you! I'll work for you.'

He felt as if his scalp was being ripped off. After an eternity in which the attacker seemed to consider his offer, the pressure on the back of his head eased. 'Work for me, eh? Well now, that's a whole new scenario.' A pause. 'The thing is, no one works for me unless they are smart. Are you going to be smart enough for me not to have to kill you, boy?'

He screamed into the pillow between sobs. 'Yes, yes.'

There was another pause. The pressure on the back of his head eased a moment before increasing savagely. 'Then you can think of me as your fairy godmother.' A harsh laugh followed. 'I can make your dreams come true. D'ya like your cocaine, boy?'

He was disoriented by the question; its significance took a moment to dawn on him. Instinct warned him his attacker wasn't a man to lie to. 'Yes.' He used it to bring some relief to a life of crushing boredom—that, and pornography. He'd found his father's collection of porn in the cupboard underneath the stairs as a child; the discovery had launched him into the world of sexual fantasy. He had no illusions as to the imperfections of his own body. His peers at school, particularly the girls, had mocked him—*a cross between a stick insect and a gibbon.* However, in his chosen fantasy world, women would do anything for him. No one ever said no.

He was currently working at a local nightclub as a cleaner. He collected and washed the empty glasses. Nothing glamorous. But it was the right environment in which to discover cocaine. He found it cooled his smouldering resentments and gave him a sense of wellbeing, a feeling impossible to find in reality. However, it wasn't easy to get the money to buy it—until he'd learned to sell it himself to known users at the club.

The eerie electronic voice continued. 'How much money do you currently make?'

Handicapped by the pillow, he gave a muffled reply.

'Son, I'm going to let you go, but don't even think of moving. Keep your head in the pillow. If you turn around, I'll kill you.' The pressure on the back of his skull eased. 'Here's the proposition. If you sell my stuff at the club, you can expect to make four times what you're currently pulling in.'

Four times! He was hooked in an instant.

There was only one disturbing note. Any failure to pay, any careless talk, anything that would upset the owner of the electronic voice would not be tolerated. He felt the silencer at the end of the pistol tapped twice between his legs. 'It would be a terrible thing for you to have a point three eight vasectomy.' There was another harsh laugh. 'The first bullet will be uncomfortable. The second one will kill you.'

Chapter 3

The train carried Adam deep into the heart of Essex through a curtain of grey drizzle. Eventually, it slid to a stop with a tired sigh and Adam alighted. He hailed a taxi that dropped him off in front of a handsome Georgian building. Fixed to the wall on one side of the imposing front steps was the school name and crest. Beneath it was the sign, *'Headmaster's Office'*. With a sense of unreality, Adam folded his stockman's coat over his arm, picked up his rucksack and entered the world of an English boarding school.

The Headmaster's personal assistant cast a covert glance at him, before speaking into a telephone. 'Dr Fairclough, Mr Hollingworth has just arrived.'

Doctor Fairclough, not Mr Fairclough—must remember that.

The assistant pasted on a smile and gestured toward an ancient stairwell. As she conducted him upstairs, she managed to convey the impression that she did not consider Adam to be a particularly sophisticated form of life. Adam hadn't shaved for thirty-six hours or changed his crumpled clothes. He reflected ruefully, he was not giving a good first impression.

She knocked on a sturdy oak door. It was opened by a slim-looking man in his fifties, who was greying at the temples. His eyes both flashed a welcome and gave warning of considerable intelligence.

The personal assistant announced in a formal tone, 'Dr Fairclough, Mr Adam Hollingworth.' She paused. 'From Australia,' she added, as if seeking to explain Adam's appearance.

A ghost of a smile played across the headmaster's face. 'Thank you, Janice.' He nodded a dismissal before turning to Adam. 'Delighted to meet you at last, Adam. Please come in.'

The headmaster settled him into a seat, made polite inquiries about his trip, and then asked about his mother with informed questions which indicated genuine interest.

Adam did not fail to notice Dr Fairclough's attire was correct in every detail. He wore a dark suit, white shirt and a tie with stripes of red, blue and yellow sloping upwards like a successful sales graph. A small crest in the centre of the tie conveyed an air of institutional respectability.

It was hard to shake the impression that, notwithstanding the affable welcome, he was being comprehensively appraised.

Adam conjured up a weak smile and gazed around him. The Georgian room with its stately fireplace and high ceiling was designed to impress. Its lofty grandeur, elaborate cornices, leather chairs and lantern windows exuded an air of security. A handsome desk stood in front of a wall of bookcases. The room was rescued from being an anachronism by the presence of a computer workstation parked discreetly in the corner and by two modern oil paintings that adorned the walls. *The ancient and the modern side-by-side.* It gave a clue to the man who had ushered him to a seat.

He felt the headmaster's gaze flit over his appearance. He was dressed in an open shirt, thermal fleece jacket and was wearing hiking boots. He wondered if he should explain that he wasn't a defiant non-conformist, it was just that he had no energy to be anything other than who he was.

Adam made a token gesture of patting down his mop of curling hair and gazed at the two oil paintings on the opposite wall. One had impressionistic outlines of an ancient bell tower; the other looked like the Bridge of Sighs in Venice. He smiled at the picture and said with rather more grimness than he'd intended, 'Where the condemned had their last view of the outside world.'

The headmaster nodded. 'You know your Venetian history. However, this Bridge of Sighs is the bridge to St John's College in Cambridge.' He paused. 'Mind you, there have been a few who have headed from St John's to the exam halls feeling like their condemned Venetian cousins.' The headmaster leaned forward at the desk, flicked on an intercom and asked Janice to bring in some coffee.

Settling back in his chair, he came straight to the point. 'Your academic qualifications are good and I particularly like the work you've done with adventure training. I say this to assure you that you are not here because of any loyalty I feel to your mother. She may have put us in touch but there are no favours owed. I need someone with your skills and energy to fill a temporary post. How much you benefit from this experience will be up to you.'

Adam said nothing.

The headmaster held his gaze and stabbed his forefinger on the arm of his chair. 'In this school, we require more of our masters than academic skill. We take our charter to teach the whole person, not just the mind, very seriously. This is particularly important given that some of our students are boarders. For most weeks of the year, we are their family. You wouldn't be here if I didn't see some evidence of a similar concern for the whole person in your work with children and outdoor adventure camps.'

Adam rubbed a hand over his face. *A lifetime ago.* 'Can you tell me how I address you?'

'Your mother calls me James. You call me "Headmaster" or "sir."'

Adam nodded and suddenly felt very tired. 'To be perfectly fair with you, er, sir, since my accident, I have struggled to find much passion for anything. All I can say is that I will try.'

The Headmaster jabbed his finger down again. 'Find that passion,' he said brutally. 'We touch too many lives to afford any passengers. We need to teach the life skills required by the next generation if we want them to have any chance of rescuing a future for themselves and society.'

Adam recognised the conviction of a true zealot. Here was a man for whom education was not merely a job, it was a mission.

'We look to our teachers to lead by example in language, conduct and dress. Amongst other things, this means we have an exacting dress code. Can you comply with that, Mr Hollingworth?'

Curiously, Adam felt some relief at the pitiless challenge, although he felt no confidence at all that he could fulfil the stated expectations. 'I won't challenge any educational standards you set. If I do fracture any dress code, it will be because of ignorance rather than design. I will, however, be constrained by the fact that my wardrobe is currently limited to one rucksack.'

The headmaster leant back. 'I understand that. We'll try and give you as much help as possible.'

Adam hung his head as he chose his words with care. 'Eight weeks ago, I wasn't even sure I could teach any more and I'm still not sure that I have the emotional strength to teach well yet. All I can say is that I will know if I am not teaching well before anyone else ... and that if I feel this, you will have my resignation the very next day.' He lifted his head and looked at the headmaster. 'Which I ask you to accept without question.'

Dr Fairclough said nothing, but pursed his lips and nodded slowly. He then excused himself, saying he needed to fetch a folder from the room next door.

Whilst he was out, Janice came in with a tray on which there were two dainty cups with matching milk jug and sugar bowl. Adam recognised the pattern on the fine china. His mother had a similar set.

Janice pursed her lips and avoided his eyes. With a sense of there being nothing to lose, he picked up a cup, turned it around in his hands and said casually, 'Royal Doulton, circa 1955.'

Janice glanced at him in surprise.

Adam sniffed the coffee. 'Wonderful! Only drinking it from my old tin mug could make it more perfect.'

'Oh, really.' She blushed and turned to leave. The door closed with a discreet thud.

The headmaster returned with a folder and handed it to him. 'Here are the practical details of what you will be teaching.'

They were going through the file together when there was another knock at the door. Janice came in, clutching, with obvious pain, Adam's tin mug filled with hot coffee. 'Here you are, Mr Hollingworth. I saw this mug strapped to your rucksack and wanted your coffee to be perfect.'

The headmaster raised a quizzical eyebrow.

Adam stood up and took the mug from her. 'Thank you.' He took a small sip, smiled and said, 'It is indeed perfect.'

Janice left.

A truce, of sorts, had been established.

Adam returned his attention to the biology syllabus. It was only one week until his first lesson. He would need to do a lot of work very quickly if he was to be ready for it.

'Your duties will involve teaching biology but you will also have sporting commitments. Rugby Union is the main sport for Michaelmas term. How much experience have you had?'

'I've never played it. I played Aussie Rules Football.'

The headmaster leaned back and looked at him. 'Let me see if I've got it right. You are not sure you can teach, you are not sure you can even dress the part of a teacher, and you've never played the major sport you are here to help teach.' He paused. 'Have I missed anything?'

Adam smiled. 'I will probably commit the occasional faux pas until I learn not to drink coffee from tin mugs in civilised surroundings. However, I can promise you that I will try. If I feel I'm not up to it, you'll have my resignation.'

The headmaster held Adam's gaze for a long time before holding out his hand. 'Mr Hollingworth, welcome to the school.'

***

The turbid estuarine water closed above Edward as he kicked wildly, seeking to find purchase against the steep mudbanks. It was futile. The relentless weight of the tool belt pulled him down. He scrabbled at the sloping mud, knowing as he did that the freshly-dredged channel banks would be almost impossible to climb. Fighting a rising sense of panic, he clawed at the mud. The fingers of his right hand found purchase inside a crevice. He pulled down hard, only to dislodge the object. But it would not shake free. His finger had jammed in it. Thrashing upwards, he tried to shake off the heavy weight. He broke the surface, gasping for air, flailing his hand back. In that horrifying instant, he saw that his finger had stuck through the back of the eye socket of a human skull. It leered at him, nodding grotesquely before it fell free. Edward sank under the water again.

Waves of terror and panic seized him. He clawed at the clay mud-bank with one hand, while trying to unfasten his tool belt with the other. Part of his brain screamed to be heard. *Don't panic! Don't panic! Conserve oxygen. Relax!*

'Aargh!'

The tool belt fell free, but still he did not float. With despair, he remembered his heavy work boots.

His hands again sought for purchase against the underwater mud slope and closed around a protruding stone. He pulled it out and used it like a dagger to stab into the steep sides of mud. It gave him just enough leverage to haul himself to the surface.

Exhausted, and trusting the stone he had stabbed into the sloping mud would hold his weight, he gasped for air.

'Edward! Hang on.'

Salvation.

A boathook banged on top of his shoulder and caught the back of his jacket.

The voice of his rescuer again broke in to his consciousness. 'I ... I think I've got you. Hold still and I'll pull you back to the pontoon.'

He felt himself being towed backwards through the water until he bumped against the tyres lashed on the edge of the pontoon. The top of the pontoon was only a half a metre above the water. It may as well have been a hundred. He had no strength left to heave himself out of the water.

'Grab hold of the tyres. Don't let go. I'll be back.'

Too spent to speak, Edward nonetheless had enough presence of mind to comply. He closed his eyes and waited.

A moment later, he felt a tickle on his forehead. He opened his eyes to see a veil of long blonde hair fall over his face.

Claire.

She was above him, face down on the pontoon, manhandling a line under his arms.

A few minutes later, he felt himself being lifted from the water. The line cut under his arms painfully. It pulled him up and away from the pontoon until he banged against the side of his boat. Claire had rigged the staysail halyard around him and was hauling him up using the anchor winch. *Clever girl. But, aargh; the line hurt.*

Slowly, he was dragged upwards until he toppled over the gunwale and flopped onto the deck.

More blonde hair.

'Edward. Are you okay?' Claire crouched over him and cradled his head.

'I ... I'm fine. Really...' His voice was a croak. 'Thanks to you.' He tried to smile. 'I tripped. Fell overboard like an old fool.'

'I heard you splashing. I was down below, making a pot of tea.'

'Sorry to cause a fuss.'

'Don't you dare do anything like that again, Edward Bryson,' she scolded. 'You're the only man I've got in my life. Certainly the only one of any worth.'

Edward reached up to touch a streak of mud on her cheek. 'You'll find a man worthy of you, Claire. Be patient.'

'What's that you're holding?'

Edward lifted his hand and discovered he was still holding the stone, the stone that had saved him.

Chapter 4

Adam hoisted his rucksack into the headmaster's car. It was only a short distance to his lodgings but Dr Fairclough had insisted on driving him there and introducing him to his hosts. 'They're the Edgecomb family. Salt of the earth. They've a three-year-old daughter with severe scoliosis of the spine. She's had lots of operations but, even so, her torso has to be permanently supported by a metal brace.' He swung the car into a narrow street opposite the abbey where a row of old terraced houses pressed against a stone pavement. 'Number four, Prior's Lane. Here's your new home.'

Adam took a deep breath. *Home?*

Elizabeth Edgecomb opened the door and was introduced by the headmaster. Adam had the brief impression of a comely, brown-haired woman in her early forties. She inspected him briefly, seemed to appreciate his tiredness and took charge. 'Call me Dizzy. Everyone does. Let's get you upstairs so you can unpack and clean up. You're in the attic room. Come down and bang on our door at six and we'll have tea. We'll talk more then.'

The headmaster left, voicing his thanks.

Adam swung his rucksack onto his shoulder and prepared to mount the stairs. As he took the first step, he heard little fists pounding on a side door. A tiny voice demanded to be allowed to see what was going on.

Dizzy opened the door. A small girl peeped out, staring at him in wide-eyed wonder.

'This,' said Dizzy, 'is Philippa Ruth.'

Adam looked at Philippa with shock. A surge of grief welled up within him. She was a beautiful child with her mother's almond eyes and strawberry-blonde curls. That alone would have melted any heart. Her body imprisoned in a brace of fibreglass and metal broke it. Adam wasn't ready for the anguish he felt.

He swallowed. 'He ... hello, Ph ... ilippa,' he stammered. He turned away, heading determinedly for the stairs. However, he was not quick enough to avoid seeing a look of pain in Dizzy's eyes ... or the reassuring hand she laid on her daughter's shoulder.

Once he was in his room, he put his head in his hands. He thought he'd let most of his grief over the sickening obscenities of life work their way through his system. *Wrong!* Eventually, his emotions subsided to a point where he was able to unpack and have a shower.

He came down stairs at six, knocked on the door and allowed himself to be ushered into a world of tasteful chaos: hanging plants, comfortable chairs, piles of fashion magazines, scattered toys ... and Philippa Ruth. Adam offered Philippa a miniature koala toy the airline had given each of its passengers. She took it shyly.

Dizzy smiled.

Philippa looked at Adam with her large eyes—and held out a giant rag doll she'd had tucked under her arm.

'That's Marmalade,' explained Dizzy. 'She was given to Ruth as a therapy doll to cheer her up in hospital.'

Adam wasn't sure what to say. He was rescued by the arrival of Dizzy's husband who brought with him an uncomplicated good nature and a losing fight to stay slim. After introducing himself as Geoffrey, he threw his briefcase into a chair and swooped up both Philippa and Marmalade into his arms.

After a hug, he headed into the kitchen.

Dizzy laughed. 'Geoff is a much better cook than me. I'm off to freshen up.' She called to her husband. 'Pour me a white wine, honey ... and Adam, too.'

By the time it arrived Adam was well on his way to feeling at home within the bosom of the Edgecomb family.

***

Later in the evening, after his final appointment, the headmaster opened Adam's personal file and looked at it again. *Am I prodding a butterfly out of its chrysalis—or am I caging it?*

Or has the butterfly died?

He closed the file and thought for a long time. Eventually, he picked up the phone and rang the boarding house.

'Gareth, Headmaster here. I've a small project for you.'

***

Over their conversation at tea, Adam learned that Dizzy and Geoffrey hadn't expected to have children as they'd married fairly late in life. Philippa had been a bit of a surprise. Somehow, Dizzy had managed to raise Philippa, help her through numerous spinal surgeries and do it all while working part-time as wardrobe mistress of a local theatre. Adam was impressed and somewhat humbled.

Dizzy told Adam that Philippa had been instructed never to go up the second flight of stairs and be a nuisance to Adam.

Adam couldn't think of what to say and simply nodded his thanks.

Philippa remained silent and watched him.

Dizzy continued. 'The only meal you'll eat with us is breakfast. I'm told you'll be eating lunch and tea at the boarding house. Evidently, its dining room is already open for staff, even though the boys won't be back for another two days.'

Later, alone in his room, the familiar black tendrils of loneliness and desolation began to tighten around Adam's heart. He fought against it by making himself read the sixth form biology curriculum. However, the heaviness of jet lag finally began to tell. He stood to get ready for bed. As he did, he heard the indignant blast of a car horn outside. A minute later, there was a ring at the front door and, a short time after that, the sound of footsteps mounting the stairs. There was a sharp rap on his door.

Adam opened it to find a slim man with over-length hair, dressed entirely in black. A red handkerchief protruded from his top jacket pocket.

''Ow do you do?' he said in a lilting Welsh accent. 'I'm Gareth Price, tutor at the boarding house—and, if it doesn't already sound too absurd, I try and teach the blighters their own language, English.'

'Umm, g'day.' Adam shook his hand. 'Adam Hollingworth. Sorry to be a nuisance. I didn't expect anyone to ride shotgun on me.'

'Don't worry, boyo. Headmaster is more concerned that you don't pollute young minds with unfashionable ideas of Australian egalitarianism, so I've got to make you safe.' He rubbed his hands together. 'I propose we repair to *The Pig and Whistle* where I will divulge the dark secrets of the British class system to you over a drop of Green King.' Gareth noticed Adam's unbuttoned shirt. 'You're not off to bed already!' he asked in a shocked voice. 'You'll shatter the Australian image that has taken years of unbridled revelry to establish.'

Adam offered him a weary smile. 'Jet lag. Give me a minute and I'll be with you.'

Gareth bounced down the stairs, saying he'd chat with Geoffrey and Dizzy.

A few minutes later, Adam accompanied Gareth out onto the front steps. In front of them, a car was parked with its front wheels mounted on the footpath and its rear protruding dangerously into the street. Gareth slapped the bonnet. 'Let's leave the beast here and walk! The pub's only round the corner.'

The Pig and Whistle was a Tudor pub that seemed to have deflated with age like a soufflé brought too quickly from the oven. Adam had to duck through its low entrance door before stepping down into the front parlour. The pub had small windows, a low ceiling and oak beams burned dark with history. A fire nestling in the inglenook filled the room with the delicate aroma of wood smoke.

Gareth made his way to the counter where a balding man with a huge moustache was placing beer mugs onto racks. 'Evening, Harold.' He cocked a thumb at Adam. 'This here is Adam from Australia. He'll be teaching at the school and is living with Geoff and Dizzy.'

Harold nodded.

Everyone, it seemed, knew Geoff and Dizzy.

Gareth placed his order. 'Two halves of Abbot, if you please.' He cocked a thumb at Adam. 'This pitiful young man has had to live to the age 'e is now without, to my knowledge, ever drinking a decent British beer.'

Harold grinned and reached for two dimple glass mugs.

Picking up their beer, Gareth led Adam to a table, nodding to a few patrons on the way. He sat down and raised his mug in a silent toast. Adam smiled his thanks and let Gareth's affable nature chase the demons away.

Gareth settled back in his chair and warmed to the subject of Adam's indoctrination. 'The thing to understand is that the school is a giant PR operation. We don't cater for reality. We cater for what fee-paying punters would like reality to be. We therefore live in the fantasy world, fondly hoped for by Generation X who grieve the loss of the stable world they could safely rebel against in their youth—a world they now want for their children.'

Adam mentally changed gear and tried to keep up with Gareth's agile mind. 'You mean a Shangri-La of conservatism holding out against postmodern deconstruction, angst and chaos?'

'Exactly. Which means, Old Bean, that symbol of repressive conformity, the tie ... always sported on duty, and preferably when you're not.'

Adam blinked, but decided to play along. 'We heard in the colonies that you had taken your lead from W.C. Grace and were only using ties to hold your pants up. You're telling me now this isn't so?'

'Worse to come. The default level of dress is tweeds and corduroy. From there, you can go in one of two directions. If you have been at the school for more than ten years and are known to be brilliant, you have earned the right to be slightly eccentric in dress. The English love eccentrics.'

'You? The ninja warrior look?'

'I've earned the right.'

'Ah.'

'Alternatively, you may have aspirations to leadership and greatness. If this is the case, wear a suit. Never a three piece; that would be ostentatious. Never anything other than grey; that would be vulgar. The deeper the grey, the greater the greatness aspired to. Quite simple, really.'

Adam noticed that Gareth's Welsh accent wasn't always in evidence. It seemed to be part of a persona he allowed to come and go. Adam found himself relaxing in the company of the irreverent extrovert. 'Simple! If dressing for work is this complicated, however many rule books do you have on the delicate art of seduction?'

'Ah. We do have a book on it, but it's written in French, so none of us can understand it. That's why we're such lousy lovers.'

Adam laughed.

'One final thing,' continued Gareth. 'Academic "show and tell". It helps prise parental dosh from wallets. Full academic rig, complete with hoods, to be worn at all chapel services and all school assemblies.'

Adam felt alarm. 'Are you serious? I haven't got an academic gown, far less a hood to go with it.'

'Hmm. That does present a small problem. The gown is no problem. There are a couple floating around the boarding house—but the hood ... What are the academic colours for your hood?'

'I haven't a clue. I was in a rehabilitation centre and missed my graduation.'

'You could find out easily enough.'

'I can't believe it's that important.'

'My son...' Gareth's sigh was exaggerated, 'you haven't learned the half of it. When can you find out the colours? We'll get the hood made up.'

'I can tell you the colours,' Adam said with a straight face. 'They're red and white'.

'How come you suddenly know?' Gareth asked suspiciously.

'I don't, but they're the colours of our local footy team, the Sydney Swans. Who'd know any different?'

Gareth put his head in his hands and groaned. He then began to laugh. 'You know ... we've simply got to do this.' He wiped tears of mirth from his face. 'And I know just the person to help us. Your landlady, Dizzy.' Pulling Adam up from the table, he propelled him towards the door.

They found Dizzy curled up with Geoff on the sofa. She was nursing a hot drink. As soon as she heard of Gareth's plan, she convulsed with laughter and dispatched him to fetch his hood from the boarding house to use as a pattern.

'If I begin tomorrow morning,' she said to Adam, 'I can have it ready for the school assembly in a week's time.'

Chapter 5

For the first month, Adam worked hard trying to catch up with his teaching preparations. He worked long hours in the school's new resource centre, searching the web for illustrations and information to augment the set texts. These he laboriously printed onto acetates for the old-fashioned overhead projector that was all the technology available in the biology department.

Gareth continued to provide his insightful and impious wisdom whenever he felt it necessary. Such an occasion occurred on the third day. The boys hadn't responded well to Adam's teaching. They were unmotivated and seemed determined to reduce all things academic into an art form of mediocrity. Their energies seemed exclusively directed at concocting the next distraction. That morning, two boys, Kevin Dixon and Seth Waterman, had set off a clockwork tortoise so that it clattered amongst the boys' feet, much to everyone's delight. Adam had picked it up, unlocked the lid of the reptile display case and placed it alongside an English adder.

No one got it out.

Adam recounted the saga of the tortoise to Gareth.

Gareth nodded, took Adam by the arm and told him to look around and tell him which school buildings were the most modern and best-appointed. Adam picked out the new sports complex, the physics and chemistry block, and the new resource centre. 'That, dear boy, should tell you where this school's priorities are. If the boys hate self-expression and literacy, they turn to science. If they are no good at the exacting demands of physics and chemistry, they elect to do biology. You sir, in your outdated Victorian laboratory, have inherited the desperate and dim, the despair of fee-paying parents.'

Adam knew he was failing the boys. His teaching was thorough but mechanical. He was emotionally distant from them and failed to inspire. While he could hide in the shadow of Gareth's extrovert personality, safe in the knowledge it made no demands on him, he didn't feel ready to allow himself to get close to his students. He didn't want anyone to depend on him—ever.

The only area in which he showed any promise was rugby. In view of Adam's ignorance of the game and Gareth's passion for it, they'd been teamed up together and allocated the school's second fifteen to coach.

Gareth nodded approvingly as he saw Adam for the first time in his sports shorts. 'Well, boyo, you sure look fit enough. Have you studied any physical education?'

Adam nodded. 'A bit.'

'Then you take charge of fitness training and I'll teach skills and tactics.'

The physical nature of the sport forced a level of engagement with the boys that Adam struggled to give in the classroom. He was surprised to discover boys began according him some respect.

After four weeks, Gareth demanded an explanation. 'You can't kick a drop goal to save yourself, but you're ruddy brilliant at a long punt. Your understanding of the game is woeful, but you're pleasingly destructive of any poor blighter unlucky enough to try and get past you with a ball. How does that work out?

'Aussie rules football, mate. Aussie rules football.'

'I haven't a clue what that is, boyo, but you've the makings of a handy fullback.' Gareth patted him on the back. 'In six weeks' time, I want you ready for the annual match when the staff and old boys combine to take on the school's first fifteen.' He trotted off after a group of boys, yelling instructions at them.

***

That evening, Adam found himself sinking again into the cloying darkness of sadness and hopelessness. Determined to shake off the demons of despair—or at least drown their voices with physical pain—he changed into his sports gear and went for a run.

The narrow, crowded streets still felt strange to him as he pounded along the footpaths.

Ninety minutes later, he returned to Priors Lane, sweating and panting. As he stood in front of his lodgings heaving in lungs full of air, he looked up at the row of three-storied terraced houses. He still found it hard to believe he lived in one of them. Dizzy had told him they'd been built for the abbey clerics in the eighteenth century. He turned and looked across the road at the soaring splendour of the abbey, delicate and beautiful, despite its impressive bulk. It seemed to look down on the town's commercial busyness with the benevolence and patience of history.

He walked across the road and through the wrought iron gates that gave access to the abbey gardens. There, he began his stretching exercises, making a token of appeasement to his much-abused muscles.

He enjoyed the peace of the place. Neatly tended grass grew where the cloisters had once stood. These, he'd learned, had burned down five hundred years earlier. Only the remains of three Gothic arches and a section of low wall remained.

Something of the antiquity and mystery of the place prompted him to investigate how the medieval walls had been constructed. He pulled himself on top of the ruined section and began to inspect the craftsmanship of ancient artisans. It was magnificent work. Very few people, he thought, were given the privilege of leaving such a permanent legacy. Certainly, he doubted he ever would.

It was from his somewhat unusual vantage point that he glimpsed something odd. He nearly missed it, but there it was. Just visible above the roof parapet between the southern transept and the abbey nave was the tip of what looked to be a human hand. With mild alarm, he watched it closely, hoping to see movement. There was none. He leaned back, cupped his hands and called out, 'Hey, mate! You, up there. Are you all right?'

There was no response.

Adam wondered what he should do next. Should he yell for help merely to discover the hand belonged to a snoozing cleric stealing time on the abbey roof with the last of the autumn sun? Certainly, he could not ignore it.

The human hand protruding from the rock ledge remained motionless, its fingers seemingly frozen into a claw, as if ready to do violence. It didn't look like the hand of someone asleep. It looked like the rictus of death.

Unconscious or dead? Adam didn't know. He inspected the wall. There was a corner wedge against a buttress that reached up for six metres. Above that was nearly three metres of vertical wall to the parapet. It would take less than five minutes to climb. Looking round, he saw the large chestnut tree nearby would screen him from the roadway. No one would see him. Adam looked around once more to check that he was alone. It was extraordinary. Around him was a peaceful, even idyllic scene.

The first chill of the evening brushed across his shoulders as he reached up to pinch a rock nodule with forefinger and thumb and haul himself up the first half metre of wall. His foot explored the possibility of purchase in a tiny crevice, but he discarded it in favour of another. He forced himself to concentrate. There was no safety rope and he was quite alone. No one would see him die if he fell. Pausing, he wondered whether it would matter. The familiar spectre of a sickening and terrible temptation washed over him. Adam savoured it for a moment before brushing it aside. However, the lingering guilt of the thought wasn't so easily dismissed. It stayed on the edge of his consciousness and continued to accuse him.

He had many reasons to feel guilty. He knew he was breaking a promise, a promise made just six weeks earlier to the person who meant more to him than any other. His other gnawing concern came from his conviction that what he was doing was illegal. Certainly, the fourteenth-century stonemasons who had worked for decades to build the soaring eastern wall of this magnificent medieval abbey had never intended anyone to climb it seven centuries later.

With heels well down, his toes fought for whatever friction the shallow face would allow as his fingers felt for holds in the tiniest of crevices. With fluid ease, he worked his way up the corner of the buttress. Greater care had to be taken on the flat expanse of wall above it as there were no adjacent surfaces to push against. All his holds needed to be found from amongst the rounded and sometimes glazed flint stones. Finally, he hooked a hand around a gargoyle and heaved himself over the parapet, disturbing the pigeons that clapped and flapped their surprise.

Throughout it all, the hand that had beckoned did not move.

As he swung over the parapet, Adam was confronted by the body of a young man dressed in jeans, bomber jacket and black tee-shirt. He lay ominously still. The waxy pallor of his face was eloquent enough.

The routines drilled in to him by his first aid training jolted him into action. Adam sprang across to the young man and felt his carotid artery for a pulse. There was none. Neither was there any sign of breathing. Did it call for mouth-to-mouth resuscitation and cardiac massage? He reached for the young man's cheek. It was already cool to the touch. Too late.

Adam sat back in shock. *Damn it.*

He looked at the young man trying to come to terms with the obscenity of death. The man seemed quite peaceful. There was no blood or any sign of violence. *What now?* Squatting alone on the roof of a medieval abbey, in the cooling twilight of an English autumn evening, with a body wasn't an everyday experience. However, his mind continued to work with detached efficiency. While there was no need to rush, clearly, there were things that needed to be done. He crossed over to the parapet. No one was in sight. It was bizarre how English towns could swallow people up in the evenings. In other countries, it was the time they came alive.

Should he yell and hope to attract attention? It seemed a little extreme.

He had just decided to climb down and fetch help when a verger in a cassock crunched along the gravel path leading from the side door of the transept. He was twirling a set of keys in his hand as he went.

Adam called out to him. 'Hey, mate. Up here.'

It took a while before the verger saw Adam. When he did, he stepped backwards in alarm.

Not wishing to broadcast his startling news around the precinct, Adam hissed in a loud whisper. 'Can you come closer? I need to tell you something.'

The verger appeared reluctant to do so and continued to stare at Adam with alarm.

Exasperated, Adam called out, 'My name's Adam Hollingworth. I'm a teacher at the school. There's a dead body up here. Please call the ambulance and police. I'll stay here until they arrive.'

The verger's mouth dropped open. He then nodded and scuttled away, leaving Adam alone with his silent charge.

As the day faded into a lingering English twilight, a chilly breeze began to cut through his tracksuit. To take his mind off his discomfort, he began to search around the body to try and make sense of what might have happened.

It didn't take long for him to find what looked like a battered tin pencil case in the gutter that ran inside the parapet. The lid was open. Inside, Adam saw the obscene agents of death. A candle, a teaspoon, a small bottle and some swabs—innocuous domestic items that belied the destructive use to which they were put in the drug culture. The body was slumped sideways with one arm flung up against the parapet. The other arm was half tucked under the body but wasn't so hidden as to completely obscure the tourniquet or the syringe still embedded in the forearm.

Adam gazed at the young face. It looked vulnerable rather than hard-bitten. Although the boy's garb was the standard uniform of rebellious youth, there was a softness to his features which did not speak of a long history of life on the streets.

Adam sighed. Such a terrible, terrible waste. A familiar wave of grief at the senseless destruction of life flooded over him. He shook his head and looked away. His internal anguish was in stark contrast to the beauty of the view from his vantage point. Lights from inside the abbey shone out of the clerestory windows along the flank of the nave. The light was welcome company in the growing darkness.

It wasn't long before he heard the strident whooping of sirens. Although he could not see any vehicles, their pulsating red and blue flashing lights bounced from the walls of the buildings huddled round the abbey precinct. He waited for some time and was wondering where the help had got to when he was startled to see the knees of a biblical saint in a nearby stained glass window disappear in a rectangle of light. A figure in a black cassock stepped through the opening. He was followed by efficient-looking paramedics and police who immediately took charge.

A flashlight played over the face of the dead youth. 'Good Lord.' The man in the cassock pushed through to have a closer look. 'That's Peter Armitage.'

'Who's he?' a policeman asked.

'He used to be a choirboy; stayed on as a tenor but not for long. He left two years ago.'

'What's he doing here?'

'I've no idea.'

'How would he know about this place?'

'You know what kids are like. The choirboys make it their business to learn as many of the abbey's secrets as possible.'

The policeman grunted and bent to examine the pencil case and the needle that Adam had pointed out. 'Looks like a classic OD, a heart attack brought on by a heroin overdose. It's sudden and usually lethal.' He looked at the young man's face. 'By the look of him, he's a fairly new user and probably got the dose wrong.' The policeman shook his head. 'This is the sixth we've had in two months.'

Names were exchanged and Adam gave a brief explanation of how he had come to find the body. It was evident it would take a while before the scene was cleared, and Adam was starting to shiver. The police suggested that the verger, who had introduced himself as Henry Harcourt, conduct Adam to the relative warmth of the vestry.

Adam followed Mr Harcourt and stepped through the stained glass window where the legs of a saint would normally have been. He found himself on a narrow stone arcade seven metres above the abbey floor. It ran clear down the end of the nave to the western wall. The view down into the abbey was breathtaking. High above the abbey floor, Adam had the impression that he was a Lilliputian walking along the second stage of a giant wedding cake. 'Wow!'

His comment was enough to launch Henry Harcourt into a lecture. Adam suspected he needed to speak to give vent to the tensions of the evening.

'This pierced triforium runs across the top of the twelfth century Norman arches. Most of the abbey was built between the eleventh and fifteenth centuries, so we have both Norman and Gothic architecture.'

Adam nodded, content to marvel at the view.

They made their way along the arcade until they arrived at a low door giving access to a narrow spiral staircase. It curled downwards inside one of the towers framing the western door of the abbey.

It was midnight before Adam was able to take his stormy thoughts across the road to the sanctuary of number four Prior's Lane. The police had taken some time to believe it possible for anyone to climb the wall. Adam eventually forestalled further questioning by taking them outside so they could see him climb the first three metres of the wall by the light of a torch held by a startled officer.

Once inside the front door, he made his way upstairs. On the final flight to his door, he discovered Philippa Ruth had left Marmalade, her therapy doll, in the middle of the third step going up to his room.

Adam stepped over it and climbed the stairs.

Chapter 6

The ensuing week wasn't a good one for Adam. He knew himself to be even more disengaged and withdrawn than usual. The interminable cycle of anger, helplessness and lethargy chased each other round and round. He was thoroughly fed up with it all and weary to the soul.

Forcing himself into action, he made his way to Highgate, the main shopping street in the town, to buy some postcards before the shops closed. After making his purchases, he headed back towards Prior's Lane. The dying evening sun highlighted the abbey tower, warming its stonework with a golden glow. Around him, the shadows lengthened amongst the jumble of rooftops that had long since settled down and become accustomed to each other's company.

He walked passed the front of the abbey and heard strains of plaintive singing coming from inside. Spontaneously, he stepped through a small side door into the cavernous interior. Inside, the abbey choir and the faithful were gathered behind the ornate rood screen to celebrate evensong. The haunting cadence of the music, combined with the settling hush of the evening, tugged at the loneliness deep within him. He crossed to the other side of the nave and stood in the shadow of one of the giant Norman arches, content to eavesdrop on the peace of aeons drifting from the service.

'*The day thou gavest Lord is ended...*'The beauty of the timeless words settled upon his soul. Unbidden, tears began to well up. Irritated at his weakness, he allowed a cynical, inner voice to mock his sentimentality—and the delicate thing that was beginning to happen in his heart vanished. Yet its shadow remained. '*Lord, now lettest thou thy servant depart in peace: according to thy word.*' Words of strange serenity lingered in the vaulted ceiling.

Embarrassed at himself, he blundered between rows of seats across to the side door. He was about to step into the aisle when his foot caught the leg of the last chair in the row. He went sprawling to the ground. As he did, he was dimly aware of some white paper taped to the floor. He fell onto the middle of it.

The emotions battling within him burst out in frustration and anger. 'Damn it!' A stab of pain shot through him from his shoulder. He grimaced as he felt for his arm to explore the damage.

'What the hell do you think you're doing? Look what you've done!'

Adam twisted around. The outburst came from a woman as she got up from a nearby seat. She was wrapped in a thick black cloak.

He kicked out in irritation at the offending chair. This action did nothing to re-establish his dignity as he lay flat on his back and served only to remind him that his shoulder did feel significantly damaged. 'Sheeesh,' he expelled between gritted teeth.

'Get off. Get off! Look at it! An hour's work, ruined.' The black phantom resolved itself into an indignant young woman. She squatted beside the paper fingering the torn ends with obvious despair.

Adam eased himself onto his side, ripping yet more paper. He groaned and struggled unsteadily onto his feet. 'Blast your wretched paper, lady!' He winced again as he sat down on a nearby chair.

Two flashing eyes under curling, dark blonde hair swivelled his way. A scowl distorted what might have been a striking face. The woman busied herself smoothing the torn paper. She glanced at him with a fleeting expression of concern. 'Are you okay?'

'Thanks for your concern.' He couldn't keep the sarcasm out of his voice. 'I've busted my shoulder.'

'And I've got a busted brass rubbing,' she retorted. 'I'd just finished it.' She sighed. 'All that work wasted. I do wish you'd been more careful.'

'If you'd finished whatever it was, why the hell didn't you fold it up, out of the way?'

'Because, like you, I was daring to listen to the music before I packed up. I hadn't anticipated a runaway pachyderm doing a reverse pike with full twist into the middle of it.'

'This particular pachyderm hadn't anticipated the abbey floor to be littered with paper.'

An abbey attendant in a blue cassock hurried over to them. Adam watched dourly as he twittered about, making placating noises.

The woman ripped up the torn remains of her work and stuffed them into a large artist's portfolio. Then, scooping up a cardboard tube, she stalked off to the side door and banged it shut behind her.

Seeing her go, Adam felt slightly free to speak his emotions out loud. 'Stupid woman!'

The abbey attendant said defensively. 'Oh, Miss Claire's okay.' He then went on to reassure himself that Adam didn't require first aid, and was not going to sue the abbey for millions.

Having satisfied himself on both accounts, he seemed anxious to see the end of the affair and held the side door open to speed Adam's departure.

Adam left, somewhat shamefaced, pondering how thoughts of things ethereal and profound could so easily be shattered by two human beings hissing abuse at each other.

He sighed.

***

Back in his lodgings, Adam thought he'd better phone Gareth and tell him his injuries would limit his involvement with rugby training.

'Dear boy, that's horrendous. I'm grooming you for greatness. How bad is your shoulder?'

'Dunno.'

'Then you'd better get over to the boarding house and let matron have a look at it. Do you need a lift or can I complete my destruction of the lower sixth's essays?'

'I'll manage.'

Adam edged a coat over his shoulders, winced, and walked through lanes and alleys to the boarding house. Coal smoke hung in the crisp night air—all so different from the balmy Australian evenings he was used to.

The boarding house was a huge, brooding affair that smelled of polish, cabbage and the fug of one hundred boys. Gareth met Adam in the entrance hall and led him upstairs to a landing which gave access to a number of old wooden doors. One of these had a small brass plaque on it inscribed *Matron*. Gareth rapped on the door and yelled, 'Maggie, are you there?'

A few seconds later, Margaret Pemberton opened the door. Her eyes swept over Gareth with the sort of exasperated indulgence Adam had seen in owners of young puppies. They then fixed themselves on Adam. Her gaze changed in an instant to no-nonsense brusqueness. 'What can I do for you?'

Gareth cocked his thumb at Adam. 'He's been falling over women in the abbey and damaged his shoulder.'

Margaret gave Adam an appraising look. 'Step across to the surgery and let's have a look.'

Inside, Margaret determined Adam had no obvious broken bones but had probably torn a muscle and quite possibly sprained a ligament. She strapped up his shoulder, fashioned a sling and organised for him to visit the local hospital for an x-ray next morning.

Adam had been introduced to Margaret Pemberton when he'd first attended the boarding house for lunch. Since then, he'd barely spoken to her. He'd found her to be quiet and to exude an aura of detachment that discouraged small talk. Although he judged her to be in her early thirties, she chose to hide what appeared to be an attractive figure in utilitarian dresses. Adam already knew that this had resulted in scurrilous rumours amongst the boys about her sexuality. He'd never seen her wear make-up and her hair was invariably pulled back into a severe bun.

Adam glanced at her as she fashioned a sling for his arm. She had magnificent auburn hair.

Margaret turned back and rummaged in a cupboard behind her until she found a packet of pills. She handed them to him. 'Take these half an hour before you go to bed. I'm afraid it's going to be a bit uncomfortable for four or five days.'

Adam nodded and rubbed his eyes with his free hand. He felt tired. Tired of everything. For just a second, he was conscious of her looking at him. In that instant, Adam saw in her eyes a flash of recognition of something that went well beyond his damaged shoulder. It was the look of ... what? Understanding?

She dropped her gaze when she saw him glance at her.

Adam said nothing but, in that unguarded moment, he'd seen in her expression something that hinted of a sadness of her own.

It was clear she knew he'd seen it. After a lengthy pause, she whispered, 'Some pain takes longer.'

'Does it ever go?'

'I don't know.'

He stood up slowly. 'Thanks for noticing.'

***

Gareth, left alone in the open entrance to matron's small sitting room, had the guilty feeling Margaret expected him to return to his study. However, never having been in her room before, he elected to make use of the ambiguity of the situation and wait for Adam. He looked around him and marvelled at the things it told him and the things it kept secret.

The room was utilitarian with simple furniture and an occasional splash of tasteful colour. A sideboard in front of a window was crowded with pot plants. He strolled over to the bookcase beside the window and was surprised by its contents. There were many books on travel. Glancing around the room, he noticed the walls were hung with photographs of exotic places. There were Aztec ruins perched amidst impossible mountain slopes, Middle Eastern marketplaces, and a herd of seals frolicking in a rock pool. Some of the best shots were of children in uninhibited natural poses. Others were of old men with faces lined by the hardships of life. Pencilled at the bottom of each picture was the date and place. With amazement, Gareth realised these were Margaret's own photos. He could not recall her ever speaking of her travel adventures.

Her bookcase also contained books on literature and philosophy—Yeats, Camus, Tennyson, Nietzsche and Keats, many of the same books he had in his own library. A book of poems by Dylan Thomas lay on the coffee table in front of her chair. 'Do not go gently into that still night. Rage, rage,' he quoted as he picked it up. *Maggie, you are indeed a dark horse.* Underneath the book was a spiral-bound notepad. He opened it and discovered it was full of hand written poems, all obviously her own. Gareth could see her editorial crossings-out and scribbles. He flicked through the pad with shameless curiosity, seeing poem after poem. Stopping at one, he began to read:

As Shakespeare's player struts and frets his hour upon the stage,

I search the stage of life for friends, to lend my patronage,

Then having chosen sect or clan, I copy all their idioms

To stay with them, and strive to keep rebellion to a minimum.

I arm myself with all the necessary personalities

And with this wardrobe act each part, accepted frivolities.

Am I doomed to forge myself on fellow beings or deity?

And if on God, must all pride change to humble, base servility?

'Whew!' said Gareth. He flicked towards the start of the pad and read another.

Janus woman, don't look back
At broken promises, now black
And stained and sour as sex-stained sheets;
Of love betrayed, the guile of cheats,
Of young buds innocent of frost,
Of desperate grieving, searing loss;
A tissue used and thrown away
And torn and bleeding, left betrayed.

Gareth blanched. This was way too personal for him to trespass further. He placed the notepad back under the book.

He had looked at Margaret with some interest when she had first arrived at the boarding house, two years ago. However, he'd soon wearied of the politely closed door whenever he sought to draw her out socially. He couldn't deny she was good at her job. Amongst the boys, she seemed quite relaxed. But amongst adult colleagues, she was very different—reserved ... closed.

Gareth felt a pang of guilt over his subsequent behaviour toward her. He'd chosen to tease her, goading her so she would react and break out of her reserve. It was now very apparent Margaret was more complex, interesting and intelligent than he'd ever appreciated.

He was startled from his reverie by the door opening. Margaret and Adam came in. She glanced at him briefly but then avoided his eye.

Gareth swallowed and pointed to a striking photograph of a pod of orcas carving their way through a perfectly calm sea. 'Margaret...' He used her full name. 'Where did you take this picture?'

After a moment's silence, Margaret replied, 'From a local fishing boat heading out to the Lofoten Islands off Norway.'

He waved his arm around the room. 'All these photos must represent amazing experiences and adventures. I'd love to hear about them sometime.'

She sniffed. 'Perhaps.'

Gareth was bewildered. He'd prided himself on living a colourful life, one garnished with romances which were highly visible, lightly held and soon over. He couldn't remember ever knowing anyone quite like Margaret. Certainly, she was a recluse, but she was also someone who loved adventure, wrote poetry that made his hair stand on end, and who had a library that reflected a keen mind.

Gareth knew himself to be in shock.

***

Back in Gareth's study, Adam sat down gingerly in an armchair and only half-listened as Gareth recounted his discoveries in Margaret's room. In truth, he felt awkward at being a party to the violation of another person's privacy. At last, he could bear it no longer. 'Gareth, you are a disgraceful perv. You should be locked in the stocks with the public invited to yell split infinitives at you.'

Gareth paid no attention. 'I tell you, our Maggie has experienced some significant trauma, and it's caused her to hide herself away. No one writes poetry like she does without good cause.'

'You didn't need to see her poetry to tell you that.'

Gareth pointed a finger at him. 'Don't tell me you already knew?'

'Umm, yes.'

'How? How could you see she'd been hurt in the past?'

Adam waved a hand in irritation, wanting to change the subject. 'Oh, I dunno. Instinct.'

Gareth paced up and down the carpet. 'There's obviously a remarkable woman up there whom I have allowed to fool me into thinking was a boring old maid.' He spun around to face Adam. 'I intend to find the real Maggie.'

'Be careful,' said Adam wearily. 'Some people don't want to be found.'

'Truth can never be a bad thing to uncover.'

'Truth can be unbearable and wounding.' He looked up at Gareth. 'This is no game, you know. You're dealing with things that are very sensitive.'

'I know that, Adam. I'm not talking about playing a game.' Gareth gripped the back of an empty armchair. 'I actually ... care a bit. In fact, I'm beginning to regret that while I have been, of course, brilliant and outstandingly witty in her company, I have also been...' He searched for the right words, '...a puerile smart-arse.'

'That's your problem, not hers.'

'Nonetheless, I'm sorry.'

Adam regarded him in silence for a moment. 'She probably doesn't want your sympathy.'

Gareth spun away in exasperation. 'Damn! I can't do a thing right.'

'You can, and you're halfway there because you care.'

Gareth turned back. 'What do you think she wants?'

'Safety ... and friends big enough to be there for her, and wise enough to give her space.'

'Hmm.'

Silence.

'I have behaved a little shabbily towards her.' Gareth slumped down into the armchair. 'I don't just want to make amends because of my guilt problem. I simply want to ... to do things right.'

Adam picked up a wooden ruler from Gareth's desk, leaned forward and tapped him ceremonially on both shoulders. 'I dub thee, Sir Gareth. Arise, and do valiantly.'

Gareth smiled somewhat sheepishly. 'And now tell me. What exactly did happen to you in the abbey? I want all the sordid details.'

Adam obliged and received, as expected, no sympathy at all, but did receive a good deal of restorative friendship.

Chapter 7

Adam arrived early at the staff common room two days later, looking for Jethro Slattery. Jethro was the senior art master, famous for his huge belly, bushy beard and collection of brightly coloured braces that held up his voluminous trousers. Adam found him reading his mail at the staff pigeonholes.

'Jethro, have you got a minute?'

'Certainly, old boy.' Jethro looked up. 'By the way, beastly business with young Armitage. Used to be a student here. Nauseous little bugger, but quite good at art. Got expelled a few years ago.'

Giles Carlingford, rummaging in his pigeonhole next to them, interrupted. 'Quite the cat burglar, it would seem.' He turned and called out, 'Lock up your valuables. The convicts are returning from the antipodes to plunder us all.' Giles taught history and seemed to delight in needling Adam at every opportunity. Adam noticed he almost always wore a suit—dark grey.

Gareth stepped over to join them, put a proprietorial hand on Adam's shoulder and said in a stage whisper, 'Never mind Giles. He's had a deprived childhood—tragic, really. He was born to rule England but got swapped at birth because of a birthmark on his arse the shape of the worker's hammer and sickle. He's never lived it down.'

Giles bit back. 'Don't seek to make your Welsh anti-royalist ravings palatable with crudity in the mistaken belief it is wit, Price.'

Adam had the distinct impression he was caught in the middle of a sparring match that had been going on for some time.

Gareth chuckled and headed off to get a coffee, yelling, 'Wally, you've got chalk dust on your fly again.'

Wally Henshaw stooped and absentmindedly dusted the front of his trousers before heading off to his Maths class.

Adam turned back to Jethro. 'Um, Jethro, would you know someone called Claire ... someone that I might ... bump into doing a brass rubbing in the abbey?'

'My dear boy, hundreds of people do brass rubbings there. What makes you think I'd know her?'

'One of the abbey staff seemed to know her, so she's probably local and she was a bit arty.'

'You make it sound like a disease,' Jethro chided. 'But go on. Describe her.'

'I didn't really get a good look. Long dark blonde hair, right handed, large brown eyes, tanned skin and a sharp tongue. Wore a black cape.'

'Black cape? That's probably Claire Sanderson.'

'Who is she?'

'She's a talented local artist. Uses masses of colour in which she hides pockets of detail, just to surprise you. She's part-owner of a small gallery called *The Borrowed Wheelbarrow* that has squeezed its way between the teashops at this end of Highgate. Why do you ask?'

'She and I had a misunderstanding when I fell over her brass rubbing. I'm afraid I didn't behave well and have been working up the courage to apologise.' He rubbed the back of his neck. 'I'm still not sure I've the guts to do so. What on earth is a brass rubbing?'

'We do them occasionally in the Art Department. You simply take a large piece of paper, tape it over a brass floor plaque of some dead medieval worthy and rub black crayon over it so you get an imprint. It's popular with tourists.'

'This particular worthy was about five metres in from the side entrance in the western end of the abbey.'

'Ah, that would be St Wilfred. He's very popular.'

'Could I do one? I could give it to her as a sort of peace offering.'

'No reason why not.'

'It's just that I'm not sure if I can do it, or do it well enough to please an artist.'

'Nonsense. A moderately deft hand, patience and care are all that is needed. I'll help set you up and get you started.'

'Could I do it this afternoon? I'm off rugby training for a bit with this crook shoulder.'

'I take it you are wanting to do this one-handed.'

'Sort of. Can it be done?'

'Dear boy, it is simply another challenge. If you are fool enough to try, come over at noon. We're still moving stuff into our new building. Just watch out when you come. There's gear all over the place and I wouldn't want you to break the other arm—not that I'm confident it would stop you.'

**

True to his word, Jethro walked with Adam over to the abbey, avoided paying the charge normally levied on those seeking to do a brass rubbing by claiming it was school business, and set Adam to work.

Adam worked carefully and methodically. He would have found it quite therapeutic had he not become self-conscious at being an object of interest to tourists.

As he was finishing, the verger, Henry Harcourt, discovered him and sat down to talk over the events of the previous week. 'There's to be an inquest. Will you need to attend?'

'No, I don't think so. They've already managed to turn what little I know into five pages of evidence, and they say that will probably do.'

'The funeral won't be for at least another two weeks. Are you planning to come? I probably shall.'

Adam shuddered. Henry nodded and to Adam's relief turned the conversation to the brass rubbing. 'You've done well.' He helped Adam unstick the paper, roll it up and slide it into the cardboard tube Jethro had supplied.

Back in his lodgings, Adam penned a small note, 'From a repentant pachyderm,' put it in an envelope and taped it to the tube.

Taking a deep breath, he tucked the tube under his arm and headed into town. Highgate was only a ten minute walk away. It was a street blocked off for pedestrians that was full of fashion boutiques and tea shops. Adam reflected on the inordinate fondness the English had for tea. They used it to bring calm in crisis, respite to tedious afternoons and to provide the necessary social oil to lubricate a conversation on any occasion.

Adam made his way along Highgate until he found a wheelbarrow hanging above a door on which was written: *The Borrowed Wheelbarrow—Art Gallery.*

The entrance was an expanse of modern glass, disfiguring the lower floor of an otherwise handsome Edwardian building. The gallery's entrance was little more than a foyer inviting patrons to go upstairs. With dwindling courage, Adam did so.

At the top of the stairs, he entered a large room with tiny, discrete spotlights highlighting a large collection of paintings. There were slashings of colour, drama and pathos everywhere he looked. The only other person present was a statuesque woman with long white-blonde hair, dressed in a floating kaftan. She was standing behind a desk, wrapping a framed picture in bubble plastic. Adam expected to see a crystal ball on the counter beside her.

'Excuse me, does Claire Sanderson work here?'

'She does,' said the clairvoyant, 'but she won't be back in until tomorrow. Can I help you?'

'May I please leave something for her?'

'Certainly.'

Adam handed over the tube.

'And who shall I say this is from?' murmured the clairvoyant, with just a hint of seduction.

'Oh, she'll know.' He edged towards the stairs.

'A man of mystery; how interesting.' She gave a low chuckle. 'Do come again.'

Outside, Adam had the same feeling people have when they emerge from an exam for which they had been poorly prepared. He threaded his way back to his lodgings, where he again stepped over Marmalade.

***

Adam reviewed his first five weeks at school. He had tried. He ran a weary hand through his hair. Goodness knows, he'd tried. He had been conscientious and kept good order but he wasn't teaching well. It was no good fooling himself any longer. This job required more than he was able to give. It was time to make a decision. He would see the headmaster during the next week, hand in his resignation and return to Australia. Perhaps he could become a climbing instructor at one of the Outward Bound schools in the Blue Mountains. Students would be with him for no more than a day. It would be safe.

Having made this resolution, Adam drifted off into a troubled sleep in which deathly pale bodies screamed Amanda's scream, while he stood helpless on the other side of a canyon.

***

Three days later, Adam found a note from the headmaster in his pigeonhole. He was somewhat perplexed at its content. There was no reference to his request for an interview. Instead, the note asked him to attend the opening of the new art department building that evening. This was no formal invitation on an embossed card, but a personal note written in the headmaster's own well-formed hand.

That evening, he visited the boarding house to show Gareth the headmaster's note. Gareth, with one leg swinging over the arm of an armchair, was rolling a small cigar between his fingers and pontificating about the idiosyncrasies of modern marketing.

'Is it just me, or do you also think it strange they promote cigars like alcoholic beverages, "rum flavoured" and "wine dipped"; washing-up liquid like citrus fruit; and coffee like ice cream, "hazelnut and vanilla flavoured?" I wish they'd bloomin' well let a smoke be a smoke, soap be soap and coffee remain as God intended it to be, coffee.'

Adam waited until he paused for breath and handed him the note. 'What do you make of this?'

Gareth read it. 'Well, boyo, all I can say is that the headmaster doesn't do anything without a reason. Pity I won't be there tonight to see what it is. I'm on duty in the boarding house.' He looked at his watch. 'You'll soon have to get a wriggle on if it begins at seven-thirty.'

'I know. I'm just off to change. I'd hoped your culturally-informed Welsh intuition might be able to prepare me for something.'

'Relax and stop your brooding. I can tell you that the headmaster does not choose gala opening nights to roast people or hang them out to dry. Push off and enjoy yourself.'

***

Marmalade was sprawled sideways on the bottom of the steps up to his room, her arms spread out in invitation. Adam stepped over her and continued up the stairs.

Chapter 8

Adam made it to the opening of the new art department building with only moments to spare. Having one arm in a sling had slowed him down more than he'd anticipated.

Other than a few staff members, Adam knew no one. He hovered towards the back, feeling self-conscious in his sling and not at all sociable. Sandy Hardcastle was crouching over a computer at the back of the small hall. His tall, thin frame made everything he wore look untidy. This wasn't helped by the fact that the pockets of his tweed jacket were always slightly distended by generous handfuls of almonds. He was always seen eating them absentmindedly, usually while prodding a computer or something electrical. Being towards the end of the day, his pockets were nearly empty. Sandy taught physics and information technology.

Towards the front, the headmaster looked up briefly from the knot of people he'd been speaking to and caught Adam's eye. Smiling, he nodded almost imperceptibly before returning to his conversation. Adam walked over to Sandy Hardcastle. 'You winning, Sandy?'

'As always, Adam, old son.' Sandy forestalled further conversation, by saying, 'Hang on, the show is getting under way.'

The guests were invited to be seated and the formalities began. There were three speeches. One was too long, one just right and the other not long enough.

The first speech was given by the Chair of the School Council. It was turgid, predictable and lurched from cliché to cliché. The next speech, by the headmaster, showed both his wit and his commitment to opening up the creative spirit of his students. Finally, Jethro gave a brilliant speech, illustrated with pictures beamed from the data projector operated by Sandy. It featured shots of the new facilities and included some ridiculous pictures—some even the wrong way up—that only made sense when they were followed by the next picture which was invariably one of

Jethro's cartoons. It was clever, over too soon and earned spontaneous applause.

Guests were then invited to enjoy refreshments and view a display of the students' artwork.

Adam had never found it easy to juggle a wine glass and plate, whilst picking up a spring roll and making polite conversation. With one arm in a sling, he didn't even try. He waylaid a glass of red wine and retreated back to Sandy's company.

Just as he was working out when it would be socially acceptable for him to slip away, the headmaster stepped up behind him. Dr Fairclough broke effortlessly into his conversation with Sandy and eased Adam away, saying that there was someone he wanted him to meet.

He led him to the far side of the hall where a collection of chairs had been placed underneath a suspended piece of clear plastic, through which the head of a porpoise was diving. A slightly-built elderly man was sitting in one of the chairs chatting amiably with Wally Henshaw, the mathematics master. At their approach, the man stood up with old-world gallantry.

The headmaster made the introductions.

'Edward, I'd like to introduce Adam Hollingworth. Adam, Edward Bryson is the nearest thing this school has to a living institution. He'll tell you anything you want to know about Viking history. He taught here for twenty-five years, was Deputy Head for twelve years, is a gentleman in every sense of the word and is the one I look to for wisdom when I need it.'

Two blue eyes looked at Adam with polite interest. Edward held out his hand. As Adam shook it, he felt the hardened calloused hands of a workman. It was at odds with the aristocratic features of a man who seemed very much at ease in a suit. 'Pleased to meet you,' said Adam.

The headmaster smiled. 'I'll leave you two to chat.' He turned to Wally Henshaw. 'Wallace, come and tell me how the mathematics of the Mandelbrot set can generate such amazing artwork. It's extraordinary.'

Wally levered himself out of his chair and shambled off with the headmaster.

Edward's smile was warm. 'Sit down with me, Adam, and rescue me from too many parents of children whose names I've forgotten.'

Adam accepted the invitation and confessed, 'I was about to cut and run myself.'

Edward glanced at him. 'But not, I suspect, because you remember too many people too poorly.'

'Too few.'

Edward nodded. 'The headmaster has told me little about you other than you like the outdoors ... and that you are needing to survive the tragic loss of your fiancé.' He paused. 'I am so sorry, Adam.' He sighed. 'I lost a young wife. It was wretched. Grief is long and lonely.'

Adam said nothing for a while. Finally, he lifted his head. 'But you survived.'

'Yes.' Silence again settled between them as Adam wrestled with hopeless blackness and disturbing images.

Edward eventually broke the silence. 'What was her name?'

Adam swallowed. 'Amanda.'

'Amanda.' Edward seemed to savour the name. Adam dropped his head.

'She must have been a remarkable woman to have left such a void. How did you first meet?'

Hesitant at first, Adam began to talk about Amanda in a way he'd not done since her death. He told of how they met, and Edward laughed. Encouraged by Edward's lack of funereal delicacy, Adam found himself talking about the wilderness adventures he and Amanda had experienced together, her silly habits and the future they had planned. Adam felt the warmth of Edward's sincere interest and continued to talk until he finally became aware of his volubility and lapsed into self-conscious silence.

'Precious memories.' Edward smiled. 'Thank you for sharing them with me, Adam. You've taken me to sacred places—and I can see that you've been blessed.'

Adam reacted with shock at the idea he had been blessed. His body stiffened. He felt anything but blessed. However, he was conscious of the kindness in the eyes of the man watching him.

Edward passed a hand over his long silvered hair. 'My wife was too sick to do anything like that with me. I'd always wanted to take her sailing.'

Adam suddenly felt guilty and selfish. He relaxed his shoulders imperceptibly, hoping that Edward hadn't noticed. The notion he'd been blessed challenged the very nature of his thinking about Amanda, and he wasn't yet ready to accept it.

'Do you sail then?' he asked, trying to change the subject.

'Yes. I live about eleven miles away in a small village where I keep a boat.' He smiled. 'Your wilderness is the high mountain peaks, mine is the estuary and the marshes. I love it.'

A distant ache tugged at Adam's soul. 'It's been a while since I've seen anything but roads and buildings. I thought this corner of England was so domesticated and built over that there would be no wild areas left.'

'That is too near the truth for any comfort but, I'm happy to report, it is not yet absolutely the case.' Edward laughed. 'How's your arm?'

'Muscle and ligament—no real drama. It should be okay for light work in a week or so.'

He gave Adam an appraising look. 'Would you like to see my wilderness this weekend?'

'What did you have in mind?'

'I want to take the boat out one more time before I lay her up for the winter. I was going to wait for the weekend because that's when my crew is normally available. Would you like to join us? It shouldn't be too demanding on your arm as I'll organise my usual team to crew.'

Adam had a sudden urge to break out of the confines of the school and see wider horizons. He'd been on a few weekend drives with Gareth in search of country pubs, but Gareth's driving was so bad, he'd had little time to admire the verdant English countryside. Adam suspected Gareth had lived as long as he had only because of the remarkable politeness and forbearance of English drivers. 'I'd like that. We've got a half-term break this weekend. I've five days without much to do.'

'Then would you like to spend those five days as my guest, "messing about in boats?" In truth, I would be grateful for the company.'

'Umm...' Adam's instincts were screaming, *No, I don't want to. I don't want anyone's company.* He looked again into the blue eyes of the older man and was surprised to hear himself say, 'Thanks. If you'd let me contribute some food, I'll come.'

'Feel free to bring a bottle of wine and no more. I have little enough to spend my money on these days, and finances are not a problem.'

Edward organised to pick Adam up in two days' time. 'Now, if we can track down one of my crew tonight, I'll get things organised.' He got to his feet and led Adam through the crowd, nodding and smiling at acquaintances as he went. 'Ah,' he said eventually, 'There's our quarry.'

A group of people was gathered around a display of scrap metal that had somehow come together on a pedestal to form an eagle, stooping dramatically with talons outstretched. Giles Carlingford was one of a number of men in the group who were failing to give the sculpture anything like the attention they gave to a beautiful shapely woman in a simple black dress who was examining it.

To Adam's astonishment, the woman smiled as Edward approached and stepped forward to kiss him on the cheek. Edward then moved aside and ushered Adam forward. 'Claire, may I introduce Adam Hollingworth. Adam, my niece, Claire Sanderson.'

It took a moment for Adam to connect the name. He knew that name. He'd heard it only recently. There was a momentary swirl of mental confusion before the excruciating memory hit him. *Oh no!* The shapeless form in a cape, the face distorted with frustration—it couldn't be. But the same eyes now looked at Adam with cool detachment. Adam died within.

'The pachyderm.' Her face showed no emotion. The two of them faced each other.

'What did you say, Claire?' asked Edward.

'Pachyderm: a large, thick-skinned mammal, usually an elephant.' Adam squirmed. 'It's a private joke. We've met before.'

Claire extended her hand for him to shake. *Was it a peace offering?* In his uncertainty, he mistimed his handshake and only grasped the ends of her fingers. *Damn!*

'Well,' Edward said, 'that's wonderful. When was that?'

'We ... bumped into each other briefly, in the abbey a few days ago,' said Claire. 'Your arm, was that...?'

Adam nodded. 'Not much wrong. Getting better.'

'I am so sorry. I didn't...'

Adam interrupted her. 'Was St Wilfred, err ... rubbed to your satisfaction?'

'He was. Not that I expected him, given my appalling behaviour.'

If Edward was bewildered, he didn't show it and organised for Claire to join him early on Saturday morning for a sail. When Edward told her Adam would be staying with him for a few days and would be sailing with them, Claire looked startled and darted a quick look at Adam. He gave the briefest of shrugs, making it clear that the circumstances were as much of a surprise to him as they were to her. For a moment he thought she'd make an excuse and cancel the engagement.

To his surprise, she changed the subject. 'Where did you get your rubbing of St Wilfred?'

'Jethro helped.'

'Ah, of course.' There was a strained silence. 'Do please thank him for giving it to you ... and thank you for giving it to me. It really wasn't necessary.'

Adam smiled and decided this was as good a point to exit as he was ever likely to get. He made his excuses and left.

Edward elected to leave with him.

***

Claire watched Adam go with a puzzled frown. Giles Carlingford stepped towards her. 'How do you know Hollingworth?'

The disdain in his voice was not lost on her. She turned from watching Adam and Edward dissolve back into the crowd. 'Oh, we met briefly in the

Abbey. I'm afraid we were rather rude to each other.'

'Typical vulgar Australian,' Giles sniffed. 'I suspect he's rude to most people.'

Claire frowned.

Giles snapped his fingers and grinned. 'I've got an idea. Let's tweak his nose a little.'

'Please don't.' Claire felt alarmed.

Giles ignored her entreaty and walked over to a computer at a nearby workstation where he busied himself on the keyboard.

Claire sighed and elected to stay close to Giles, to check he would not do anything untoward. Five minutes later, he stood up, holding a computer memory stick. Claire gave him an enquiring look.

'I've downloaded a brilliant picture of a man's hands gripping prison bars ... and attached the convict's song of lament, *Botany Bay.* The trouble is, I can't access the data projector from that computer. Evidently, it's only hooked in to the computer where Sandy is.' Giles chewed his lip. 'And he can be a bit prickly.'

Claire reached out and took the memory stick. 'I'll take it. Sandy won't refuse me anything.'

Giles guffawed.

Claire eased her way through groups of people and found the table where sticks of charcoal and white paper had been placed to encourage guests to draw something. With confident, economic strokes, she began to do so.

Jethro Slattery, the art master, came alongside her and looked over her shoulder. 'You know you're better than me, don't you, Claire, darling.'

'Rubbish.' Claire shook her head. 'You're brilliant.'

Jethro smiled and made to move off but Claire held him back. 'Jethro, tell me about Adam Hollingworth.'

'You've not turned him into another of your aspiring suitors, have you?' He chuckled.

Claire shuddered. 'Anything but. It's just that Edward's organised for him to come sailing with us and I want to know what I'm letting myself in for.'

'Adam is broody and quiet. He's an introvert but has flashes of humour. He tends to see things others don't.' Jethro paused. 'There's some personal tragedy lurking in the background somewhere, but he's a nice guy. He told me he tripped over your brass rubbing in the abbey. Did you get your replacement St Wilfred?'

'Yes, thanks for giving it to him.'

'Darling, I didn't give it to him. He insisted on doing the rubbing himself with one arm in a sling, the daft blighter. I just got him started.'

'Really! He did it?'

Jethro nodded.

Claire groaned.

'What's the matter?'

'Too long to explain. But now I really do need to fix something.' She nodded her thanks and set off across the room.

Sandy looked up from his computer through thick glasses as she approached. When he recognised who it was, he smiled. Claire bent over and whispered in his ear. A few seconds later, Sandy nodded, took out his mobile phone and photographed Claire's picture. Plugging the mobile into his computer, he fiddled for a few minutes before giving her the thumbs up.

Claire brushed a kiss of thanks on Sandy's cheek. 'Sandy, can you return this memory stick to Giles? This was his idea but I'm afraid his offering was a little less gracious.'

Sandy snorted. 'I can well imagine.' He returned his gaze to the computer. 'Want me to do this now?'

She nodded.

The giant screen above the crowd came to life.

***

From the other side of the room, Adam and Edward looked up at the screen.

An introductory slide simply said, 'By special request.' However, it was the next slide that had Adam choking on his drink. It was a cartoon of an elephant sitting on a stool with a front leg in a sling, looking forlorn. As he looked, the words to the song, *I Never Meant To Hurt You,* began to play.

Adam looked across at Sandy, who simply shrugged and pointed to Claire standing beside him. She picked up Sandy's glass of champagne and raised it in a silent toast.

Strangely moved and deeply grateful, Adam reciprocated and raised his own glass.

Feeling as if the evening had given him all that he could cope with for one night, Adam decided to take his leave. Edward insisted on walking with him to the door and shaking his hand. 'It has been a pleasure to meet you, Adam.'

'I can well understand the headmaster valuing you as his mentor.'

Edward waved dismissively. 'He exaggerates. He doesn't often need my wisdom. But he's a good friend.' He smiled. 'I'll pick you up on Thursday.'

Adam walked slowly back to his lodgings, reflecting on the evening. Edward had drawn him out in a way that had amazed him. He'd even managed to laugh at some of the crazy antics he'd gotten up to with Amanda.

Adam didn't think Edward completely guileless and wasn't entirely sure of his innocence in choosing to construct his sailing invitation to Claire in the way that he had. And what an extraordinary girl she was. It was all ... bewildering.

***

Marmalade was sitting in the middle of the steps with her head falling forwards, as if in deep contemplation. Adam stepped over her and went up to his room.

Chapter 9

Adam emerged from the main school gates with his rucksack over his shoulder. He spotted Edward leaning on the front of a battered Land Rover, talking with some of the senior boys as they waited to be picked up for their half-term break. He waved to Adam, opened the tailgate for him to throw his rucksack in, and they both climbed in. Edward patted the dashboard. 'Economy class, I'm afraid. Uncomfortable as anything but it tolerates abuse and for the most part, doesn't rust.'

They drove past the council estates and industrial areas at the edge of town, out into the English countryside. Narrow roads, bordered by hedgerows, wound their way through villages with charming names—some sounding slightly French, revealing their Norman ancestry. Eventually they trundled into a small village. Edward drove past an old church with a lychgate leaning on a yew tree, turned down a side street at the village common and pulled into a gravel driveway.

Adam saw that Edward's home was a small two-storey cottage. It was made of old brick and exposed baulks of timber. The tiled roof was covered in lichen. Edward explained the cottage had once been the village forge. Only the house now remained. He grew hollyhocks in the remains of the old furnace.

Edward opened the door and ushered Adam through its low entrance. It led straight into a front parlour.

'I only light the fire for special occasions. The central heating system is pretty good.'

Multi-paned windows peered out from under the low eaves. They looked out onto a front garden that was beginning to surrender to the stilling hand of winter.

Inside, some of the wattle and daub had been removed from an internal wall to leave the dark supporting posts and beams. These, together with a wooden breakfast bar, divided the front parlour from the kitchen. Beyond the kitchen, a modern sunroom extended into the back garden.

Adam was charmed by the house. It was so English. Edward pointed upstairs to Adam's bedroom. He climbed the stairs and entered a tiny room with a sloping roof and a dormer window. Outside, he could see the thin silver ribbon of the estuary beyond a line of trees.

When he came back downstairs, he found Edward busy preparing a packed lunch. Edward asked Adam to slice some cheese and tomato while he unearthed some home-made cake. The simple act of preparing lunch together helped Adam feel more at home.

After fetching some tools from the garage, they drove the short distance to a boatshed. It stood next to the hard. The open space beside the slipway was littered with marine flotsam. Smart sailing boats held upright by wooden stanchions, nestled between old boats that would never sail again. Some were leaning sadly on their broken cheeks. Piles of rusted chains, discarded timber and weather-bleached dinghies lay scattered about.

Edward unlocked a gate into a fenced compound, retrieved a wheelbarrow, dropped his bag of tools into it and the two of them set off across the duckboards into the saltings.

It was a strange, bleak, untidy place. Boats with masts leaning drunkenly in different directions, sat down in the culverts and mud hollows. Gulls wheeled and squabbled overhead. Crabs scuttled sideways under protective fronds of seaweed—and everywhere, the mud surface was pockmarked with marine wormholes, bird tracks and a thousand other mysterious marks.

'The saltings are probably the marine equivalent of the rainforest. The diversity of organisms living here is fantastic. Sadly, there are not a lot of the saltings left any more. Miles and miles of earthen sea walls were erected years ago by local landowners to reclaim much of it for sheep grazing.'

'That's an all-too-familiar tale.' Adam looked around. 'It looks amazing. I had no idea places like this existed.'

'It'll be high tide in five hours. It looks a different world then. Wait and see.'

They reached the mud hollow where *Sanderling* nestled. Adam looked down at the stolid, ancient sailing boat and was captivated. 'She's lovely.'

Edward was soon at work re-caulking a small section of decking around the Sampson post. Adam sat on the forward end of the deckhouse roof and watched.

Edward patted the post. 'It's really just a bollard. It passes through the foredeck and is bedded into the keel, so it is hugely strong. The trouble is, anything that penetrates a deck has a habit of letting in water.'

'She must take a lot of work to maintain,' Adam said.

'She does. *Sanderling* had a major refit five years ago to get her ready for my retirement. Her old deck was a mess. The old planks had been joggled together and caulked with oakum—that's a tar-impregnated rope.' Edward prodded at some grout with a screwdriver. 'Then they poured molten pitch over the cracks. It was messy stuff. Always sticking to your feet. Pass me that chisel, will you?'

Adam did so and Edward began prising away some black rubberised material from the joints between the post and the deck. 'Nowadays, we use modern synthetic caulking compounds but, as you can see, it doesn't always do a better job.'

Adam insisted on being allowed to do some work. Edward handed him a sanding block and asked him to rub back the paint on the forward hatch cover. 'She's a fairly wet boat, without a lot of freeboard, so it's important I keep her sealed up tight.'

As they worked beside each other, Adam told Edward a slightly edited version of how he had first met Claire, not mentioning how he damaged his arm. He was, however, honest about how badly he'd behaved.

Edward grunted. 'From what I understand, you've made ample amends. Not everyone would have done that.' He smiled. 'I can tell you, it caught Claire by surprise. And that's not easy. It's usually Claire who springs the surprises.'

'How's that?'

'Oh, she's fairly colourful in her ways...'

'In what way?'

'Oh...' he said vaguely. 'She's always searching for things worthy of her passion—often getting hurt in the process.' He rested back on his heels. 'She is the only daughter of my youngest sister, who used to live in town until she moved to Vancouver two years ago with her new husband. Claire now shares a flat with two other girls, but she quite often comes to stay with me and go sailing. She's very special to me. The nearest thing I have to a daughter.'

For the next two hours they worked together, saying little. To the west, threatening clouds began to build up. Edward glanced at them. 'I think we'll postpone varnishing the hatch. The cold front is nearly upon us. Let's have lunch.'

Adam followed Edward down the companionway ladder and stepped into a cramped world of bunks, benches and cupboards.

The first spattering of rain fell as the kettle boiled and lunch was being set out on the chart table. Adam looked out of a porthole and watched the heavy rain shatter like sparks on the deck.

'The rain that comes with a cold front is often heavy and squally,' Edward said. 'We may be stuck here for a bit.'

The two of them applied themselves to a leisurely lunch.

Afterwards, Adam put the kettle on for another cup of tea while Edward pulled some old rope out of a locker. He hooked two pieces of thick marlin twine on a nail in a deck beam and braced the two strands apart by a small wooden spreader. Edward then unravelled the old rope and began to cut the loose strands into four inch lengths. 'I'll show you how to make baggywrinkle,' he said.

'Sounds like something from a nursery rhyme.'

Edward chuckled, 'It's those fluffy things you saw halfway up the rigging. They stop the shrouds from chaffing and wearing holes in the sails.'

Outside, dark anvil-shaped clouds grumbled and showered the saltings with heavy rain.

Adam stood up and again looked out of the porthole. 'It certainly is a bleak and lonely place.' He paused before laughing derisively at himself. 'Perhaps appropriate.'

'Have you ever contemplated suicide?' Edward asked matter-of-factly.

Adam was shocked at the question. but Edward's good nature robbed the question of any offence. Adam marshalled his thoughts. 'I flirted with the possibility for a while.'

Applying himself to knotting a piece of rope around the twin marlin stands, Edward continued in his straightforward manner. 'Grief is lonely. And no one can grieve your grief for you.' He glanced at Adam. 'So, let yourself grieve it through. It always takes longer than people think. Grief is a visitor that takes its leave most reluctantly.'

Adam tried to digest what he had heard. 'It's wretched. Sometimes I don't even want to get out of bed.' He paused. 'It's affected my teaching.'

'How?'

'Um ... I just don't want the emotional complication of committing to people any more.'

'Then why did you agree to come with me this weekend?'

'I nearly cancelled it a dozen times, but you seemed safe.'

'Hmm.' Edward stopped and regarded Adam from under his bushy eyebrows. 'Grief is a mechanism our bodies use to cope with loss. Whilst it is never pleasant, grief can and should be healthy, not self-destructive.' He turned back to his work. 'I would be deeply saddened if you allowed your grief to do you harm.'

Adam was surprised to learn his wellbeing mattered to Edward. The realisation both warmed and disturbed him.

Edward glanced at him. 'The trauma you are facing concerns things much more fundamental than you may realise.'

Adam said nothing.

Edward pointed to him with the short piece of rope he held. 'You, of all people, being a biologist, should understand what an outrageous miracle life is. There are billions of ways in which this universe could have been chaotic if it were simply the product of blind chance. But it isn't. It hangs together with mathematics that is as beautiful as it is profound.' He waved his hand with passion. 'Why are the physical laws of nature both beautiful and universal? Why are they comprehensible to us?' Edward put the piece of rope between his teeth, but still managed to say, 'If you need a miracle to persuade you life is sacred—then look in the mirror.'

He took the piece of rope from his mouth and hitched it round the two lengths of marlin. 'If there is a God, then you have a purpose to fulfil. And if there is no God, then you have the responsibility to live and make the most of the most preposterous, unlikely event it is possible to imagine and make it mean something.' He pointed at Adam. 'You need to recover your sense of wonder and discover your part in it all. Because unless you do, you will hold your life lightly and be foolish with it. You certainly won't have the drive or passion to teach well.'

Edward picked up another piece of unravelled rope. 'Now watch. Put a piece of rope behind the twin lines of marlin and fold the ends around and through the middle in a cow hitch. Pull it tight and slide it up to the top.'

'You think life has a purpose?'

'The real point is, do you?'

Silence followed.

Adam shook his head slowly. 'You think we all have some sort of obligation to fulfil in life?'

Edward, now with a knife between his teeth, nodded as he hitched on another small piece of rope.

'What if I reject that obligation?'

Edward took the knife from his mouth, 'It would be an unconscionable waste. And anyway, it's not just your decision, so you don't have the right.'

Adam was unable to suppress a smile at Edward's audacity.

'None of us lives in isolation. We belong to each other, and so each of us needs to bear the pain, joy, fallibilities and foibles of love.' He waved a hand. 'Despite the current fad of people trying to live only for themselves, the fact remains: we can't.

We are all inescapably trapped in relationships in which we have a claim on others and they have a claim on us. You are simply not yours to dispose of as you will. You don't have the right.'

Adam felt *Sanderling* lurch and bump gently as the water began to bear her afloat.

Edward reached for his mug of tea and looked at Adam with a hint of challenge. 'You will make some good friends as you go through life. But tell me, if one of them falls sick and dies, will you regret ever having been their friend?'

'Is that why you said I'd been fortunate having had my time with Amanda?' said Adam slowly.

Edward nodded. '*Sanderling* was not the first boat I have owned. Thirty years ago, I had a lovely twenty-four foot yawl called *Vanda.* We sailed together for six years before she was driven ashore from her mooring in a storm and broke up. I have to say to you that losing her was a grief but it did not stop my love of sailing or cause me to regret the fun I had with her.'

Adam shook his head in irritation. 'Bad analogy. Boats are inanimate objects. Amanda was not.'

'Tell me the difference.'

'Don't be absurd. You give your heart to one in a relationship that is infinitely more important than bits of wood connected together to make a boat.'

'You're angry I should so demean the value of human relationships?'

'Yes,' Adam said savagely.

'But I'm not seeking to destroy one. You are.'

Adam was silent.

Edward smiled. 'It is not relationships you need to fear or flee; it is those things which destroy them, you need to rage against. It's not noninvolvement you need. You need to be passionately involved in order to protect "non-inanimate" objects from meaningless waste. You need to value the miracle of life. You need to value your relationships. You need to fight for your students like a tiger fights for her cubs and rescue them from anything that destroys their potential.' He slapped his hand on the chart table. 'So, fight meaninglessness and waste wherever you see it. Hate it. Wage war against it. Don't let destruction, chaos and meaninglessness win.'

Adam was stung by his words. In just a few minutes, Edward had tossed his beliefs and values into the air and they hadn't yet had time to land in their new places. He said nothing for a long while. Eventually he asked, 'Why is there pain and suffering?'

Edward hitched up another strand of baggywrinkle. 'You'll never ask a more profound question. Let me be the first to say that I don't know all the answers.' He reached for a knife to cut a fresh piece of old rope. 'The insights I do have are influenced by my faith so they may not be helpful to you.'

'Don't tell me you believe it's God's plan that bad things happen. Quite frankly, if that's the case, I want nothing to do with him.'

Edward's equanimity was not in the least disturbed by Adam's tone. 'I wouldn't blame you. No, it's more complex than that.'

'Well?'

'The world is an imperfect place. It's bearing the consequences of us having the free-will to damage ourselves.'

'So we just grin and bear it. What's the point of being religious, then?'

Edward leant back from his baggywrinkle. 'If you simply want a God to wear around your neck like a good luck charm to stop bad things from happening to you, forget it. Christianity never was intended to make life comfortable.'

'Belief in God seems pretty useless then.'

'It would be, if my faith didn't also compel me to address suffering wherever I come across it.'

'You don't have to be a Christian to do good. Plenty of people do good.'

Edward frowned. 'Think bigger, Adam. It's not just a question of doing good. It's the reason why good is good. It's what guarantees what is good. Fundamentally, it's not just about morality. It's about what is true.'

Adam was completely unused to this type of conversation. He had sought to protect his own freedom in the past by not thinking much about spiritual responsibilities and had been content to justify his position by holding on to a number of preconceptions and generalisations. Having his grief-induced self-absorption challenged was unsettling. For the first time in many months, Adam caught a glimpse of the sort of person he had allowed himself to become, and wasn't sure he liked what he saw.

Edward broke into his reverie. 'What's the weather doing?'

Relieved to be distracted, Adam looked through the porthole. 'The horizon's dropped away and I can't see much over the edge. It's stopped raining and there's some sunlight breaking through.'

'Right, let's get going. We'll take *Sanderling* round to the hard, pick up the dinghy and moor in the river so we can cast off any time we want to tomorrow. If you could stow the mugs, I'll coax the "iron staysail" into life.'

Edward folded up a section of the companionway ladder and opened a hatch to reveal the diesel engine. He fiddled briefly, replaced the hatch and pushed a button above the chart table.

The peace was shattered as the diesel chugged into life and settled into a steady, vibrating rumble.

When Adam came out on deck, he was amazed. The entire vista had changed. The muddy gullies were now filled with water. *Sanderling* and the boats nearby were floating, nudging and testing their mooring lines. It was now a flat landscape with the water almost level with the low scrubby vegetation on top of the mud-banks. To the east, the rain shadows were retreating. To the west, the lowering sun shone optimistically, lending warm highlights to the boats and channels.

Edward became businesslike. 'I'll take in her stern line and the aft spring. We'll single up on the bowline and forward spring. Would you be able to unhitch the last bight on the cleat with your good arm, and pull in that line when I give the word?'

Adam understood enough to nod.

Edward gave the engine a burst so that the stern kicked away from the pylon. He then gave the word for the remaining mooring lines to be brought aboard. Leaning on the long, curving tiller, he reversed *Sanderling* out of her snug into the channel. Once in mid-channel, he swung the tiller over and eased the throttle forward, aiming the long bowsprit towards the village.

A few minutes later, *Sanderling* nudged gently alongside the wharf beside the slipway. Adam sprang ashore and fastened the bow-line around a bollard. Edward made the stern fast and walked across to a small pier where several dinghies were moored. After some minutes, he appeared from behind a gaggle of boats, standing up in a dinghy, sculling it along with practised ease using a single oar over the stern.

With the dinghy in tow, they motored *Sanderling* back down the main channel.

Some moments later, Edward nosed *Sanderling* against a pink mooring buoy and clambered forward with a boat hook to haul it inboard. After making the line fast to the Sampson post, he made his way back and switched off the engine. A hush descended and both men sat on the deckhouse roof, nursing mugs of tea.

Twilight came and the light of the day filtered away like a reluctant lover.

'You were pretty tough on me today, Edward.' said Adam.

'Perhaps you're worth fighting for.'

Chapter 10

Next morning, Adam crept downstairs from his cottage bedroom, unsure whether Edward was awake or not. He needn't have worried.

Edward was sitting at a small table in the sunroom, inspecting what looked to be maps of building sites. He smiled, rose to his feet and gestured to the maps. 'A little hobby of mine: the historian in me refuses to die. These are modern plans of the abbey and school precincts. I'm superimposing on them the position of the ancient Roman settlement that once existed there. I've been collecting the information about it for years from various archives.' Edward clapped his hands and rubbed them in anticipation. 'Now ... breakfast. My standard is coffee, fresh fruit, toast and ginger marmalade. Will that do?'

'Sounds great.'

'I suggest we pack a haversack, walk down to the hard, varnish the forward hatch on *Sanderling,* then go for a walk along the sea wall. There are ruins of an old fort on the point. We can have lunch there.'

They walked through the village, stopping to buy two crusty pork pies for their lunch. Adam eyed them with some suspicion. A pie had been cut in half for display purposes and Adam wasn't sure it was actually a selling point.

Edward took Adam across to a large boatbuilder's shed that flanked one side of the hard. 'I'll just get another tube of joint sealant while I'm here.' They walked into a front office that obviously doubled as a small chandlery. No one was there. Edward pushed through a door behind the counter into the boatshed following the sound of loud music coming from inside. Adam trailed behind.

A young man was standing beside a partly rebuilt wooden hull. Adam watched as the man pushed a loose-armed bevel up each wooden rib so it banged against the last plank put in place. He then transferred the angle on the bevel to a piece of thin board with a pencil.

'Hi Stan,' yelled Edward.

Stan looked up and reached over to switch the radio off. Edward introduced him to Adam.

'An Aussie, eh.' Stan grinned. 'We won't talk about the cricket, then. Too depressing.'

Adam nodded to the hull. 'What are you doing here?'

'This is *Eleanor.* She's just about a total rebuild. The ol' darlin' was built locally ninety years ago, so we probably can't complain.'

'Wow. How long does it take to rebuild? It must cost a fortune.'

Stan laughed. 'If you 'ave to ask, you probably can't afford it. But sadly, the money don't all go to me.'

'How long does it take?'

'We do about one plank a day. We need to measure up, shape the plank, steam it and fix it into place. It's a long job.'

Adam couldn't help but feel glad there were at least some boat builders still in existence using traditional methods.

Stan showed Adam round the hull. '*Eleanor*'s about eighteen tonnes and draws about six feet. She's twelve feet wide and forty-four feet long, so she's nearly ten feet longer than *Sanderling.* That means she could fish deeper waters. They could fill her with four hundred bushels of fish and sail her back to port with 'er decks awash.' Stan pointed to the keel. 'She's got an oak keel, grown oak ribs and is planked with pitch pine. I've got a bit of yew which I'll use for the planks near the keel because it resists water well.'

'Can you still get the wood?' Adam asked.

'It's difficult. We have to use imported exotic woods more and more these days, because the local wood is so hard to get.'

As they walked out of Stan's shed, Edward said, 'Life is full of fascination, isn't it?'

Adam didn't reply.

Soon they were in the dinghy, wiggling side to side towards *Sanderling* as Edward stood up in the stern, sculling over the back with an oar.

'One day, you'll have to show me how to do that,' Adam said.

***

Two hours later, they were walking along the earthen sea wall, away from the village towards the point. Flocks of dunlin were standing on a low mud-bank and a pair of oystercatchers was strutting in the shallows with their bright orange beaks. Out in the estuary a number of sailing boats could be seen leaning to the wind.

Edward pointed to the thin, wooden poles that could be seen protruding from the water. Some were wearing tufts of seaweed which blew out like flags. 'They're called withies. They mark the position of old oyster beds. There were three main species cultivated in this area. The best was the "Native". It is said that one worthy gentleman once swallowed eleven dozen in a single sitting at an oyster feast years ago—which I guess is testimony enough to their quality. But, sadly, an imported disease wiped out the oysters years ago.'

Inland, a heron stood hunched and still in a drainage channel.

'This area has a fairly savage history. The Norse, Saxons and Danes all fought over it when the Romans left.

Some of the stones in the ruins we're walking to came from the remains of an earlier Roman fortress.' His voice became wistful. 'If only they could speak.'

'What do you think they'd say?'

'They'd tell tales of Viking invasions; of graceful, lightweight boats crossing the stormiest seas to plunder, extort and trade.' Edward ran his hand through some dried stalks of grass. 'The Vikings were deservedly feared. Courage in battle was embedded in their very culture and beliefs. Only the finest warriors were summoned to dine in Odin's banqueting hall after their death. As a result, they scorned fear—and pillaged and enslaved wherever they went.' He paused. 'Did you know that the Viking slave market in Dublin was once the largest slave market in the world?'

Adam shook his head. 'I know next to nothing about them, other than they wore horned helmets and had an uncommon fondness for violence.'

Edward chuckled. 'The Vikings certainly loved a fight. Many became mercenaries. They formed the backbone of the Varangian Guard, an elite unit of the Byzantine army between the ninth and fourteenth centuries.' He paused a moment before continuing, 'Vikings put a high value on loyalty and so, were the only ones considered trustworthy enough to be the personal bodyguards of the emperor.'

'Good people to have on your side.' Edward nodded.

An hour later, they arrived at the end of the point jutting out into the estuary. It had a small beach of shell grit, sand and mud. Inland were the tumbled remains of old stone walls, their bases rubbed bare of grass by sheep seeking shelter from the freezing north-easterly winds. Adam and Edward sat with their backs against one of the walls, admiring the view over the estuary and eating lunch.

Rather to his surprise, Adam enjoyed his pork pie. 'How did you know I was thinking of packing-in teaching and leaving?'

Edward ignored the question. 'Are you?'

'I don't know.'

'You can choose to be a casualty all your life or you can choose to take control. You can deal with the pain of life by becoming less human and cutting yourself off from people, or you can live the glory of being human and play your part in making things better.' Edward waved a piece of pie in the air as he emphasised his point. 'Life is so terribly, terribly precious. You only get one shot at it. So, will you pursue the best for those who come across your path, or will you run?'

'It's all very well for you to hand out your challenges, Edward, but it's not that easy.' Adam crushed the paper bag that had held his pie into a tight ball. 'Do you think I enjoy being like I am? Do you think I don't care? I see kids in my class who need so much extra help; I'm appalled. Some still need to learn to write basic English and they're in the final two years of their schooling, for goodness' sake!' He screwed his eyes shut in anguish. 'I live in a house with a little girl whose body is encased in fibreglass and metal. It tears me apart. You tell me to charge in and risk more heartbreak. It's easy for you to say, but where will you be, Edward? Because it's me who has to risk it.'

'Where would you like me to be?'

'Out of my face!' said Adam angrily. 'No ... no.' He was instantly contrite. 'Sorry. I would like...' He paused, searching for words to describe the indescribable. 'I need someone to show me the roses.' He sighed. 'My head tells me I can't live in isolation from others, but my heart may take a while to agree. It's the best I can say right now.'

'That's good enough for me.' Edward placed a hand on his shoulder. 'Don't think for one moment I underestimate what it has cost you to get to this point.'

The shadow of something large appeared from behind the wall where they were sitting. 'Wow! Look at that!' Edward turned around.

A majestic east coast sailing barge was easing its way around the point under full sail. Adam could clearly hear the rush of water being pushed aside by its bluff bow. The huge mainsail was braced by a long sprit-boom sloping backwards from the foot of the main mast. They watched it sail past, leaning over her lowered leeboard.

Edward eased himself stiffly onto his feet. 'That's probably as good a cue as any for us to wend our way back for a pint at *The Plough.*'

That night, Adam slept soundly.

Chapter 11

Next morning, Adam woke to the delicious smell of hot toast. Clumsy with sleep, he looked at his watch. It was early. *Whatever time does Edward get up?* The morning was cold and the sun had not yet risen.

As he was getting dressed, he heard a car pull up in the driveway. The front door banged, voices greeted each other cheerfully and then dulled to a murmur. A woman's laugh reminded Adam that Claire was joining them for the day. A pall of apprehension gripped him. In the peace of this place, he was conscious he'd been through an emotional wringer and wasn't sure he had enough energy left to cope with the cool Miss Claire. He determined, however, to do what he could to allay any tensions between them. He smiled grimly. Let this be the first test for his new resolve to embrace life. 'Sheeesh, it's cold.' He wrapped a blanket around his shoulders and descended the stairs.

Edward was seated with Claire at the breakfast bar. His eyes were dancing as Claire recounted some story with extravagant gestures. 'Good morning, Adam. How did you sleep?'

'Pretty good, thanks, but remind me to send you some insomnia pills. G'day, Claire.'

'Hello,' Claire said.

'I sleep well enough, thanks,' said Edward. 'The heating's only just come on. It should warm up soon.'

Adam shivered. 'No wonder Britain went in search of Australia. They needed a place to thaw out.' He turned to Claire. 'Your uncle is quite a guy. You anticipate a gentle weekend straight out of *Wind in the Willows* and end up being bullied mercilessly in the most charming way. He's dangerous.' Adam pulled the blanket tighter around himself.

'Would you like some coffee?' Claire asked.

Adam nodded. Claire reached for the plunger and poured his coffee. He accepted it gratefully, noticing her long artistic fingers.

'Edward isn't always as benign and innocent as he looks.' Claire smiled.

Adam was intensely relieved that Claire was showing no signs of awkwardness in her reunion with him.

Edward interrupted his thoughts. 'Claire's brought two vacuum flasks of soup but I'm hoping to put in to a pub for lunch, so we won't be needing too much in the way of victuals.' He noticed Adam shivering. 'Dress warmly. *Sanderling*'s decks are very exposed.'

***

Adam sat in the stern of the dinghy, feeling slightly helpless as Edward rowed them all out to *Sanderling*. As they breasted against *Sanderling*'s quarter, Edward brought one oar and rowlock in at the last moment to avoid damaging her side. They climbed on board as the first blush of dawn began to kiss the marshes with gold.

Adam loved it.

Edward and Claire moved around the boat with practised ease, not allowing Adam to do much because of his damaged shoulder. This frustrated him, as it soon became apparent that hoisting sail on a gaff-rigged smack was an intensely physical activity that needed every hand available. Edward explained the sequence and the nautical terms they'd be using, as *Sanderling* was made ready. The sail ties were removed, and Edward and Claire hauled on the mainsail halyards, being careful to keep the gaff horizontal. The huge mainsail climbed into the air. When the throat was as high as it could go, Edward asked Adam to help 'swig' up, by heaving on the halyard one-handed in a series of rhythmic jerks, as Edward pulled the slack rope in around a belaying pin, before making it fast. The gaff peak was then hoisted up so that it cocked up high behind the mast.

Adam asked about the bottom section of the mainsail that remained rolled up and tied along the length of the boom. 'Ah,' said Edward. 'She's a little self-willed and prone to steering into the wind, even in a moderate breeze. If we reef the main, she stays balanced. You'll appreciate it when you get on the helm.'

'Me?' exclaimed Adam, surprised.

'You,' Edward confirmed.

The jib was run out to the end of the bowsprit and hoisted with a block and tackle so that it flapped languidly in the early morning breeze. This was followed by the staysail. It was heavy work. 'Haven't you guys ever heard of winches?' Adam asked.

'Winches! Sacrilege. This, my boy, is the real thing.' Edward turned to Claire. 'We've got wind and current going in the same direction, so it'll be easy enough to sail her off the mooring without using the engine.'

He pointed to the bow. 'Adam, cast off the mooring line and throw it and its marker buoy clear when I give the word. Claire, stand by to back the jib. Right, here we go. Adam, cast off ... Claire, back the jib.'

Slowly, *Sanderling*'s bow edged away from the wind. 'Bring her over,' yelled Edward. The jib snapped across to the other side. *Sanderling* leaned to the wind and came alive as the sound of water began to chuckle down her side. They were sailing.

Claire eased and trimmed the sheets before sitting beside Adam on the deckhouse roof, panting for breath.

'Don't get too comfortable,' warned Edward. 'We'll need to put in a few short tacks before we get out into the estuary.' He turned to Adam. 'Gaffers don't much like tacking into the eye of the wind, but the smack design let's her do it better than most.' He patted the long, curving tiller with affection. 'You just need to be patient and free her off enough to get a bit of speed. Tacking is a fairly leisurely affair on *Sanderling*.'

They butted their way out into the estuary and then bore away with the wind. Adam was surprised at their speed. *Sanderling* was now boiling along in spectacular fashion.

Adam caught Claire looking at him. She looked away. He smiled, rummaged in his haversack, took out his camera and took a photo of her as she turned back round. He caught her as she laughed in protest, her hair streaming in the wind.

Edward then surprised him. 'Come on, Adam. Take the helm.' Then he turned to Claire. 'Teach him.' He walked away from the tiller, leaving it completely unattended, stretched himself out on top of the coach roof and closed his eyes. *Sanderling* sailed on without deviating from her course. It was clear he had implicit faith both in Claire and in his boat.

Adam wasn't sure he shared it. Months of fierce independence and avoiding the need to trust anyone caused him to stiffen with apprehension. While he wanted the experience of controlling the bucking living thing that was *Sanderling,* he struggled with the idea of engaging with anyone who might teach him—particularly someone as disturbing as Claire.

He saw Claire flash him a quizzical look as she shifted over to the helmsman's bench and took hold of the tiller. With a neutral expression back in place, she began to teach. 'Sailing in a straight line requires you to steer in the same direction relative to the wind. This means you must always know where the wind is coming from.'

Adam nodded dumbly.

'Where is the wind coming from?' Claire asked.

Adam moved his head from side to side, feeling the wind on his cheeks before he pointed over the port bow.

'Right. Now come and hold this tiller with me and move it to keep the wind in the same position on your cheek.'

Adam did as he was told. He was intensely aware of her physical presence as he took his place in front of her at the tiller. Her chest and thigh occasionally touched him gently from behind as she guided his hands to help him steady the boat. He could detect the scent of her perfume. It was disorientating. He pulled himself together and applied himself to the task in hand.

After a few minutes, Claire nodded in approval. 'That's good. Now, roll down your woollen hat over your eyes so you can't see, and then steer the boat so you keep the wind in the same position on your cheek.'

He glanced at her in alarm. She smiled. 'Don't worry, I won't be far away.'

Despite the cold, he was conscious of feeling slightly flushed and sweaty.

'You're very tense, Mr Hollingworth. Are you finding it difficult to trust me?'

'No, I'm sure you're ... um...' He tried again. 'It's just that right now, I don't know how to trust myself.'

Claire's voice was a murmur just behind his left ear. 'Then we'll just have to teach you how, won't we?'

Two hours later, Edward announced they would "heave-to" for morning coffee. 'We'll drop the peak and trice up the clew to scandalise the main and take the power out of the mainsail. Then we'll back the jib.'

Adam had no idea what he'd said.

Edward seemed to sense his bewilderment. 'We're setting *Sanderling*'s two sails so they sail against each other. That way, she'll sit balanced and still in the seaway. Should allow us to have morning coffee in relative peace.'

Adam was amazed.

Sitting on the deckhouse roof, eating a muffin, Edward explained, 'They used to dredge for oysters like this. Every fisherman needed to perfect the art of sailing slow. Sometimes they'd even stop. In the off-season they'd go staw-boating for sprats and they'd do that at anchor.'

'Staw-boating?' Adam queried.

'Staw-boating, or stand boating. They'd anchor and drop a net over from the bow. They were pretty big nets with a fifteen foot boom top and bottom held apart by twenty foot garps.'

Adam decided not to ask about garps.

'The tide carried the sprats backwards into the net.' Edward appeared to lose himself in thought for a moment. 'They were hard men in those days ... and they knew their stuff. I don't think I'd fancy doing that in the freezing fog in the midst of the shipping heading into London.' He sighed. 'The old masters knew a thing or two. All lost now, sadly.' He looked up towards some gulls following them optimistically. 'They used to know the depth of the sprats from looking at the seagulls. If they flew close over the water, they were shallow. If they flew high, the sprats were deep. If you understood the signs, you made a living.'

'Extraordinary.' Adam shook his head.

They set sail again, and the wind that had been building in strength throughout the morning began to kick the estuary into steep, spiteful waves. Adam looked at Claire on the helm with some apprehension. Edward dismissed the waves. 'Don't worry about the waves. *Sanderling's* a sea kindly boat, and with her heavy displacement, she'll push straight through without noticing them. And Claire is very good.'

Adam nodded and felt guilty. It soon became apparent that Claire was, indeed, very good. She seemed to relish being on the helm in such weather. He watched her long honey-coloured hair dance in the wind. She was grinning, exulting in their wild ride through the sea.

Towards midday, they surged into an arm of the estuary and headed towards the wharf of the town where Edward planned to stop for lunch. Still some way from the town's moorings, he turned *Sanderling* into the wind and they dropped the mainsail and staysail. Then they ghosted against the tide into the wharf, sailing with the jib alone.

Claire smiled at Adam. 'You do realise that Edward is showing off, just a bit.'

'Just practising basic skills in case the engine should ever fail,' he said loftily.

'I bet you wouldn't, if half the people in Scotty's bar weren't looking at you right now,' she laughed.

'Preposterous insinuation.' Edward smiled. 'But if we're being watched, you two had better look smart with the mooring lines.'

Safely moored, the three of them trooped into the pub by the foreshore. A huge elderly man stood behind the counter, chatting to a patron. When he saw Edward, he raised his voice. 'I 'ad to teach Edward to sail o' course. Forever doing things wrong, 'e was. Kept wanting me to shake out the reef in me sail one calm day, so I says to 'im, "Blast ye boy, you let things be as they are. Don't you change nothin'. There ain't enough wind for what little sail we 'ave got."'

'Afternoon, Scotty.' Edward maintained a straight face. 'Three of your steak and kidney lunches if you please, but only if you can promise that you didn't make them.' He turned to Adam. 'I once used his gravy to caulk my deck planks. Didn't leak for ten years and killed the rats into the bargain.'

More good-natured banter followed and the three of them were soon ensconced at a table by the window enjoying an excellent lunch.

***

Adam was still finishing his pie when Edward got up to have a brief chat with Scotty. He came back a short while later. 'I might just have a look behind Emmerson's boat shed. Scotty tells me there's a salvaged top-mast there. I'll meet you outside in a couple of minutes.' He headed towards the front door.

A minute later, Adam and Claire got up to join Edward, but chose first to detour via the toilets. As they walked down the corridor, Adam paused to inspect the darkening clouds through a small window. He noticed four youths wearing rolled up balaclavas, making their way across the vacant block outside. He would have dismissed the sight, but one of them started trailing off behind Edward round the back of a flat-roofed warehouse on the far side of the waste ground. Adam's concern gave way to alarm when the others followed, rolling down their balaclavas to cover their faces.

Adam grabbed Claire's arm. 'Claire, get help. Edward may be getting mugged.' Claire's face froze in surprise as he leapt for the side door and sprinted across the waste ground with the loop of his sling flailing around his neck like a scarf.

Adam ran straight at the window of the warehouse, leaping at the last second to plant a rubber-soled foot on a window ledge and bounce into the air. He caught hold of the roof parapet with his hands. A searing pain in his left arm told him his already-traumatised limb had been further damaged. He ignored it and pulled himself up onto the roof. Once on top, he crept to the far edge.

He was too late.

Below him, two youths had Edward pinned against a rack of old timber behind the boatshed, and a third was holding a knife to his throat.

Below Adam, the fourth youth was standing, apparently on guard, at the end of the warehouse. Adam dropped on top of him from three metres. As he landed, he crashed his good elbow between the youth's neck and shoulder. The youth collapsed onto his back. He was thickset and powerfully-built. Adam knelt across his neck, pushed his thumb into the bottom of his eye socket and yelled to the young man with the knife, 'Back off, or your boyfriend loses an eye.'

The man with the knife turned. 'What the...?'

Adam snarled. 'You can't afford the trouble. Leave the old man alone and you're free to fight another day.'

Underneath him, the youth started to squirm, attempting to heave him off.

Keep the initiative. Adam pushed his thumb into the youth's eye socket. 'Don't move, you bastard, or you'll die.' The youth went still.

The young man with the knife stepped back from Edward and closed his flick-knife with defiant showmanship.

'Keep well clear of me when you go...' Adam yelled, '...and I'll let the kid go.'

The youth nodded to his accomplices to move off. As they did so, the youth with the knife spun round and hit Edward in the stomach with a vicious blow. Then, he turned to circle around Adam, pulling his knife out and holding it in a way that betrayed a degree of competence.

Adam was beginning to think he was losing control of the situation when Scotty, in all his massive bulk, rounded the corner brandishing a heavy walking stick. Claire was close behind.

The youth with the knife backed away.

Adam stepped off his victim and allowed him to crawl towards the other two youths who pulled him to his feet. Together, they set off in a stumbling run. The knife-wielder slashed in defiance at Scotty as he ran past, but he was well out of range.

Adam leapt across to Edward who was doubled over on his knees, retching. 'Are you okay?'

Edward wheezed, coughed and then retched again.

Claire dropped to her knees and took Edward's head in her hands. 'Edward, Edward, what happened? Are you all right?'

Scotty lumbered up behind muttering an impressive list of invectives. 'Damn and blast, but they gone 'afore I could swear at 'em.' He turned his attention to Edward. 'You need an ambulance?'

Edward shook his head. 'I'm fine. Just need...' He retched again. '...a bit of time.'

Adam rocked back onto his heels. 'Look after him.' He sprang to his feet, looked round the corner of the warehouse and started to run. He burst out onto the street, searching for the attackers. He spotted them diving down a side street. Adam sprinted after them, jinking left and right to avoid pedestrians.

As he came to a corner, he saw his quarry run into a space between two rows of terraced buildings. Adam raced down the narrow street until he reached the dirt driveway. Cautiously, he edged down it. Adam could see that it opened out into a vacant block used as a car park.

He heard car doors slamming shut. A white sedan was reversing out of a row of cars.

Adam glanced sideways. Parked beside the driveway, behind one of the buildings was a large industrial waste bin. It stood on four small metal wheels. He jumped round to the end of it and started to push. It was heavy and reluctant to move. Adam heaved with all his might.

A scream of tyres told him he'd been seen. However, the bin was now rumbling into the driveway beginning to block it off. The car roared towards the closing gap. Adam had a fleeting impression of fat tyres, mag wheels and a snarling modified exhaust.

He pushed with every fibre of his being. *C'mon, c'mon.* The car sped forward. Six metres away, the driver stamped on the brakes. The car skidded in a pall of blue smoke and crashed simultaneously into both the bin and the brick wall of the adjacent building.

The bin jerked sideways under the force of the impact, teetering on two wheels before crashing upright again. The car revved and spun its tyres, reversing backwards before skidding to a halt. The four youths began scrambling out of the car.

Stay in control. It's all or nothing. Adam ran at the front passenger door, leapt into the air and crashed against it with two feet. The youth getting out had one foot on the ground and was pushing the door open with a hand holding a knife. The door smashed shut against his leg.

Adam bounced up from the ground and looked desperately for something to arm himself with. He snapped off the car aerial and vaulted onto the top of the waste bin. It was the only place where he could defend himself.

The youths had all removed their balaclavas and he could see the human face of rage and hatred in all its rawness. He could also sense their fear and desperation and knew it to be a highly dangerous mixture.

Two of them began to push the bin, with Adam on top, back from the entrance. The third youth crept around it, seeking a way to attack. Adam bounded forward and slashed with the aerial at the two who were pushing, opening up the cheek of one of them in a deep cut. They fell back.

One of the youths ran back to the car and returned with an extendible steering wheel lock. He flailed at Adam's legs while the others pushed the bin backwards. Adam stayed on top, dancing and swinging his aerial like a monkey on a barrel organ. Once the bin was pushed to one side, the youths ran back to the car to join their wounded comrade.

In their zeal to start the car, they stalled the engine but soon had it revving again. Adam wasted no time. He jumped down and once again pushed the bin forward to close off their escape route.

However, he wasn't quite quick enough. The bin crashed into the side of the car as it accelerated forward. The vehicle scraped its way between the bin and the side wall until it broke free and roared up the driveway.

Adam raced forward to try and read the number plate. The car skidded to a halt. The engine howled as its wheels spun in reverse. It surged backwards at him.

Adam leapt sideways behind the protection of the building, as the car smashed into the bin.

He lay sprawled on the ground. Beside him a downpipe ran from the roof guttering into a drain. The drain was covered by a metal plate. He snatched up the steel plate, got to his feet and hurled it through the rear side window of the car.

He had the momentary impression of it crashing into a face.

The battered car accelerated back up the drive, swung into the roadway and sped off.

***

A police car arrived, with lights and sirens blaring, moments after Adam's attackers drove off. The officers checked that Adam didn't need immediate medical attention and satisfied themselves with the essential details of what had happened. One of them retrieved the knife dropped by one of the attackers.

Pain and depression began to sink chilly fingers into him as he came off his adrenaline high.

The police sergeant asked Adam to tell him again what had happened as he checked the salient details off on his notes.

'The car will have sustained significant damage to its front end. Both sides of the car will also be badly scarred. The rear end will have some damage ... and the aerial will be missing.'

The policeman nodded towards Adam's sore arm. 'Did they do that to you?'

'No, my arm was in a sling before.'

'Let me get this right. You tell me one of these guys will have a damaged leg—quite possibly broken, the driver will have a deep cut on his right cheek.' He checked his notes. 'One possibly has a smashed face ... and you did all this with one arm?' He looked at Adam sharply. 'What do you do when you're really pissed off?' He pursed his lips. 'I suggest you let us catch the bad guys next time. It might result in less collateral damage.'

The sergeant went on to say that, in view of the damage inflicted, and what was known about the assailants, there was some chance they would be caught. The likelihood was, however, they would go to ground somewhere, probably in London. Their details would be circulated around local doctors and hospitals.

An hour later, Adam was driven to the local doctor's surgery. He was surprised to find Edward and Claire still there.

'Edward's refused to go to hospital but the doctor has insisted he stay here under observation for a while.' Claire held Edward's hand as he lay with his eyes closed on a gurney.

Adam noticed a brief spasm shake his body. He was obviously still in shock. Adam picked up a folded blanket beside him and pulled it over him. Edward opened his eyes and acknowledged him with a tired wave. 'I'm as right as rain. Just a bit sore.'

Claire sniffed. 'The doctor wanted Edward to stay in the local hospital overnight but Edward insisted that he would sleep better on *Sanderling*.'

'Of course I will,' said Edward. 'We'll spend a quiet evening here and sail *Sanderling* back to her berth tomorrow.'

Before Adam could voice his opinion, he was summoned to the surgery where his arm was examined and re-strapped. The doctor told him he had put back its healing by at least two weeks. Adam grunted. He could only imagine what Gareth might say about that.

When he returned to Edward and Claire, he discovered Scotty had arrived to collect them from the clinic. 'I'll take you back to *Sanderling,* but you'll be eating in my restaurant this evening—on the house.' He snorted. 'My apology for not 'itting any of them bastards.'

***

They had a quiet meal. Adam watched Claire occasionally put her hand over Edward's, as if to reassure herself he was still there.

Edward turned to Adam with an appraising look. 'What triggered you?'

He shrugged—then wished he hadn't. Pain shot through his shoulder. 'You needed help.'

'You were...' Edward paused. 'You were very convincing.'

Adam smiled tiredly. 'Are you concerned that you've created a monster?'

'No, no. It was all just ... a bit sudden.'

After their meal, they walked back to the wharf where *Sanderling* was moored, and prepared for the night. Bed linen was found and the beds were made up. Claire and Edward prepared their beds on the two bunks in the main salon. Adam was tucked into the narrow cot that ran aft beside the engine bay.

When they had finished, Edward went up on deck to secure the halyards so they wouldn't bang in the wind during the night. Claire sat on her bunk with her knees drawn up under her chin. She watched as Adam poured hot water into a coffee plunger. 'Thanks for helping Edward. He's very special to me.'

'I know.'

The golden glow of the gimballed oil lamp turned the deck beams the colour of dark honey ... *the colour of her—*

She interrupted his thinking. 'You deceived me.'

Adam raised an eyebrow.

Claire continued. 'You let me continue in the mistaken belief that you were given the brass rubbing. Why?'

'It wasn't important.'

'Why?'

'Things were complicated enough.'

'I must have sounded like an ungrateful prude.'

'I didn't think so.'

Edward came back down the companionway steps.

Adam picked up the bottle of Tia Maria he had bought and handed it to Claire. 'Here.' He reached round for some mugs. 'Can you open that?'

Claire opened the bottle and returned it. Adam poured three mugs of coffee and topped them up with generous slugs of the liqueur.

Edward nodded gratefully as he passed him his drink.

Adam picked up the other two mugs in one hand and followed Claire up on deck.

Claire sat on the end of the curving thwart and wedged herself against the bulwark. She accepted one of the mugs from Adam and folded her arms, hugging the jacket around her.

The clouds had passed. It was a clear night.

Content with silence, they sat together watching the moon-silvered wavelets of the estuary.

Chapter 12

Edward returned Adam to his lodgings two days later. After waving farewell, he drove at a leisurely pace back to the saltings. Preparations needed to be made for laying up *Sanderling* for the winter. However, when he climbed back on board his boat, the aches in his body protested so much that he gave up and slumped into his chair at the chart table. Seeking an excuse to distract himself, he rummaged in the drawer under the table and withdrew a package wrapped in tissue. Two folded letters sat underneath the package.

One was a report of forensic tests that determined the skeletal remains uncovered by the recent dredging of the channel were centuries old. The other was a letter from the geological department of the University of London. He'd read it many times. It told him what this strange stone was, the stone that had saved him. The semi-precious stone was cordierite. The Vikings had called it 'sunstone' and used it to help them navigate on cloudy days.

He unwrapped the stone and gazed at it—his very own Viking stone. Then, with a grunt of pain, he heaved himself up and clambered out of the hatchway. He crossed the deck to the pontoon and made his way across the saltings.

Alone on a marshy hummock, Edward held the crystal up to a leaden sky and turned it slowly. The blue of the crystal reflected the chill of the day. A bitter Siberian wind was gusting over the marshes and the boats themselves seemed to huddle deeper into their mud berths. Standing with an arm upraised, Edward knew he must look like an ancient priest making oblation to the gods. But he was intrigued. He wanted to find out. He recalled the Halfdan Saga:

'The weather was thick and stormy ... Leif the Navigator looked about and saw no blue sky. Then he took the Viking sunstone and held it up, and saw where the light beamed from the stone.'

Was it true? Would his Viking stone work?

He thought of Adam and asked himself again: Would it work? Had he done enough to rescue a future for Adam?

He turned the stone some more as he held it aloft. Nothing happened. A pall of disappointment was beginning to form when, suddenly, the crystal changed from chilly blue to liquid gold.

Edward stared at it with delight. Yes, it worked. He smiled, lowered the Viking stone and trudged his way back to *Sanderling*.

***

Adam followed Janice into the headmaster's study and heard her close the door behind him discreetly.

Trapped.

The headmaster rolled himself back from the computer desk on his office chair. He swivelled round and asked 'Adam, how can I help you?'

Adam wasn't looking forward to this interview. Nothing about it was going to be easy. He swept a hand over his unruly hair as he accepted the proffered chair.

The headmaster waited for him to speak. Adam began moving his mouth as if sucking on a collection of marbles. *For goodness sake, spit it out, man.*

He swallowed, and tried again. 'I believe the school is failing the boys I teach, particularly those in their final two years of study. I, most certainly, am failing them.'

The headmaster remained silent.

'They choose biology so they can hide from literary self-expression, abstract concepts and their smarter peers.' Adam felt his passion starting to rise. He waved a hand in exasperation. 'Most of them think in simple concrete ways and don't really fit in to the school's current academic set-up. As a result, they band together to encourage each other in their underachievement.' He passed a hand wearily across his face. 'For my part, I've played the game and trotted out the prescribed academic syllabus while they serve out their time at school. I teach them in an antiquated Victorian building with the minimum of modern facilities and I'm furnished with lab equipment handed down from the last refurbishment of the physics laboratory.' He shrugged. 'I don't want to do things this way any more.'

The headmaster retained the guarded expression of a poker player. 'Over half our buildings date from before Queen Victoria, but I hear what you are saying. What do you propose?'

'I want to suggest we change the current examination curriculum in favour of one from another examining body, one that places more emphasis on practical research projects and continual assessment. These boys would do better with practical assignments they can get their teeth into.' Adam took a deep breath. 'I'd also like to address their literary difficulties. The boys would have more confidence if they could type their assignments on a computer that flags wrong spelling and grammar. Then they wouldn't be intimidated by poor handwriting and copious amounts of red ink correcting their English. It would also help develop the computer skills needed in the workplace these days.' He stopped.

Only the ticking of the clock on the mantelpiece broke the silence. *Tick tock, tick tock.*

Eventually, the Headmaster said, 'What would this mean?'

Hardly believing his outburst was being taken seriously, Adam pressed on. 'It would mean sixteen networked computers on the benches of the second biology lab. These would need to have Internet access and be networked to my computer at the front desk. Because they are not in the main teaching lab, they can be available for use in free periods. This will encourage the boys to do their assignments in school hours when help and facilities are available.' He drew a deep breath. 'I've had to make use of transparencies and an overhead projector. This means I can't easily access the excellent multimedia resources that are now available on the Internet. So, I'd also like to have a data projector in the main teaching lab linked with a computer. That's a minimum. An electronic whiteboard would be a help as well.' He tapped a fist into a hand. 'Multimedia would be such a help in teaching these boys.

They, more than most, gain information visually rather than through the spoken word.'

'It takes more than advanced technology to teach a boy,' said the Headmaster. 'How committed will you be to them?'

This was the key question. *How much does it matter to me?* Adam was surprised to hear himself say, 'I want these tools to help me motivate them to take up the challenge of new possibilities.' He straightened in his chair. 'There is no reason for you to believe that I will be committed to them on the basis of my teaching up until now—but I believe I can ... that we should ... do better.'

The headmaster regarded him for a long time. 'Do you have the costings of your proposal in writing?'

Adam handed a folder across to him.

The headmaster raised an eyebrow, took it and placed it on the desk. 'Leave it with me and I'll let you know.'

Adam exhaled slowly to release his tension, nodded, and took his leave.

***

Half a minute later, Janice was surprised to hear what sounded like a whoop coming from the headmaster's office.

***

The young man woke to the familiar sour smell of his dingy room. He hated the place. It was a converted storeroom at the back of a fish and chip shop. It was all he could afford, but that would soon change. Everything would change. In fact, things were already changing. He reflected back on the previous evening, dwelling pleasurably on what had happened. The woman had been small, gaunt and thin, her face hard and pinched—a wreckage of once-good looks. She had harped on at him over and over to give her the stuff. He'd have the money next week, she promised.

The young man shivered. No way! Never again.

In the early days, he had been two hundred pounds short because he had given stuff to a long-term local on credit. He remembered the horror of learning the long-term local had abruptly decided not to remain local. He'd disappeared from the area, leaving a string of debts. That's when he'd made his only mistake.

He'd tried to pass on the bad debt to his supplier. He'd written a note laboriously in his simple block handwriting at the bottom of the "order form", explaining that someone had not paid. The money would be two hundred pounds short. He'd placed it in the small self-sealing plastic bag with the rest of the money, more money than he would ever have imagined himself handling the year before. Surely, the man wouldn't begrudge two hundred pounds. He himself couldn't pay it, at least, not without selling his bike. He'd just done a lot of work on it. He didn't want to lose it now.

The young man shuddered as he glanced at the racing-car sticker on the middle of his bed head. It advertised motor oil. He'd used it to cover the single bullet hole he'd found there three days after he had delivered his note. On his pillow was the small piece of paper torn from his own note. It only contained three words: 'Two hundred pounds.'

He'd sold the bike the next day.

No, he would never get caught like that again. But she had kept on and on at him. He was telling her to piss off when she'd offered him sex as payment. It dawned on him that a whole new range of possibilities now lay open to him. After assuring himself he had the funds to cover her small shortfall, he'd tormented her by a protracted show of reluctance until grudgingly agreeing to the contract.

He'd brought her to his room and ordered her to strip. She'd wanted to take things slower. Making a half-hearted attempt to fake affection, she'd tried to kiss him. This had simply irritated him, so he'd slapped her.

He knew she was desperate for the stuff. He'd watched her eyes dart to the package he'd left to tantalise her on the chest of drawers. She'd cried, then wheedled ... and then complied.

***

A persistent drizzle floated from a leaden sky to soak the already saturated turf of the playing field. Adam was glad of his oiled stockman's coat. His head, however, was uncovered. He wiped the rain from his face as he stared speculatively at the rough ground falling away from the playing fields behind the groundsman's sheds.

He was disturbed in his reverie by the sound of someone squelching through the soggy turf behind him. Turning, he discovered Margaret Pemberton coming towards him, huddled under an umbrella. 'I saw you from the path. You make a melancholy picture standing in the rain. So, in the interests of avoiding you queuing up at my surgery with pneumonia, may I share my umbrella with you?'

'Ah, Margaret. Thanks. What's the time?'

'Teatime.'

'You call dinner, "tea"; and you have dinner at lunchtime. Your supper can either mean dinner or a bedtime drink of Horlicks and Scotch Finger biscuits. It's all very confusing to an Australian.'

'From a nation with furry animals that lay eggs, I'd air such bemusements with restraint.'

'Ah, our platypus. One of nature's more playful inventions.'

Forced close together under the umbrella, Adam helped guide Margaret through the muddy turf towards the path to the boarding house. Nothing was said until one incautious step caused Margaret to slip and start toppling backwards. Adam caught her, winced with the pain in his arm, and restored her balance. Without a word, he offered his good arm and continued to escort her to the security of the path.

He expected Margaret to pull free once they had escaped the soggy turf, but they walked arm in arm until they reached the foyer of the boarding house. There, he helped remove her steaming coat.

The dinner bell rang and she made to move off.

Adam said quietly, 'Thanks Margaret ... for caring, and being safe.'

She looked at him and nodded before joining a stream of boys jostling into the dining hall.

***

Adam was preparing to don his coat for the walk back to his lodgings when Gareth intercepted him and steered him into his study.

'Why am I already beginning to worry about the reason for this?' Adam sank into one of Gareth's armchairs.

'"Prick me, do I not bleed?"' Gareth quipped. 'I am shocked and deeply wounded you could think for one moment I would have anything but your best interests at heart.' He set about pouring Adam a cup of coffee from a percolator he seemed to have permanently in use. 'Merely a small case of subterfuge in the cause of freedom and emancipation.'

'Whose freedom and emancipation did you have in mind?'

'Ah,' Gareth played a drum roll with his forefingers on his desktop. 'The elusive and immutable Miss Pemberton.'

'Has it occurred to you that Margaret may be perfectly happy eluding you and being immutable?'

Gareth considered this for a moment. 'Not possible. Not only would it be too wounding to think that my charm could be so ineffectual, but I think, I really do think, it would be good for her to break out a bit and have some fun.'

'If Margaret is hurt in your quest for fun, I shall rearrange the giblets in your abdominal cavity in alphabetical order.'

'I'm talking about her fun, not my fun,' Gareth protested.

Adam shot him a sharp look.

Gareth sighed. 'Seriously, boyo, I'm not such a dunce as to fail to understand that fun can only happen if she feels socially secure. In fact...' His tone became more serious. '...I suspect that winning trust is the key issue—and that it will take some time to win.'

'Hmm. What were you planning?'

Gareth returned to his ebullient self and rubbed his hands. 'It's great. I'm very proud of it. We've discovered she is a closet-reader of poetry, and I...' He gave another drum roll ... 'have discovered a fantastic evening of drama and poetry in London in two weeks' time. The trick will be to get her there. I will make sure she sees the advert. She will, I'm fairly sure, fill in the coupon for a ticket. Your job is to intercept the letter to the booking agent. It won't be hard.'

Adam rolled his eyes. Gareth pressed on. 'You take the boarding house mail to the mailbox every evening. Just look for a letter addressed to the agent and give it to me. I will open it and put a postscript to her order-form asking for another ticket to a seat next to Margaret's, append my credit-card details and then send it off asking them to send both tickets to me. When they come, I'll transfer her ticket to another envelope and address it to her. I'll smudge some black ink across the stamp to make it look as if it's been franked. Can you imagine what she'll think when I come and sit beside her in London. We'd have to talk about poetry, perhaps go for a small meal somewhere and *voilà,* the ice will begin to thaw.'

'The trouble with the scheme is that I can imagine exactly what she would think if she found herself sitting, "quite by accident", next to you in a London theatre. It's outrageous, Gareth. There's no way I can be an accessory to you tampering with other people's mail.' He paused and massaged his forehead. 'Where's the advert for this poetry thing?'

Gareth protested. 'But...'

'But nothing. Where is it?'

Gareth, sighed, reached over to his pin board and unpinned a flier. Adam took it and waved Gareth away from the desk, so he could gain access to the telephone. After scanning the internal phone directory, he found Margaret's number and rang it. A few moments later, she answered.

'Hello, Margaret. It's Adam. I'm with Gareth and am trying to forestall one of his more hare-brained schemes. I think I might do it, if you can tell me you would like to attend an evening of Welsh poetry with Celtic drama themes presented by the Ballinger Players, Friday week, seven thirty, in London. The cost is thirty-five pounds. Would you like to attend, even if Gareth went along? It's his idea. It's just he feels he has been such a galah towards you, he's finding it hard to ask you in the conventional fashion.' He paused. 'Trust me, you don't want to know about his unconventional fashion.'

Adam was vaguely aware of Gareth pummelling his arm—fortunately, his good one. He listened carefully, before replying. 'Yes. He's serious.'

More uncertainty and another question.

'No. He's sincere and it's well meant. I can...' He cleared his throat. '...vouch for that.'

Adam closed his eyes and massaged his forehead as he continued to listen to Margaret. 'Yes, well, why don't we do that then. I'll...' He swallowed. '...find someone. Um. Thanks, Margaret. Good night.'

Looking up, he found Gareth hanging onto the doorknob, apparently in an apoplexy of anguish. Adam rose to his feet, eased him away from the door and patted him on the shoulder. 'She said yes. The bad news is that I'm coming too—with someone.'

***

Back at number four, Marmalade wasn't simply sprawled across the bottom of the stairs but was sitting up straight in the middle of the first step up to his room as if waiting to speak with him. Adam stared at the doll for a moment. It had become a familiar sight. It was little Pippa's calling card. She routinely left it on the step to let him know she'd been there. He swallowed down the lump in his throat, stepped around it and went up to his room.

Chapter 13

Adam was conscious that something within him was beginning to change. While he still had to battle with feelings of bleak unreality, he discovered he was engaging his students with a good deal more energy. His teaching style also changed. As much time was spent splodging along the brackish river bank in gumboots, digging up mud at different levels above the low tide level to examine the organisms within it, as was spent in the classroom. Before long, Adam noticed even the most reluctant student was caught up in the novelty of it all. They seemed to enjoy it.

He conceded these outdoor activities were not universally appreciated. He reflected ruefully on the occasion he had talked a local farmer into giving him an orphan lamb born out of season for the boys to care for and monitor. The farmer had placed this small bundle of legs and kicking sinew into Adam's arms one morning at the start of a school day. As he carried it into the staff common room to pick up some papers, the hitherto quiescent lamb began to 'baa' pitifully at a decibel level, quite at odds with its diminutive size. It was perhaps unfortunate Giles Carlingford happened to be on hand when it happened.

'Good God, Hollingworth, this isn't some filthy sheep pen. In case you hadn't noticed, we have moved beyond subsistence farming here, even though this may not be the case in that culturally-benighted penal colony of yours.'

It was perhaps equally unfortunate that Adam's resilience level was not great at the time. Uncharacteristically, he reacted. 'Anyone who boasts a cultural heritage that has included Gary Glitter and the Spice Girls probably needs to think twice before trumpeting their cultural elitism.'

'This is a school, not some stinking zoo.'

'When this animal craps, at least I know it's alive, which is more than can be said for your moldy history books.'

Giles stalked off in apparent disgust.

Adam wasn't proud of his outburst. His irritability was in no way helped by the realization he'd been hoist by his own petard in organising for Gareth to spend time with Margaret. Whilst his presence was the only thing that persuaded Margaret to agree to the evening, it had forced him into a social scenario he viewed with some trepidation.

Much against his will, he made his way along the ancient flagstones of Highgate to *The Borrowed Wheelbarrow* and climbed the steps into that dim, hushed world of colour and creativity.

Both Claire and the clairvoyant were seated behind the counter where they looked to be engaged in some sort of paperwork.

'Hello,' said Claire.

Adam was relieved not to hear any hint of reservation in her tone.

'Well ... hello again,' purred the clairvoyant. 'Come with any more brass rubbings?'

Adam wondered how anyone could say 'brass rubbings' in such a way as to make it sound like a sin. This unbidden thought was in no way discouraged by the clairvoyant's tight yellow dress from which her well-endowed figure was in imminent danger of overflowing. He took a deep breath. 'No. Perhaps I should have, I normally bring them for times when my craven self needs to grovel in abject, sniveling servility and plead for a favour.'

The clairvoyant laughed. 'Claire, who is this guy, and why isn't his groveling at all persuasive?'

'Oh!' Her tone was airy. 'This is Adam Hollingworth, a teacher at the school. Adam, this is Andrea Dalesford.'

Adam nodded to Andrea and turned back to Claire. 'May I have word?'

Claire led him to the back office that was cluttered with picture frames, packaging material and filing cabinets. She waved him to an office chair and sat herself on the edge of the desk.

Adam recounted the story of Gareth's attempt to begin a more sensible relationship with Margaret, and how Margaret wasn't ready to accompany any male to a social function without the security of other safe people around her—in this case, Adam. This meant that he needed a partner to attend a show with him in London. He swallowed. 'Would you like to come?'

Claire appeared lost for words. 'What's the show?' she asked, eventually. 'When is it?'

'Welsh poetry and Celtic drama. Friday week.'

She wrinkled her nose. 'Not quite my thing.' Nonetheless, she pulled across her desk diary and flipped over a few pages. 'Oh dear. I've an appointment to visit my agent and discuss details of my first London exhibition.'

'Of your art?' Adam managed to ask, despite the stab of disappointment he felt.

She nodded. 'Something I've dreamed of and worked towards for years.' She turned the desk diary round so Adam could see the engagement clearly written down. 'I'm so sorry.'

'Nah. Please don't be. It was a long shot.'

An awkward silence hung between them.

'Why don't you ask Andrea?' Claire blurted out.

Adam blinked in shock. 'I have the distinct impression she would eat me alive. Please spare me that.'

Claire laughed. 'She is...' she paused, '...a lot of woman, but she is nothing if not discriminating about those upon whom she bestows her favours. Don't worry, she may be a bit assertive but she has a heart of gold.'

Adam was not at all assured by her comments, but Claire took events out of his hands by walking out and explaining the situation to Andrea.

The clairvoyant put her hands on her hips. 'As I understand it, you are asking me to help chaperon a lady's virtue by playing gooseberry with you, whilst she makes up her mind whether or not he is a complete prat. Have I got that right?'

'Close enough,' Adam admitted.

'The show sounds as boring as hell, but if you promise to be in scintillating good form and can assure me of some fun, I'll come.'

'Those are exacting terms but I'm forced to accept them.' Adam smiled. 'I'll do my best.'

Andrea agreed to meet him in the entrance hall of the boarding house on the appointed day.

***

Adam had worked long hours preparing the term's lesson plans and was becoming conscious of his need for a break from the all-consuming demands of the school. He ached to be back in the wilderness where he could breathe the bigness of the world again. The possibility of doing this was severely limited by his lack of transport. Adam recalled seeing a motorbike showroom near the railway station. The upshot was that, the following Saturday, he arrived back at number four Prior's Lane astride a second-hand motorbike.

Dizzy was on the doorstep with bags of shopping, about to enter when he arrived. She was impressed. 'A 500 Honda, twin cylinder. Don't show Geoffrey—he fantasises about bikes.'

Adam removed his helmet. 'I thought I'd take it for a run tomorrow as I'm free of boarding duties.'

'Where will you go?'

'No idea; to the coast, probably. I'll buy a map.'

'Don't bother. I've got a local ordinance survey map you can borrow. I'll tuck it under your door tonight.'

As they walked inside, Philippa Ruth came into the hallway and hugged one of Dizzy's legs as she stared at Adam with her wide eyes. Adam glanced at her. She really was a beautiful child, and seemed to be completely unconscious of the obscene fibreglass shell that imprisoned her.

He lowered his head and turned to go upstairs.

Dizzy wagged a finger at him. 'Don't forget: you're welcome to join Geoffrey and myself on Friday evenings for a restorative glass of wine around eight. Open invitation. Life can be a bit ordinary on your own sometimes and we'd welcome your company.'

Adam had looked back at the guileless, candid eyes of Philippa Ruth and forced a smile. 'Thanks, I'll try and make it when I can.'

***

Next morning, Adam crept quietly downstairs dressed in his new bike jacket and let himself out the front door.

Dawn was someway off as he drove through the town's early morning chill. He passed an electric milk cart humming and rattling its way on its morning rounds. The steady growl of the bike took him down the winding lanes flanked by naked trees, stark in their winter filigree.

It had been a few years since he had ridden a bike and this, coupled with the patches of treacherous frost that reached across the road from the lee of the hedgerows, meant that Adam drove carefully. However, he soon grew in confidence and pushed through the sleeping winter countryside towards the coast.

A watery dawn made a reluctant appearance as he parked his bike beside a wooden sail loft on the foreshore. He stretched and coaxed his chilled muscles into life as he tried to decide whether to head into the village for a warming cup of coffee, or to go immediately into the saltings to explore its secrets.

He chose the saltings and spent two magical hours meandering over the maze of mud hillocks, observing its life with a naturalist's keen eye. Occasionally, he hid himself in the reed beds to watch the birds on the mudflats. Eventually, hunger drove him back towards the village. He began to retrace his steps when he recognised the junction in the duckboards that led off to *Sanderling.* Impulsively, he made a detour and was soon looking at her snugged down in her mud berth. A thin wisp of smoke from the funnel of the galley's charcoal heater told him Edward was on board.

He climbed down and clumped over to the hatchway in his riding boots. As he got there, the hatch slid open and Edward's weather-beaten head appeared. 'What a welcome surprise. Come down below and warm up with a brew.'

Edward made Adam a mug of coffee and followed it up, inevitably, with several rounds of toast and ginger marmalade.

Warmed and replete, they began dismantling wooden pulley blocks so the axles could be greased and the blocks coated with linseed oil. As they were working, a small motorised floating pontoon, complete with derrick, pushed its blunt nose into the channel in which they were berthed. A cheerful hail came from a shapeless form, enveloped in a battered sou'wester, at its helm.

Adam recognized Stan from the boatyard.

'Mornin' Edward. I was worried you mightn't have enough to do an' wondered if you could 'elp me lay a mooring up on the North Arm. Lenny's missus is expectin', so 'e's frettin' about in 'ospital. Poor bugger. You'd think that after five kids, he'd've worked out 'ow it 'appened.' He waved to Adam. 'Mornin', Aussie.'

'G'day, Stan. I thought you built boats.'

Stan edged his ungainly vessel alongside until it nudged the fenders along *Sanderling*'s hull. He grinned. 'I build boats for a livin' and I park 'em to earn a few of life's luxuries. Don't tell the taxman.'

'We're just finishing here, Stan,' said Edward. 'I'm free to lend a hand. What about you Adam? There's no obligation for you to come.'

'No worries. I'm happy to lend a hand.' Adam shrugged. 'I've not got much on today.'

The rest of the daylight, brief as it was, was spent organising and dropping the massive ground tackle and concrete block for a mooring big enough to tether a ten-tonne yacht.

Stan ferried them back to *Sanderling* in the early twilight. Edward packed his haversack, hoisted it on his shoulders and walked with Adam across the saltings to the hard. 'The community here is pretty close-knit and we tend to rely on each other.'

'Sounds nice.' said Adam, thinking it would not be nice at all.

'Yes, it is.'

Adam forced himself to sound interested. 'Do you work for Stan often?'

'Just now and then.' Edward smiled. 'We've found we need each other. Not much money exchanges hands on the marshes. Stan simply sees to it that my chandlery bill is viewed sympathetically. I've had to learn it's the way things work here.' He turned the conversation. 'Your heart and your morale: how are things going?'

Adam breathed in slowly and pondered the question for a few moments. 'Good days and bad ... generally better. I have moments of energy, then times of despair when everything seems meaningless. But I'm learning that these periods don't last.'

Edward nodded his approval before looking at his watch. 'You've not really had lunch and now it's nearly teatime. Why don't you stay the night and join me for dinner? The bed's always made up. You can drive back to school tomorrow morning.' He smiled. 'Besides, you haven't got a chandlery account, so think of it as payment for services rendered today.'

Adam protested. 'You know that's not necessary.'

'Then let me be more honest and invite you to stay simply for the fun of it.'

Adam rubbed his forehead. 'Hmm.' His instincts, born of self-protection, still screamed 'no.' But now he understood the demon and challenged it. 'Thanks. I'll come.'

His bike crunched through the gravel of Edward's driveway and growled to a halt near the front door. He removed his helmet and unzipped the front of his jacket as he passed into the house. It was a full ten seconds before he noticed Claire sitting in the gloom of the lounge room behind a laptop computer. She was wearing an oversized pullover and had hitched the sleeves up to her elbows. Her sun-bleached hair was highlighted from a distant kitchen spotlight.

Seeing her there, looking slightly pale and guarded, triggered an emotion in Adam that was as powerful as it was incomprehensible. She was breathtakingly beautiful. His spirit lifted briefly ... before he cursed himself for his folly and allowed the pitiless blanket of grief and despair to crush him again.

***

Claire had had the advantage of seeing Adam for a few seconds longer. The bike jacket casually swinging open, the blue jeans and the businesslike riding boots accentuated his physicality in a startling way. She had already seen that Adam was obviously very fit. In fact, she'd been slightly surprised he hadn't showed this off to her when they were last together—in that not-so-subtle way men usually employed. As it was, he'd seemed to be completely unaware of his physical attributes and hid his body in warm, loose-fitting clothes. However, in his slim-fitting riding gear, Adam's true shape could not be hidden. He presented an impressive, even intimidating, sight.

Something deep and primal stirred within her. She shook her head in irritation and dismissed it. What she didn't need now was another failed relationship. It wouldn't work anyway. Teachers were altogether too institutionalised. She was looking for someone with more life. The ones she courted were the wild ones.

She compressed her lips as she reflected on her experience with men. Once or twice she'd thought she was in love, but invariably she'd found her passions were fueled by perceptions that outstripped reality. Inevitably, her boyfriend's neuroses and self-destructive habits thrust their chilling swords through her heart. Claire shook her head. She'd had enough of male egos and foibles. It was time to concentrate on her career. She had her first exhibition in London coming up. Preparing for it would take up all of her time. In fact, she admitted to herself, she was already exhausted.

Now this strange man—someone who disturbed her, alternately by his rudeness and then by his sensitivity; whose face could be as bleak as the North Sea, but whose eyes could light up with pleasure—how could this person now transform himself from a teacher dressed in shapeless corduroys into an Adonis in leathers? It was deeply disturbing.

Warmth flooded her, a symptom that betrayed her unspoken thoughts.

Adam's eyes regarded her steadily for a moment. His gaze seemed to lay bare her soul.

She had to re-take the initiative. 'Mr Hollingworth. What a surprise.'

He closed his eyes, massaged his forehead and looked at her with an expression of—was it bewilderment?

'Claire...' His voice was hesitant. '...equally a ... surprise.'

Edward began to bang about the kitchen, ignorant of the shouting silence. 'Lovely to see you, Claire, m'dear. We'll be three for dinner.' He turned to Adam. 'Claire has her own key. She treats this place as her bolt-hole and doesn't seem to mind gladdening an old man's heart by doing so.' He turned back and called over his shoulder. 'Claire, are you here to work, rest or play?'

She rose and joined him in the kitchen. 'I had a call from rehab to say they were releasing George this afternoon. I'd said I'd pop in with some groceries for him and check that he's okay. He's very shaky. I noticed his toenails when he took off his slippers. Horrible, so I stayed and cut them.' She shrugged. 'As I was down here, I thought I'd stay the night and do some more preparation for the art show.'

Edward nodded at Adam. 'Old George lives on *The Sapphire Maid,* a dilapidated houseboat in the saltings. He's ex-navy, never married and battles with alcohol. He's a lovely old guy but he's only just managing on his own. Claire and I keep a bit of an eye on him.' He pulled out some sausages from the fridge. 'Both of us have become the nearest thing he has to a family.'

Claire hoped Adam would open up a little more during dinner so she could learn more about him. However, although socially polite, he seemed withdrawn and tense. At one point, the conversation touched on whether or not the police had made any progress in tracking down Edward's attackers. Claire remembered the horror of that afternoon and bristled with indignation. 'I wish those wretches would have got at least a little of their just desserts.'

'Hmm,' said Adam.

After a moment's silence, Edward gave a small cough. 'My dear Claire, I feel fairly sure that my assailants are now heartily wishing they had slightly less than their just desserts.' He turned to Adam. 'If I remember rightly, one almost certainly has a broken jaw; another, a broken leg; and the other two significant facial lacerations.'

Adam said nothing.

Claire looked shocked. 'How...?'

'I'm sorry, dear. I thought you knew. They attacked Adam ... and, um, came off rather badly.'

Claire looked at Adam open-mouthed. He looked down and chased some errant peas around his plate with a fork.

'Oh.' she said, weakly.

She was thoughtful for the rest of the meal and got up as soon as she had finished. 'Do you guys mind if I get on with my work? I need some undisturbed time.'

Edward waved her away, saying that he and Adam would do the washing up.

She retreated to her computer in the gloom of the unlit front room and began to peck away at it in desultory fashion, occasionally casting a covert glance at Adam in the kitchen.

She was downloading a series of web pages advertising art shows in America, but couldn't concentrate. On impulse, she typed 'Adam Hollingworth' into her search engine ... and pushed the button.

The result shocked her. There were two pages of entries from various rock climbing organisations and magazines featuring extreme sports. Scarcely believing they would relate to the Adam Hollingworth she knew, she clicked on an entry.

She was rewarded with a picture of what was indisputably Adam, hanging one-handed from under a rock overhang with a drop of several hundred metres beneath him. The caption read: *Adam Hollingworth free climbing at Mt Buller.*

Appalled, she continued to explore. More pictures came up. One of them caught Adam in mid-air as he had leaped from the side of a vertical rock face across a chasm, to grasp a handhold on another. The photographer had appended a title of masterful understatement: *Leap of Faith.*

Adam seemed oblivious to the camera in all of the photographs. If his face could be seen, it was invariably a picture of intense determination.

Claire switched on a table lamp and got up to fetch her sketchbook, along with a stick of charcoal. She glanced at Adam in the kitchen. Then, with deft strokes, she sketched a young man with his head in his hands in deep despair. She drew him again with eyes screwed shut and his head tilted back in anguish ... and then drew another ... and another.

***

Edward ignored the washing up and sat with Adam at the kitchen table, waiting to see what was on his mind. His only contribution was to oil the way by pouring him another glass of Shiraz.

Adam sighed and looked at him with a grim smile. 'It still seems pretty pointless at times.'

'Yes, I suspect it does.' Edward watched Adam pinch the top of his nose and screw his eyes shut. He looked very tired.

'Hard to stay positive.'

'Hmm.'

A long silence followed.

Adam slumped back in his chair. 'Why? Why all the ... crap?'

Desperately hoping he had the words to help, Edward said, 'Life is a process of coping with loss. It is an imperfect thing.' He shrugged. 'As I've said, it is a good thing spoilt.'

Adam lifted his head. 'You mean we've spoilt it?'

'We've been asked not to, but have been given the choice.'

More silence followed.

'Who chose Amanda's death?' Adam asked quietly.

So this was it. Edward sighed, feeling the grief of centuries settle on his heart. He picked his words carefully. 'Suffering that comes from humankind's bad moral choices is perhaps easier to understand. It's simply the fault of humankind exercising freewill poorly. But the suffering that comes from natural disasters, like Amanda's death, is harder to understand. It seems creation itself is fundamentally flawed.' He rocked a teacup around slowly on its base. 'The Apostle Paul spoke of all of creation waiting to be rescued by God.'

Adam hit out savagely. 'So, we're caught like rats in a cruel maze made by some distant God who hasn't yet got round to rescuing us from it.'

'I didn't say that.'

Adam was clearly far from mollified. 'Then what do you say?'

'I say that God is not a God who remains distant from us but has come to us to share our pain.' Edward pointed to a small crucifix hanging on the side of a wall cupboard, 'God understands.'

And so the conversation drifted on, touching on things profound, mysterious and sacred.

***

The next evening, Marmalade was again propped up on the bottom of the steps. Adam stared at her. Philippa Ruth had obviously been playing with Marmalade and her toy dinner set. It appeared she was determined to make contact. He pictured the beautiful girl encased in her brace. Impulsively, he squatted down and tidied up the toys, positioning Marmalade so that she held one of the tea cups. He stood back up and surveyed what he'd done. *You win, Pippa.*

Chapter 14

Adam's arm was almost fully healed but he had been advised not to play rugby for another week. He was therefore dressed in his stockman's coat, supervising the fitness training of the second fifteen. Twenty minutes later, Gareth took over and organized the boys into a practice match. Adam strolled over to the groundsman's shed and banged on the door. 'Ted, have you got a moment for a chat?'

Ted Jarrow was simultaneously holding a huge mug of tea, puffing at a pipe and grumbling at a newspaper. He had built a little nest for himself in the corner of his machine workshop, consisting of two condemned armchairs, a kettle, an ancient brown teapot and a collection of football posters.

'Mr 'ollingworf. Dunno what the world is comin' to.' Ted threw the newspaper down with disgust and, unbidden, unhooked a mug from a nail and poured Adam a cup of thick, dark tea.

'Thanks, Ted. What's the matter?' Adam picked up the newspaper. It was the local *Tribune* and its lead story concerned a spate of deaths from drug overdoses. Adam read the opening lines: 'Police suspect new operators are carving out a market for themselves by targeting schoolchildren. Schools have been asked to be vigilant.'

'In my day, we 'ad a few beers an' carried on like ruddy 'oodlums but didn't need no drugs.'

'Yeah, but West Ham United were winning in those days, Ted.'

'Cheeky blighter.'

'Ted, I've got some hoodlums of my own I want to sort out and I've got an idea that might help. I need you to tell me if it's doable. I want to know if it is possible to turn the rough ground at the back of this shed into a miniature arable farm ... and for my kids to farm it.'

When he had finished expanding on his idea, Ted puffed out his cheeks. 'You wanna turn this place into a bleedin' farm! You're barmy, you are. Wocher fink the toffs are gonna say about that?'

'More important, Ted, what do you think about it? It's not a go-er unless you're behind it.'

Adam knew Ted to be a well-known walking contradiction. He shared his working class socialist views with conviction to anyone who would listen, but was also one of the most passionate and loyal supporters of the school. His fierce pride in the establishment meant he never missed a first fifteen rugby match, and his hoarse voice could often be heard above the crowd offering pithy advice to anyone on the field unlucky enough to warrant it.

'I fink it's bloomin' marvelous.' Ted cackled. 'The little darlin's will get their lily-white 'ands dirty. Might learn somefink useful.'

'Ted, I'd need a tractor.'

Adam's comment brought Ted up with a start. He took off his cap and scratched his head. 'I don't fink you can 'ave me John Deere. I fought two year to get that. It'd be no bloomin' use to you anyway 'cos it's got smooth grass tyres on it. But you could use me old grey Massey. I've put ridged tyres back on 'er for rough work. She's 'ardly used now but is still in pretty good nick. Yer can use that.'

'I couldn't have wished for anything more, Ted. Thanks.'

''Ow much of the rough do ya want?'

'Most of it, but you must still have space to dump your soil and sand. I reckon I'd use about a half a hectare.'

'What the hell's that?'

Adam smiled. *So much for compulsory metrication.* 'Bit over an acre.'

'Right. Grab four of them metal posts and that mallet. I'll get the measurin' wheel and we'll see wot yer bleedin' farm might look like.'

Together, they went outside.

***

Next day, Adam surprised his lower sixth biology class with a request. 'Before you go, boys, I've a favour to ask of you.' This was not the sort of language the boys were used to and it successfully got their attention. They listened with curiosity. 'Some of you blokes are from surrounding farms. I'm looking at the possibility of making this subject more interesting for you but what I need from you country boys is any information on how I can get hold of a small mouldboard plough and a set of light harrows that would fit behind a tractor. If you have any suggestions, I'd be pleased to hear them.'

The result of this wasn't entirely what Adam expected. Next morning, he received a phone call asking him to come to the boarding house. He arrived as the boarders were finishing breakfast. Some were directing good-natured jibes at a day-boy, Kevin Dixon, as they filed out past him in the hallway where he stood waiting for Adam.

Kevin grinned as Adam approached. 'Dad's outside with a plough and a set of harrows. Where do you want them?'

Adam hurried outside to see a Range Rover double-parked on the road in front of the boarding house. It was towing a trailer with a plough and a set of harrows roped down. A large florid man climbed out of the front seat and introduced himself. 'Geoff Dixon. Will these do ... a three bladed plough and harrows?

Adam cast a quick eye over them. 'Yes, I think so.'

'Try them out. If they're no good, I'll take them back and get rid of them for you. Our rigs have gone up several sizes since these were last used, so I've no more use for them. They might as well be used by you, as rust outside my shed. Have them for as long as you want.'

Adam expressed his heartfelt thanks and drove with him across to the groundsman's sheds to unload. Mr Dixon did this with singular efficiency. He tied a rope around the implements in the trailer and fastened the other end around a large beech tree beside one of the sheds. He then drove the trailer out from under its load so that they crashed to the ground. He was evidently not a man to waste time.

As he was coiling the rope, Mr Dixon nodded at Adam. 'Mr Hollingworth, Kevin has never found schooling easy ... but you've somehow got him keen on your subject.' He struggled to find any more words. After a few attempts to clear his throat, he said, 'Thanks.' He shook Adam's hand and drove away.

Ted Jarrow came clattering up on his bicycle, He dismounted, leaned the bike against the shed and walked over to the plough. 'Should do nicely,' was his verdict.

Gareth had evidently witnessed Adam's hurried departure from breakfast because he came ambling across the playing fields from the boarding house. He stared at the farm implements. 'Does the headmaster know about this, boyo?'

'No.'

Gareth sighed and put a hand on Adam's shoulder. 'Your stay here will be most interesting ... possibly brief, but definitely interesting.'

***

Adam had to promise Ted a bottle of whiskey in order to persuade him to come to the interview with the headmaster. 'Relax, Ted, I'll tell him it's my idea. Just be on hand in case he asks if you are happy with it. You're the only one who uses the ground, so he'll want to hear from you.'

The headmaster welcomed them into his study and calmed Ted's obvious nerves by offering them both a cup of tea. After polite small talk in which the headmaster asked Ted's opinion on recent performances of the first fifteen, he asked the purpose of their visit.

Taking a deep breath, Adam began to explain his idea. 'The new biology syllabus I've chosen for the boys has a huge emphasis on a research project. There is no doubt this will suit the boys, but an academic research project still risks remaining a purely academic exercise, unless it can be made to live.' His passion for the project gave him eloquence. 'If we were able to begin an arable farm in miniature on the school premises, the boys could be engaged in everything from tractor handling, ploughing, sowing, disease and weed control, right through to harvest. They could investigate the effect of sowing depths and crop varieties.' He waved a hand. 'Everything they did would be intensely practical and would require physical work as well as brains. And having a school farm would mean all the boys' projects would have a common theme and would encourage co-operation between them. I think it would make a big difference to their learning.'

The Headmaster asked carefully, 'Where would you site this farm?'

'It would be an acre of the rough land behind Ted's sheds.' Adam nodded towards Ted. 'We've already marked out its possible boundaries.'

'Wouldn't the cost of machinery be unrealistic for such a small area?'

Ted butted in. ''Ee's already got most of it.' Ee can have me old Massey. She'll have enough puff in her for this sort o' work. A plough and a set of 'arrows got give him this mornin'.'

The headmaster raised his eyebrows in surprise. 'Really?' He paused. 'How can you ensure safety?'

'We'd employ the best practices set for agricultural colleges. Some of these are already in place for Ted's machinery shed and chemical store.'

'You haven't a seeding unit. How would you sow the crop?'

'Ted hires a small seeder when he wants to over-sow the playing fields. He says it should suit our purposes.'

The headmaster regarded him in silence for a while. 'When do you want to start?'

'Soon as possible. Now. We'd have to if we want to get any winter wheat and barley in. We'll do a second sowing when the weather warms up after Christmas and put in some spring barley.'

'Hmm.' The headmaster thought for a while. 'Adam, would you be kind enough to help Janice organise another cup of tea for us all?'

Adam took the tray of empty cups down to Janice and explained his errand. Janice smiled at him. 'The headmaster wants ten minutes alone with Ted. We don't have to rush.'

Ten minutes later, the headmaster buzzed them on the intercom and asked Janice to return with Adam ready to take down a few notes. As they entered, both Ted and the headmaster were obviously very much at ease. In fact, Ted was in the middle of a wheezy chuckle.

'Janice,' said the headmaster. 'Would you be kind enough to take down a list of things we require in order to begin the Hollingworth School Farm?' He turned to Adam. 'Right, Adam, what do we need?'

Adam repressed a grin of delight and forced himself to think. He ticked off items on his fingers. 'Eight garden hoes; a knapsack sprayer with a two metre spray boom with eighty degree flat fan nozzles; four safety masks with spare filters; one hundred wooden marker pegs; a fifty metre measuring tape...' Janice continued to write down Adam's list in shorthand. 'It's a pity we can't get a better system for harvesting than taking sample quadrats from each patch of crop. If the worst comes to the worst, we may have to forget harvest and simply turn the crop in as fertilizer, particularly as the boys will be on summer holidays during harvest time.'

'Mr Hollingworth, may I volunteer a possibility that could overcome that problem?' Everyone looked at Janice with surprise. With just the faintest hint of self-importance, she smiled. 'My son-in-law, Rowan Eastman, works as a research scientist for an international chemical company. He has to test all sorts of crop protection products on farmland around the place. The point is, they have the cutest little harvester that they tow all over the country harvesting trial plots. I've seen it.' She tapped her pen on her notepad. 'If the boys were to conduct one of the chemical company experiments on your farm, well ... they would harvest it all for you, weigh the grain and do all the other clever things they do to measure its quality. I could give you his telephone number, if you wish.'

There was a moment of awed silence, pregnant with new possibilities. Adam's head was spinning. 'Janice, you're a genius. Thank you.'

She smiled.

As they were leaving, the headmaster called Adam back. 'Ah, before you go, may I have a brief word.' Adam stepped back into the study.

'Two things,' said the headmaster. 'First, you will have your computers for the start of next term. Use them well. Second, you will find a new bottle of whiskey in that cupboard to your left. I'd be obliged if you would take it and

use it for the furtherance of this project
of yours.'

Chapter 15

Adam knew Gareth was not his usual easygoing self, despite the charade he was putting on. He was pacing up and down the grand hallway of the boarding house, quoting Shakespearian sonnets. He had dressed himself in his usual black attire, augmented for the occasion with a white silk evening scarf.

Adam put a hand on his arm to still the performance. 'Gareth, you don't have to burrow into the persona of literary giants. Your own self is quite good enough.'

Gareth deflated. 'But that's just it, old boy, I don't have one—a persona, I mean. I've played everyone else's part but forgotten my own. "Man is an eternal mystery to himself."'

Adam sighed. Gareth's gift for drama was irrepressible. 'Fortunately for you, you are less of a mystery to others.'

'Who am I then?' Gareth wailed theatrically.

'Gareth, you are an overacting dill. Happily, quite a likeable one. You are also a nervous bloke who is, unfortunately, about to stuff up a perfectly pleasant evening because you can't decide whether to be Don Juan, Shakespeare or yourself. If you are seriously entertaining the possibility of any long-term relationship, might I suggest the latter. You'll find it more profitable.'

Gareth's antics had the effect of distracting Adam from any misgivings of his own. However, he was reminded of them when Andrea pushed her way through the front doors into the stately hallway. She was looking striking in a stylish black coat which, although voluminous, still manifestly failed to conceal her figure. She was at her alluring best.

Adam introduced Andrea to Gareth, who instantly adopted the demeanour of the perfect host.

After a few sentences of small talk, Gareth excused himself so he could collect Margaret from her room. As he passed, he hissed in Adam's ear, 'Wow!' before bounding up the stairs.

A few moments later, he came back down with Margaret. She was wearing a plain tweed skirt and cardigan, underneath an unbuttoned duffel coat.

Andrea leaned over to Adam. 'Our gallant suitor has not yet inspired her to impress with her dress.'

'This is merely a recce,' Adam replied quietly. 'Merely a recce.'

***

The party took their places on the train in facing pairs of seats. The fuggy warmth of the rail carriage was in stark contrast to the biting cold on the platform. There, they had stood hunched inside their coats, breathing clouds of white through muffling scarves. Adam, at least, had been grateful for the semi-darkness and was debating with himself how much he should involve himself in the social pantomime that must inevitably follow. He was far from certain how events would unfold.

The harsh carriage lights stripped away his privacy and the regimentation of the seats forced him to make his first social decision—where to sit. Adam and Andrea faced Gareth and Margaret. Margaret had made to sit next to Andrea but Andrea had adroitly, and apparently innocently, stood to unfasten her scarf, making room for Gareth to take her place.

Adam was relieved Gareth was astute enough not to be overbearing. He maintained the conversation and involved them all with attentive questioning and flashes of humour. The easy-going atmosphere was shattered, however, when the warmth of the carriage required Andrea to unbutton her coat. The stretching fabric of her low-cut dress presented, rather than contained a stunning cleavage. Smooth, white skin ballooned provocatively a metre in front of Gareth's nose. Adam experienced a giddy heave of primal sexual tension that he successfully wrestled to a standstill. Rather disturbingly, this was followed almost instantly by a feeling of intense emptiness.

After what seemed like hours, he struggled to the surface to note that, in the milliseconds that had passed, Gareth had blinked and had his mouth open in readiness to say something totally disastrous.

With a sense of heading off Custer's doomed last charge, Adam leaned over to Andrea. 'You know, of course, you will be sent straight to hell for wearing such a beautiful dress. It will make the worthy burghers of London insanely jealous of me. I'm looking forward to it.'

Andrea looked at Adam with a smile. 'That pretty compliment ought to get you a black eye. But it's still one of the nicest I've had. I shall accept it and expect many more throughout the evening.'

Margaret retreated into observer mode, adopting a distant, almost sardonic expression that discouraged conversation.

When they arrived at London, matters did not improve. The poetry reading and drama production was not the delightful treat Gareth had anticipated. The actors strutted their introspections and attempted levels of sophistication that completely eluded most of the audience. Margaret looked sad, Gareth looked frustrated, Andrea looked bored. Covertly, Adam looked at them all.

Afterwards, true to his promise to give Andrea some fun, Adam steered the party into the elegant lounge bar of a nearby hotel. A poster outside advertising a band had persuaded him to investigate. They arrived as the band was resting after the first set. After organising outrageously priced drinks and two large plates of antipasto, the tensions and disappointments of the evening gave way to humour as Gareth embarked on a wicked parody of the evening's performance. Margaret, while polite, remained withdrawn.

Andrea's irrepressible nature soon began to spark off Gareth's extrovert antics. Whilst Gareth tried to craft his responses to include Margaret, it was a losing battle. Adam certainly felt himself no match for Gareth's sparkling humour and so he too retreated to making just the occasional comment. Gareth and Andrea were soon locked in a combat of mirth, wit and sexuality that have been the stuff of friendships and flirtations since gin and tonics were first invented.

When the band assembled again, it launched off into a brassy swing number. Andrea started swaying in time with the music and couples began to fill the small dance floor. Only Adam noticed Gareth steal a lingering glance at Margaret, whilst she was helping Andrea fish under the table for a lost shoe. He saw Gareth's eyes soften but also noticed his grimace of frustration. By the time Margaret returned upright, brandishing Andrea's shoe, Gareth's lazy grin was back in place.

'Would you like to dance?' he asked her.

She was visibly taken aback. 'Why ... why don't you ask Andrea? I'm not ... quite ready.'

Gareth masked his disappointment and repeated his invitation to Andrea. The two of them were soon dancing to the pulsating rhythm of a jive. It was evident Gareth was very much at home on the dance floor. His natural sense of co-ordination and skill meant he gave Andrea all the confidence she wanted to explore the physicality of the dance to the full. While she danced with rather more enthusiasm than finesse, Gareth was able to accommodate her inventiveness so that they made a striking pair.

Adam fixed Margaret with a level look. 'That was unkind, Margaret.'

'What! Why? It's obvious he's more interested in Andrea.' She added with a touch of bitterness. 'Any man would be.'

'No!' Adam sighed. 'What is obvious is that Andrea isn't so self-protective she can't entertain the possibility of having some fun. Gareth is trying to give you a good time, so why have you opted to play the ugly duckling when you manifestly are not one?'

Margaret said nothing.

The band began the next song. 'Margaret,' he said gently. 'I will ask you this only once.'

Margaret stiffened with apprehension.

'If you promise not to step on my broken wing ... and I promise not to step on yours, will you honour me with this dance, which I believe to be a fairly safe waltz?' He paused. 'You can dance?'

After some seconds of hesitation, Margaret nodded.

Taking advantage of the ambiguity as to whether the nod referred to her ability to dance or her acceptance of his invitation, Adam rose and held out his hand. She trailed after him, but halfway to the dance floor, she broke away and hurried back to the table. He thought all was lost but she simply slipped out of her cardigan and returned to him.

Adam nodded in approval. A woman in a tweed skirt and cardigan on a dance floor might be the object of derision. However, a slim, shapely woman in a crisp white shirt and a tweed skirt, who danced with an easy fluidity, was quite another matter. She was a skilful dancer. Her simple movements betrayed the feminine in her. Adam suspected she had probably studied ballet in her youth.

Whenever he could, Gareth shot glances over towards Margaret. Adam saw him with his mouth open in delight. He swept past Adam, mouthed 'Wow!' and lunged back to Andrea, who was in imminent danger of spinning out of control.

Adam didn't let Margaret rest after the first song, and led her seamlessly into the next dance. Margaret's confidence in her social setting had risen to a point where she was just starting to move to the rhythm of another jive number when Adam deftly stepped sideways to take charge of Andrea, leaving Gareth to partner Margaret.

Gareth spun her into the opening bars of the jive before she realised it. Once launched into this highly physical dance, there was no turning back.

Adam wasn't greatly skilled at the jive but got by with a good deal of improvisation from his enthusiastic partner. Out of the corner of his eye he noted the delight on Gareth's face. It was obvious each was acutely aware of the other but both were oblivious to the impact they were making on the dance floor.

Adam guided Andrea back to the table and sat watching. She directed a measured look at him. 'Mr Hollingworth, you've shown me a whole new dimension to matchmaking'.

Adam smiled. 'Thanks for making it possible, Andrea. Want another dance?'

'Normally, yes. But I'm as intrigued as you are. I want to watch what happens.' They sat together like conspirators sipping their drinks. Adam distinctly saw a small smile of mischief flit across Margaret's face as she executed a daring dance move, much to Gareth's delight. Both of them stayed on the dance floor a long time, neither apparently wanting to leave.

'This should be interesting,' purred Andrea as the dance changed to a slow "smoochy" number. Gareth and Margaret, after a second of self-conscious delay, came together to dance circumspectly but intimately. Adam noticed Gareth was looking slightly nervous, but his eyes were soft. Margaret looked at ease.

'Bingo.' Andrea winked at Adam mischievously.

***

When the train pulled back into their station well after midnight, the four of them disembarked. Gareth drove them back to the boarding house with uncharacteristic care. There, they dropped Margaret off and said their goodbyes.

'Adam is walking home so I'll drop Andrea back,' said Gareth.

Andrea said huskily, 'Now there's an offer I can't refuse.'

Only Adam saw Margaret blanch and clench her fist to her stomach. She turned and walked swiftly up the stairs.

Chapter 16

The following Saturday, Adam took his chest-high waders and headed to the estuarine river. Soon, he was pushing his way through the muddy water, working his way along the pylons of the jetty that poked its stubby nose out from the shore. A small waterproof bag containing a digital camera, notebook and numerous sample bags hung around his neck. He began identifying and examining the bands of barnacles and seaweed that grew at different heights up the pylons, depending on the length of time they needed to be submerged by the tide. His research would form the basis for an upcoming field trip for his students.

The water compressed the waders tight against him as he pushed on waist-deep to the last pylon he wanted to investigate. As he collected his samples and was jotting down notes, Adam ruminated over the bewildering behaviour exhibited by Margaret over the last week.

The previous weekend was, in spite of the disastrous poetry reading, a success by almost any standard. Friendships had blossomed, hilarity had been enjoyed, and Margaret had begun to make her first timorous steps towards social engagement. Her tentative smiles held out the first glimmers of friendship towards Gareth who had not, at any time, overplayed his hand. Only at the end had Margaret left abruptly to return to her rooms.

Since that time, she seemed to have regressed. Tragically for Gareth, she seemed to distance herself from him in particular, leaving him mystified and perplexed. Her dialogue with him in the dining hall during mealtimes was minimal to the point of rudeness. Gareth, nobly, was blaming himself.

'I pushed her too hard. I was too stupid. I've frightened her back into her shell.' He'd turned beseechingly to Adam. 'What did I do that was stupid? Tell me.'

Adam had poured his friend a glass of pre-dinner sherry. 'No, my friend, you did nothing stupid. You were, rather surprisingly, your normal splendid self.

I suspect something else is to blame for Margaret's behaviour, something we don't yet understand.'

His assurances had failed to put Gareth at ease.

'Damn, damn, damn.'

Adam tried to analyse the evening once more as he threaded his way through a gaggle of tethered boats to reach the final pylon. A few of the boats had cabins on to afford their occupants some shelter during a day's fishing. One of these also had a canvas boat-cover over it. Adam could hear a murmur of voices resonating through its fibreglass hull. The sounds were surprisingly clear. Taking no real notice, he started to push on to the last pylon when he was brought short by a voice he recognised. It was the distinctive, cracking, half-man, half-boy voice of Seth Waterman, one of the boys in his sixth form biology class.

'How long before this Ecstasy stuff makes me feel good, man? I'm sweating like a pig and feeling shitty in my stomach.'

Another person laughed. 'Can't even take your E. You're such a dweeb.

Relax. It takes twenty minutes before you "feel the luurv."'

'You're the dweeb, Gibbo. I'm a darn sight tougher'n you are.'

'I don't think so. If you're really tough, you don't go the tablet. You inject the stuff—and that leads to all sorts of interesting possibilities. But that's big league stuff. Not for kids.' There was a pause. 'Do you want to try it?'

'Sod off, Gibbo. I'm not one of your smack-heads. This is enough for me. Got to do something in this boring shit-hole.'

Laughter ensued, followed by Seth urging his companion to be quieter. His friend scoffed. 'Who the hell is going to hear us in here?'

Adam considered carefully what he should do. After a few moments, he elected to finish taking his samples and making his notes. However, the notes he made included a verbatim of the conversation, a description of the boat, together with a record of the boat's registration number. He made no attempt to hurry as he waded back towards the mudbank. Once there, he settled himself on a loading platform behind some pallets. It afforded an excellent view down the short jetty. Fifteen minutes later, Seth Waterman and a lanky young man with a shaved head climbed up from the boat to the jetty and made their way back to the foreshore.

Adam lifted his camera and took three photos.

Back in his attic flat at number four Prior's Lane, Adam pondered the situation. He elected not to share his problem with Gareth for fear of compromising him. What really irked him was Seth Waterman had been beginning to show real evidence of improvement in his studies. He'd been the class show-off. This, coupled with his athletic abilities, meant he was usually leading the mischief the boys were engaged in. Seth was a natural leader who was just beginning to amount to something academically. He had discovered he learned better by doing, rather than being told, and Adam's new teaching style was allowing him to flourish.

Whilst Adam was bitterly disappointed in Seth, he did not want Seth's academic progress to come grinding to a halt because of a school expulsion.

Eventually, a plan suggested itself. He made his way down the stairs and knocked on the Edgecomb's living room door. Dizzy opened it.

Before she could ask Adam how she could help, a little hand pushed a small jar up into her mother's waist and demanded her attention. 'Mummy, Mummy, see ... I really have got fairies in my jar.' Philippa Ruth was obviously not allowing the awesome event of Adam's arrival to divert her from her stupendous triumph.

Without looking at Philippa, Adam squatted down and looked into the jar she was holding. Inside were five fragile dandelion seeds. 'Wow! Are those fairies?'

'Yes. I caught them in Dad's greenhouse.'

'May I have a look?' As Philippa Ruth thrust the jar out for him to inspect.

'Hmm,' Adam said. 'I thought so. 'These are a special type of fairy.'

'What sort? What sort?' Philippa demanded.

Adam sat on the floor in the doorway. 'Let me have a closer look.'

She handed the jar to him. 'Yes. Do you see those winged feather things on top?' He turned the jar slowly. They tell me something. And do you see the tiny little package on the end of the stalk underneath? That makes it quite clear.'

'What is it?' Philippa bobbed forward stiffly to look closer.

'These are "travelling flower fairies". They are quite common in your gardens in spring. Each "travelling flower fairy" carries a secret.'

'What secret? What secret?' She grabbed the jar to take a closer look.

'Well, those winged feather things on top are to allow the wind to blow it wherever it wants. So these fairies get blown to new places by the wind. See that little lump on the bottom of the stalk? That is a secret package with all the plans to build a beautiful flower. That's why they are called "travelling flower fairies".'

Philippa Ruth gazed in wonder and swayed stiffly in her fibreglass shell across to Geoff at the sink. She held out the jar to him, bubbling over with excitement.

Dizzy smiled at Adam. 'That was well done. Come and join us. There's a "chateau cardboard" on top of the fridge.' She pointed to a two-litre cardboard wine cask. 'Help yourself.'

Eventually, Adam returned to his room, clutching the phone directory. With some trepidation, he made a call.

The phone was answered after the sixth ring. 'Waterman here,' a deep, gravelly voice growled.

'Mr Waterman, my name is Adam Hollingworth. I'm one of Seth's schoolteachers. I've got a concern about Seth that may affect his future at the school. I'd like to talk with you about it confidentially without Seth knowing—in the hope we can work it out. Can we meet?'

'Has Seth done something stupid? If he has, just tell me. I promise you he won't do it again.' Mr Waterman's voice gave every indication of the truth of his statement.

'I'd rather talk with you face to face, without Seth knowing at this stage.'

'Yeah, yeah ... I suppose.' There was a pause. 'We've sacrificed a lot so he could go to that school. He's our only kid. I want him to have a better chance than I did. Where do you live?'

Adam told him.

'Can you find *The Cooper's Arms,* the pub on Jackson Street by the docks? I live just round the corner. I can see you there in half an hour. Ask for me at the bar.'

'Okay,' Adam said, as the phone clicked dead.

***

After getting directions from Geoff Edgecomb and a warning that he'd be walking in a none-too-salubrious area of town, Adam began the twenty-minute walk down to the docklands pub.

He found it easily enough. It was an uncompromising workman's pub that had yet to discover European wines or political correctness. As Adam asked for the whereabouts of one Mr Waterman, a large hand placed itself on his shoulder. Its owner was a huge man, well-muscled and prematurely balding. He presented a formidable sight. 'I'm Alan Waterman. You must be Hollingworth.'

'Call me Adam. Let me buy you a beer.'

'Next time. I invited you here.' Mr Waterman ordered two pints and remained grimly silent until they were poured. He then steered Adam to a secluded table and eased his bulk onto an ancient and much-abused bench seat.

He picked up his pint of stout and took a long drink. 'What's Seth done?'

Adam told him.

Waterman scowled. 'How do you know it was Seth?'

Adam took out his notebook, gave him the details ... and showed him the photos on his camera.

'Shit! He was in my bloody boat.' Waterman wiped his huge paw across his face. 'What will this mean? Expulsion? Dammit. I'll have his hide. Bloody fool! Throwing away the chance we gave him.'

'I am hoping that expulsion won't be necessary. It all depends on Seth, how hardened he has become to drugs and whether he has it within him never to touch them again.'

The beginnings of hope flickered across Waterman's face. 'I'll damn well find out,' he growled. 'All kids are a mystery to their parents but I reckon I know my kid better than most.' He looked directly at Adam. 'He's got a good heart. He's got a lip on him and balls bigger than he's any right to have at his age, but he is basically a good kid.'

Adam nodded. 'I agree. He's been doing well with me recently and I'd like to see him succeed.'

Mr Waterman turned an appraising eye on him. 'You're the biology teacher. He talks about you.' He reached for his beer. 'He's got time for you.' If the comment fell short of conferring a knighthood, Adam suspected that it was only by a whisker.

Waterman banged his empty beer mug on the table. 'We'll sort it tonight. Come home with me. You stay in the kitchen while I talk with the lad in the drawing room. You'll be able to hear what's said and form your own opinion.'

Adam stared at his barely-started pint of dark brown stout and its silky pale froth. Instinctively, he knew it was important to finish the drink. He managed to down the earthy brown liquid without gagging. Mr Waterman nodded his approval, stood up and threaded his way across the pub, before pushing through the door into the evening chill.

Outside, a girl with heavily applied make-up was kissing a man passionately against the pub wall. Mr Waterman barely looked at her. 'Piss off home, Cindy. He's twice your age and he'll give you the clap.' Cindy tried a sulky pout but nonetheless wasted no time in flouncing off down the road. Waterman paused and turned to the man. 'She's underage. Don't let me see you here again.' The man had the sense to lower his head and remain mute. 'Bloody kids,' Waterman growled, as he and Adam set off.

In the short walk along the street and down a side alley, Adam learned that Waterman had, in fact, a good deal of compassion for kids. In a few pithy sentences, he explained to Adam that, when work at the port had dried up, he had applied for a grant to start up a local gymnasium. The venture had gone well and the gymnasium, in an old converted warehouse, had become the centre for a good number of community projects involving children. 'I know a lot of the kids around here,' he confided.

They came to a back gate in a row of modest terraced houses. Adam was ushered up the short path to the back door and into the kitchen. Inside, a careworn woman, still showing evidence of past beauty, was kneading some dough.

Mr Waterman kissed her on top of her head. 'This is Michelle. She seduced me at sixteen, fights for me like a she-wolf and is the only one I live in fear of.'

Mrs Waterman slapped him on the arm in mock affront and began to fill the kettle as Waterman explained Adam's presence. 'Seth's done something stupid. Mr Hollingworth here is trying to stop it getting him expelled from the school. I'm going to talk to Seth now.'

Mrs Waterman was not the sort to be satisfied by such a perfunctory explanation. 'Alan Waterman, you will do nothing of the kind. You're a bull in a china shop. Sit down while I make us all a cup of tea and you can tell me what is going on.'

Mr Waterman sighed, sat down and told her what had happened. Halfway through the account, Mrs Waterman sat herself down on a kitchen chair and covered her face with her hands. Adam got up from the kitchen table, poured the hot water into the teapot and carried it to the table, together with three mugs he rescued from the draining board. He poured the tea, handed out the mugs and pushed the milk and sugar towards Mrs Waterman. She helped herself to both mechanically.

'Mrs Waterman, please understand that this isn't a police matter.' Adam adopted a tone he hoped would reassure her. 'In fact, I reckon they wouldn't even look at it. The real trouble is that Seth is sabotaging his future. That's not something I feel happy about because I can see real potential in him and I want to do all I can to help him realise it. But, first I need to be persuaded Seth isn't influencing other boys with his drug use. If I have any doubt about this, I will have to give evidence that is likely to result in Seth being expelled.'

Mrs Waterman stiffened in readiness to defend her son.

Adam held up his hand. 'I don't for one moment think he is a bad influence. Mr Waterman has brought me here tonight to show me that my faith in Seth is well-founded.'

'Let's not muck about any longer then.' Waterman put his hands on the table and heaved himself up. He walked through to the hallway and bellowed up the stairwell to a bedroom from which the sound of booming music was coming. Seth soon came down.

Waterman led his bewildered son into the drawing room, leaving the door slightly ajar. Adam could see a thin slice of him from his vantage place in the kitchen. Waterman placed his hands on his son's shoulder and looked him in the eye. 'Son, plenty of kids lie to their parents and many get away with it. They choose to be dishonourable. I have always taught you to be a man of honour. If you haven't got honour, you're nobody. Right, Seth?' There was silence for a moment. 'Right now is an important moment in your life. You can either do it right, whatever the cost, or do it wrong and regret it for the rest of your life. Did you take Ecstasy with Gibbo in my boat this afternoon?'

There was a pause. 'Yes, Dad, I did.'

'Have you ever used any drugs besides Ecstasy?'

'Just marijuana. Twice. But that's all. I didn't like it.'

'How often have you taken Ecstasy?'

'Today was my first time. Gibbo came along and I was bored. Dad ... I'm sorry.'

Muffled sounds followed and Adam guessed Seth was struggling a good deal to keep his emotions under control.

Waterman said gently, 'The trouble is, Seth, the school knows about it. You will be expelled if you can't convince them you aren't encouraging other boys to take drugs.'

Seth's voice rose to an outraged, almost hysterical pitch. 'No Dad, I never. I never would get other kids into drugs. It would only take one of them to blab...' He left the sentence unfinished. 'Gibbo wanted me to pass the word around but I wouldn't. He's a no-hoper. I should never have had anything to do with him. Dad, what will happen? Will the school kick me out? Dad, I'm sorry. What can I do?'

'You've been a bloody idiot but you are not without friends at the school. That's how we found out. They care about you and have promised to put in a good word for you, if you show you are worth it.'

'Dad, I'll do anything. I want to stay.' There was more muffled sobbing. 'Two months ago I wanted to leave but now I want to stay and finish my studies.' There was a sniff. 'Do you suppose it'll be possible?'

'That depends on you and it depends on the support of the school. Now, go out the front door to your grandmother's house and make yourself useful there for an hour, while I talk to your Mum.'

Adam heard the front door open and close and presently Mr Waterman entered the kitchen. His face was soft with emotion.

Adam nodded at him. 'He stays. Tell him to report to me at morning break on Friday every week, so he can tell me how things are going. No further action will be taken unless he does something stupid—and I very much doubt that will be the case.'

He rose to leave. Mrs Waterman rose with him and surprised him by hugging him briefly. She had tears in her eyes.

Waterman, however, remained seated. 'Not so fast. What about Gibbo? The bastard is supplying drugs. He nearly got Seth.'

Adam sat down again. 'What do you know about this Gibbo character?'

Waterman stroked his whiskery chin. 'I know the bastard is afraid of heights.'

Chapter 17

Adam was working hard. The school farm was taking shape and he had even managed to sow some winter wheat and barley before the frosts took hold. In the classroom, he had taught the boys the art of using the mouldboard plough. The genius of the mouldboard plough was its ability to turn a layer of soil upside down to suffocate the weeds and loosen the soil. However, this had to be done gently so the soil didn't shatter but preserved its natural structure.

He had then delighted the boys by showing them the tractor, and instituting a ploughing competition with prizes for the straightest and neatest set of furrows of the right depth and width. They quickly became each other's sharpest critics.

Over the last three weeks, they'd been introduced to the safety and handling of tractors under the tutelage of Ted Jarrow. Adam had written out a roster of tractor-driving lessons with Ted. Most of the boys had not yet driven a car, let alone a tractor, so it was the cause of some excitement.

Adam scored a bonanza when he contacted the research scientist, Rowan Eastman, Janice's son-in-law. Over a series of phone calls and emails, he had agreed to the school conducting a powdery mildew research trial for him on spring barley. Rowan had promised that if the trial was laid down and assessed according to specifications, he would come with his team in summer and harvest not only the mildew trial but all the farm's research plots. Adam was delighted.

As a consequence of implementing all these new programs, Adam felt exhausted and in need of a rest. The end of the school term was drawing closer. Choir rehearsals in the Abbey now punctuated the normal school routine as preparations were underway for the Christmas Carol Service.

Adam turned his mind to how he might spend the holiday break. The Edgecombs had made it clear he was welcome to stay in his flat and join them for Christmas, but he felt the need to get away. Gareth was returning to Wales for Christmas, then heading up to Edinburgh to attend a conference. He had said he refused to inflict his family on anyone but strongly urged Adam to join him in Edinburgh. Apparently that city's many hostelries warranted attention.

Adam wasn't at all sure he had the energy for the trip and had declined. He thought he might take the Eurostar to Paris for Christmas but rued the fact he would be visiting that beautiful city at the chilliest and darkest time of the year ... and alone.

As the momentum of Christmas gathered pace, the day of the rugby match between the first fifteen and the old boys—supplemented by some of the staff—was upon them. As Gareth had planned, Adam was down to play fullback.

The game was a one-sided affair that wasn't without its lighter moments. Most of the old boys had met at the local pub for lunch and reminiscences. The consequences of their imbibitions became evident in their game. Adam, at fullback, had to face appalling odds as onslaught after onslaught of fit young men from the first fifteen sprinted down on him. True to Gareth's predictions, Adam tracked and brought to ground anyone unwise enough to be still holding the ball within his reach. In fact, it was only his singlehanded endeavours that constrained the losing margin to a respectable loss rather than a humiliating rout.

Gareth was philosophical about their defeat. He, himself, had been carried off the field in the first half with mild concussion. 'I think we'll leave the stupidity of playing against these fit young boyos to the Old Boys next year.' He refused to countenance any suggestion he should go easy on the festivities because of his concussion and set about joining in the revelries of the Old Boys.

Adam tried to slip away but was caught by Edward. 'Well played, Adam.' His eyes swept over the gathering merriment in the pavilion. 'Not joining in, I see.'

'Ah, no!'

'Hmm. What are you doing for Christmas?'

Adam said nothing.

'Truth to tell, it gets a bit lonely in the cottage in winter, so I wondered if you would like to spend the Christmas break with me. I also need to change the stern gland in *Sanderling*'s prop shaft and would welcome a hand. How would you feel about spending some fairly undemanding time on the marshes with me?'

Adam had an instant mental picture of the marshes with its grasses and sedges bending to the wind, a scene made melancholy with the dim light of winter. It exactly matched his mood. 'I'd like that very much.'

'Fine, I'll expect you for lunch on Thursday week.'

That evening, the phone rang. The unmistakable voice of Alan Waterman growled without preamble. 'What are you doing tomorrow morning at 9:30? Can you get time off? I've invited Gibbo to the gym, and I thought you and I might like to have a chat to him.'

***

Gibbo had hung around the gymnasium in the docklands from time to time and found it a useful place to make new contacts. Occasionally he would even manage to sell some bags of weed. He was making good money now and had managed to buy himself another motorbike. This time, it was almost new.

He had, however, always been intimidated by Alan Waterman and tried to steer clear of him at the gym. Nonetheless, he derived some pleasure in thinking he was grooming the Hulk's kid as a user and was enjoying his growing sense of power. However, he did envy Waterman his impressive physique. His own poor body image still rankled.

So it was that he'd felt surprised, even grateful, when Waterman invited him to begin a weights program in the gym in order to bulk up.

'Great for pulling the chicks,' Waterman had said. 'Why not come in tomorrow at ten and try out a few exercise options. I'll give you some free personal training for half an hour and you can see if you like it.'

Gibbo wasn't used to doing anything much in the morning. His cleaning job began in the afternoon. However, on his arrival at the gym, he discovered a sign on the door: *Closed for maintenance.* Before he could utter a curse, Waterman opened the door.

Gibbo was taken into the weights room where he tried out some of the exercise machines. There was only one other person in the gym, a fit blond-haired man doing bench presses.

Waterman led him to an eight-metre high climbing wall at the end of the gym. Multicoloured projections pockmarked its face. Waterman explained that these provided footholds and handholds when climbing. However, he didn't recommend climbing for Gibbo. He just needed to work his way along the bottom, trying to keep his feet from touching the floor.

'It's great exercise. A bit like doing chin-ups, but much more interesting. Good for the pecs. I'll put you into a climbing harness as a safety precaution. The Workplace Health bods don't want you twisting an ankle if you drop down to the floor. I'll just keep a bit of pressure on the top rope to give you confidence.'

Gibbo looked at the climbing wall with alarm. Ropes dangled down from pulleys on a roof beam. The beginnings of fear prickled his conscience.

Waterman chivvied him on. 'Come on, you'll never be more than a metre from the ground.'

Gibbo stepped hesitantly into the harness and allowed himself to be buckled up. Loud dance music suddenly blared out from the gym's loudspeakers and he wondered if an exercise class was beginning somewhere. *But why so loud?*

Waterman stepped back and hauled on the rope.

With a jerk, Gibbo soared into the air. He screamed in terror and flailed his arms and feet, scrabbling for the wall. He was hoisted up to within a metre of the roof beam, where he hung, spiralling slowly, high above the floor. Paralysing fear and nausea swept over him. He was dimly aware he'd wet himself. Screaming and whimpering, he begged to be let down.

Waterman was completely unmoved.

However, Gibbo saw hope come in the form of the fair-haired man. He was running to the rescue. The man ran past Waterman and began to climb the wall with astonishing speed and agility. He wasn't even using a safety rope. Gibbo reached out towards him and screamed for help.

In just a few seconds, the blond man joined him high above the gymnasium floor. Gibbo whimpered and blubbered, begging to be saved.

The man's chilling answer shattered any hope he had of succour. 'There are three things you should know. The first is that Mr Waterman knows you've been selling drugs to Seth. The second is that my sister died from a drug overdose. The third is that both Mr Waterman and I are going to enjoy watching you die.'

Gibbo screamed.

The pulsating exercise music mocked his terror.

The terrible calm voice of the blond man continued. 'Let me tell you how you will die. We'll drop you to the ground. The top of your legs will break out of the hip joints and the base of your spinal column will smash against the floor, driving your spine through the base of your skull.' He smiled—the smile failed to reach his eyes. 'The drop will feel like this.'

The man nodded to Waterman. An instant later, Gibbo found himself free-falling towards the ground. He screamed. As he was about to smash into oblivion, his fall was abruptly halted. He found himself bouncing up and down on the rope, just a metre above the ground.

Any sense of relief he was still alive was instantly shattered. He was immediately hauled back up to the roof.

He came face to face with the fair-haired man again. The man shook his head. 'You see, we hate drug pushers. You hurt people we love. So think of us as Joe Public, fighting back. And now, unless you give me a good reason why it shouldn't happen, there's going to be a terrible accident and you will die.'

'Don't kill me. Get me down,' wailed Gibbo. 'I'll do anything you want.'

'I don't think there is anything you could offer that would stop us killing you.' The fair-haired man seemed to reflect a moment. 'Maybe if you told me who your supplier was, we could let you live. Maybe you're not the main dealer we're after.'

Gibbo was beside himself. 'I'm not, I'm not,' he screamed. 'But I don't know who he is. I've never seen him. I'm not allowed to see him, not allowed to even hear his voice. He's got a machine that disguises it. He just gives me the stuff. He phones and tells me the pick-up places.'

'What sort of places? How often?'

'Once a week, maybe twice. The places vary...' Gibbo was astonished to see the man take a pencil out of a top pocket and write the details on a pad taped just above his right knee. He looked as cool as an ice cube, completely at ease holding on to the wall with just one hand.

'Not enough,' came his chilly reply. The man put the pencil back into his top pocket and reached across to the rope.

Gibbo screamed.

'Who do you sell to? I want names.' The interrogation was remorseless.

Gibbo blubbered out every bit of information he could think of. His cries of terror gave way to pitiful cries for mercy.

At another nod from the fair-haired man, he was lowered to the floor.

Waterman unclipped his safety harness and hauled him to his feet by the hair. 'Come with me, son,' he growled. 'Your day has only just begun.'

Chapter 18

Back at the boarding house, Adam was sitting down to lunch when Margaret, tray in hand, walked past. Gareth called out to her to sit by him, saying he wasn't at all sure he had recovered from concussion and needed her medical opinion.

'I'm not sure you really want any help from me.' Margaret walked past him and sat at the next table beside Adam. Gareth took it good-naturedly but Adam could see he'd been hurt.

Adam said nothing and ate his meal, biding his time. Towards the end of lunch, he asked quietly, 'Why Margaret? What's the deal? Why hurt Gareth?'

She blanched and looked away from him. Adam waited. She shook her head, turned back to him and hissed, 'Because he's aggravating and not to be trusted.'

Adam was surprised by her venom.

He finished his meal and collected Margaret's plate. 'Why not join me in a walk around our new farm? My first lesson is free this afternoon.'

Margaret looked at him suspiciously.

Adam smiled, waiting.

'Very well.' She said grudgingly.

He helped her into her anorak and donned his stockman's coat. Together they walked across the playing fields to the groundsman's hut. Adam was acutely aware of Margaret's simmering defiance, hurt and guilt, so he elected to speak casually about the farm. 'The winter-sown barley and wheat plots have already started to germinate. The boys have sown the wheat at three different depths, and the barley has been sown at two different sowing dates.' He pointed to the plots. 'You can see the effect now that this has had on the germination rate.'

Ted Jarrow came bustling out of the shed as they approached and nodded to Margaret. 'Ow ya goin' then, Miss? Olright?'

'Fine,' she snapped.

Ted turned to Adam. 'We got a bit o' bird damage at the northern end. Got to go now and meet a geezer wots come dahn to flog me some herbicide. See ya'.' He bustled away, leaving the two of them together.

They strolled between the strips of crop. Some plots were almost bare while others had seedlings with two leaves on. Without looking at her, he said, matter-of-factly, 'Why the feelings of irritation and lack of trust towards Gareth?'

Margaret dropped her head and took a moment to reply. 'Wouldn't you?' she said defiantly. 'He comes on all hot and strong, with all the right words, and then can't wait to finish the night with another woman.'

'And when did this happen?' Adam asked.

She looked at him with evident exasperation. 'When we got back from London. He couldn't wait to take Andrea home and make a move on her.' She looked away. 'I happened to hear him drive that dreadful car of his back at three o'clock in the morning. I'm not a fool.'

'No, Margaret, you are not a fool. Mistaken perhaps, but certainly not a fool.' He paused before challenging her. 'Is it possible you exposed enough of your heart to allow it to be hurt?'

She drew back from him. 'Certainly not! What makes you think so?'

'No one has a reaction against someone like you have shown, unless their heart has been a little bit broken.' Margaret made to interrupt but Adam held up a hand to forestall her. 'And no one stays awake until three in the morning without being motivated by strong feelings.'

'Feelings of scorn.' She compressed her lips.

'Feelings of hurt,' corrected Adam. They were silent for a while. 'What do you want from Gareth, Margaret?'

'I want nothing from him.'

'Then what sort of person do you want him to be?'

She waved an arm irritably. 'Is it too much to ask for some sort of integrity? Someone who is dependable. Someone ... someone like you.' She turned and hid her face from him.

Adam blinked but managed to keep his composure. 'I'm not sure that's the whole truth. I think you naturally like people who are full of colour. I suspect you like romantics.'

Margaret remained silent.

Adam pressed on. 'Your dowager dress and antisocial manner are just masks. I've seen you dance. I've seen the pictures on your wall. I've seen the books in your bookshelf ... and I saw sparks of the real you in London.' He stopped until she was forced to turn and look at him. 'I suspect you love to laugh and that it will be important to you to find someone who makes you do so.'

'Provided they don't make you cry.' Margaret's hands were clenched into fists.

'You need someone with integrity but you also need someone who will call the best out of you—the real you. Isn't that the case?'

Margaret was silent for a long time. 'Yes.' She took a deep breath. 'But it's just a dream. It never happens.'

'And someone who cares for you enough to go to great lengths to win your approval?'

'Yes,' she snapped.

'Someone who remains faithful despite significant other temptations?'

'Yes.' She threw up her hands in exasperation.

'Margaret, I think it is time I told you a story. Once, a young man realised the woman who lived next door, whom he had taken for granted for so long, was, in fact, a lovely and remarkable woman. He longed to see her laugh because he suspected there had been enormous pain in her life. So he began to go to great lengths to give her a happy time and win her approval. He was determined to woo her properly and made careful plans for her to have a wonderful evening out.' Adam paused, waiting to be sure she was listening. 'Even when the object of his affection dressed like a sixty year old spinster in order to protect herself from any overtures from him, he was delighted with her company. Rather surprisingly, she also enjoyed his. Her tight reserve and self-protection began to fall away. But there was a hitch. Another woman, exuding raw sexuality from every pore, crossed his path. Would he remain faithful to his first love who had been, at best, sparing with her favours, or would he drive the other woman home in order to get his hands on her?'

Margaret turned away from Adam. He took her gently by the shoulders and turned her back. She moved her head sideways—away from him.

'I'll tell you exactly what happened next, Margaret. He drops the other woman off at her home, then hotfoots it across to my place where he is as high as a kite in his excitement over his time with you.' Adam dropped his hands. 'It took me over two hours to talk him down and throw him out.'

Margaret's eyes widened but she still said nothing.

'Margaret, the characteristics you described as wanting in a bloke? They exactly match Gareth. It's not anyone like me at all. You have confused understanding with affection. I'm safe because I like you as a friend. But real affection...' Adam shook his head. '...that's something else. Real affection can't help but be a bit dangerous.'

Margaret paled. All traces of defiance had evaporated. 'He ... he was at your place ... all the time?' she stammered.

'Yes, Margaret.'

'Oh.' She turned away, put one hand over her heart, bent over and began to weep. Heartbreaking, mewing sounds escaped her.

Adam let her cry for some time. Eventually he put his arms around her and comforted her. 'I suspect these tears are long overdue.' He rocked her gently.

***

That evening, Adam was again sitting at Alan Waterman's kitchen table. The two of them were nursing mugs of tea and reviewing all that had happened in the gym.

'Gibbo didn't exactly have a comfortable day,' Alan said with evident satisfaction.

Adam decided it might be propitious not to enquire too much about what had happened to Gibbo once he had left the gym. He settled for a vague enquiry. 'What sort of shape is he in?'

'Sore. The boys in the pub took an interest in him. It'll be hard for him to push drugs now everyone knows he's a dealer.' Alan looked at Adam speculatively. 'You certainly put the wind up him. What did you say?'

'Just a little bit of exaggeration.' Adam changed the topic. 'The trouble is, we can't very well go to the police and say we have a list of his customers and a list of the places where the drugs have been dropped off. He scarcely volunteered the information without duress.' Adam grimaced. 'The law frowns on our sort of escapades. There could be consequences.'

Alan was unconcerned. 'We've got a sort of understanding with the police. We work with them.' He jabbed his finger at the piece of paper in front of him. 'And I got the list. I know over half of 'em.'

Adam decided not to explore the nature of his relationship with the police. 'What else do we know? Do the drop-off places mean anything to you?'

Alan picked up the list from the table and looked at it, grunting with scorn. 'Basically, it's the club, places around the docks or along the river.' He slapped the piece of paper on the table. 'It tells us nothing.'

Adam picked up the piece of paper. The list included boat tenders, mooring buoys and loading crates. 'Do you know where these places are?'

'Some. The boats I know, and I can pretty much guess which mooring buoys. Most are round the docks and the loading yard by the marina where the new chandlery's been built.'

'Could the drugs be coming in by boat?'

'It certainly looks as if those involved know their way around the river.'

Adam nodded. 'Well, whatever is going on, I don't think Seth is going to be troubled any more by Gibbo.'

Alan's smile was almost feral. 'I can guarantee it.'

***

Next morning, Adam was in the staffroom to pick up his timetable for the Lent term. Gareth pushed past without giving him the benefit of his customary banter. Adam gazed at his retreating back, puzzled by his out-of-character behaviour. It was almost as if Gareth were giving him the cold shoulder.

Some of the staff were rifling through the morning paper and chatting about what they were going to do for Christmas. Their conversation made him realise he hadn't given any consideration to buying anyone a Christmas present. He would organise for a big bunch of flowers to be delivered to his mother ... and, as he would be staying with Edward, it would be reasonable to buy him a small gift. What about Claire? Would she be joining them?

His mind dwelt again on the windswept, honey-blonde hair and the laughing eyes. It was an image never far from his mind. He found himself thinking of her, even at the most inopportune moments.

He realised he very much hoped she would be joining Edward for Christmas.

After the final lesson for the day, Adam walked down to Highgate and made his way to *The Borrowed Wheelbarrow.* He bounded up the stairs and entered the gallery. Claire was on some folding steps trying to hook a large painting onto an aluminium picture rail. He hurried over and took the weight of the picture, while she hooked it in place.

'Thanks.' She looked him over. 'You seem to have a knack of turning up at the right moment.'

'Hmm. Not yours?' He indicated the picture. It was a stark, highly stylised work with bold brushstrokes, faintly indicative of Chinese writing, except the characters appeared to have become tangled in a nightmare.

'No, it's not.'

'I didn't think so.'

'Oh.' Her voice held a slight hint of challenge. 'And what sort of painting do I do then?'

'I don't know what you paint, but I can tell you what you should paint.'

Claire laughed. She folded the stepladder away, put her hands on her hips and faced him. 'And just what do you think I should paint?'

Adam was quiet for a moment, watching her. 'There's a restlessness about you, a searching, but you haven't surrendered to hopelessness and chaos.' He indicated the picture they had just hung together. 'You wouldn't naturally paint something like this. Your pictures would have unanswered questions in them, things left unfinished.' He looked at the light dancing in her eyes. 'Your greatest friend is colour, warm colours. You love life and embrace it. There has to be movement, restless movement but not senseless movement. You need the safety of enough order to make your pictures beautiful, not just striking. Order is important to you, or needs to be.' He smiled, embarrassed at having said too much.

Her voice was a quiet whisper. 'Do go on.'

He searched her eyes. 'And a touch of pain. The pain of things matters to you—and you've probably experienced it.'

Further conversation was interrupted by the sound of footsteps coming up the stairs. Adam turned to see Andrea push through the door, holding two takeaway cups of coffee.

'Well, hello stranger.' She beamed at him. 'Have we come to recruit some more cavalry to rescue damsels distressed by tweed and uncertainty?' She brush passed Adam and gave him a kiss on the cheek. 'I had a lovely time in London, by the way.' She placed the coffee cups on the counter. 'It's our caffeine happy hour. We always have one at the end of every working day. Do you want me to get you one? It's only from across the road.'

'No, please don't bother.'

Claire blurted out, 'We still have some fruit cake in the cupboard. At least have a piece of that. I'll get it.'

As she walked out into the back room, Adam turned to Andrea. 'Actually, I, umm, do need your help again. I've been asked to spend Christmas with Claire's Uncle Edward. I'm not sure whether Claire will be there.' He smiled sheepishly. 'The thing is, I need Christmas presents for them both ... in case. Are you able to take digital pictures off my memory stick and frame them? I've only put two shots on it, so you'll know which ones they are.'

'Sure,' said Andrea. 'It's one of the things we do. Just tell me what size, what frame and what border you want.'

'I think you know Claire pretty well—Edward too, probably. Can I leave all that to you? The pictures need to fit into a rucksack. Other than that, just make them ... as special as you can.'

'No problems.' She took the memory stick from Adam. 'I'll keep them from Claire's prying eyes and have them wrapped for you to collect in two days. Come about this time.'

Adam nodded his thanks as Claire returned holding, not only a plate of cake but also a mug of instant coffee for him.

She smiled. 'No milk or sugar. Isn't that right? Sorry it's not gourmet. Best Sainsbury's.'

Adam nodded his thanks. He was absurdly grateful she'd remembered how he took his coffee.

***

Back at school, the term began to wind down for Christmas. Adam caught himself reflecting on his previous Christmas. He'd spent it in a rehabilitation ward, surrounded by a severe, utilitarian ugliness no amount of tinsel could disguise. Familiar waves of melancholy stole over him as he remembered. The stabs of pain and searing anguish were still there.

Then he remembered Edward and, curiously, Claire. Thanks to them, life had become bearable again. Edward had warned him it would probably take two years before the worst of the grief left him. He reflected ruefully that he was over halfway. The grief was still raw, but at least he could now dare to face the pain, and even operate within it to a degree. After a moment of reflection, he concluded he was now able to wear the pain as an undergarment, not as a topcoat. He sighed. It wasn't much, but it was something. Perhaps he was making progress.

It was a revelation to Adam how seriously the school took the tradition of Christmas. It was certainly a contrast to his home in Sydney, a city that seemed to rejoice in its secular status. It only allowed a few days of sentimentality at Yuletide, before it engaged again in unbridled hedonism. Sydney seemed to put on Christmas like a fancy dress costume. But this English town was different. It seemed to put on Christmas like a comfortable, well-loved sweater.

The abbey was full for the school's annual carol service. There was the burble of conversation and polite 'excuse me's' as people filed into their seats and sat down, coats steaming in the abbey's warmth. In the background, the organist played a fugue.

Adam watched the gold light from the candles on the choir stalls dance with the shadows on the immense gothic columns.

Suddenly there was silence and a lone choir boy, standing in the opening of the rood screen under the great organ, began to sing in a clear, reedy voice: 'Once in Royal David's city...'

For some reason, Adam found his eyes filling with tears and a faint hope he might enjoy this Christmas with Edward ... and Claire.

Chapter 19

Claire kicked off her gumboots and shook the drips from her raincoat before ducking through the front door of Edward's cottage. She stepped into the parlour to find Edward dozing but Adam awake. Both were ensconced in armchairs close to the fire. Edward snorted to life and gallantly pushed himself to his feet.

Claire had seen Adam's motorbike parked next to Edward's battered Land Rover as she came up the driveway. She was glad it was there—had been anticipating it being there, if she were honest. She stood inside the doorway, a little breathless. It had obviously been a steeper climb up to the cottage than she had remembered.

What a strange man, she thought, as she stowed the gumboots. *A man of contradictions. Self-possessed, yet vulnerable. Perceptive but blind; gentle but courageous. A teacher who looked out for the welfare of his students but who climbed mountains in the most dangerous way imaginable.*

She turned to find him standing in the hallway—watching her. She faced him, not trusting herself to say anything. 'Hello,' she managed eventually. She noticed he was wearing jeans again, but this time he had exchanged his bike jacket for a woollen jumper. His hair was still unruly but neater than she'd ever seen it before. He'd made some effort. He was smiling but looking very tired.

'Hello.' He just stood there, looking at her. Expressionless—almost. Diffident? Certainly ... but also ... pleased, she decided. Yes ... pleased.

She was glad.

Claire allowed his inspection, conscious she wanted to be known by him, to be understood, to be noticed. She searched for his eyes and for a fleeting second found him. Then he blinked, turned away and rubbed his forehead.

Come back!

'It's wet,' she said. *Lame.*

'Yes.'

Feeling as if she'd said too much, Claire made her way into the kitchen and settled her nerves by putting the kettle on. *It's wet. All I could say was, 'it's wet.'* She chastised herself furiously. *He'd stood there looking exhausted, vulnerable and ... good ... very good ... and all I could say was, 'It's wet.'*

Pulling herself together, she called over her shoulder to Edward. 'I've been over to see George on *Sapphire Maid.* He said he'd love to come for Christmas, and even wants to go with us to the service. I've said we'll pick him up at nine fifteen. Is that all right?'

'That's fine,' Edward said.

She came back into the parlour as the kettle heated and leaned on the doorway. She reflected on her visit to George—and how disquieting she'd found it. 'He's getting frail, and I'm worried for him.' She sighed. 'I made him some scrambled eggs, and he took my hand in that shaky old hand of his, put it to his cheek and, for some reason, cried. He was so amazingly grateful. You'd think I'd cooked him a banquet.'

Edward looked up and seemed to set his gaze on some distant thing. 'But you had, Claire.'

She shook her head in disbelief. 'How long will *Sapphire Maid* stay afloat? She's a wreck.'

'He'll die first. Quite soon, I suspect,' Edward said, matter-of-factly.

Claire walked over and put a hand on his shoulder. Edward reached back and squeezed it. 'Don't worry, he won't die alone.'

***

Adam watched and wondered what it would feel like to put his arms around her, just to comfort her.

Edward jolted him back to reality. 'Now Adam, what do you want to do on your first afternoon off? A walk? Fiddle around on *Sanderling?* Stay by the fire? Claire has an appointment in town but will be back for tea.'

What Adam wanted to do was to talk with Claire for as long as possible. What he wanted to do was hold her hand to his cheek. Aloud, he said, 'What I would like to do is have a few hours' sleep, then drive with you and Claire to Scotty's pub where I will buy you both dinner. How does that sound?'

Edward rubbed his hands together in anticipation. 'Capital idea. Thank you, Adam.' He waved a remonstrating finger. 'But I warn you, that's the last meal you pay for this holiday.'

Adam smiled. 'We'll see.'

Edward eased himself out of his armchair and walked into the kitchen, 'I'll ring the old reprobate and book a table. It gets crowded around Christmas.'

A short time later, he came back, chuckling. 'I had to suffer the usual abuse but he's reserved a table for us at seven-thirty.'

Adam mounted the steep stairs, and ducked through the low doorway into his attic bedroom. He barely noticed the uneven floor, or the steeply sloping roof, or the raucous cries of the gulls outside the dormer window. However, he did notice the lingering smell of Claire's scent on the extra pillow on his bed.

He smiled. The pillow had come from her room. She'd probably made up his bed and put an extra pillow there so he could read.

An altogether new and wonderful feeling stole across his heart. It was like the first rays of dawn. It was the experience of peace.

He slept deeply for four hours before Edward woke him with a cup of tea.

***

Adam greatly enjoyed the meal. When they'd finished, Scotty came over and joined them. 'Now Edward, you aren't agoin' to tell me that weren't the best beef you ever 'ad.'

Edward smiled. 'Tolerable, very tolerable.'

'Tolerable!' said Scotty with indignation. 'Now you listen here ol' boy, that were the best beef you ever tasted.' He sniffed derisively and turned to Claire. 'Ah, my lovely lady, I ain't never afore seen you in me pub with the same boy twice runnin'.' He jerked a thumb at Adam. 'Wot's 'e got that I don't, if it ain't too much a secret?'

Claire lowered her head and coloured deeply. 'About forty years less wenching, I'd say Scotty.'

'Just forty!' Scotty burst out in wheezy laughter.

Adam listened to the easy banter, which quickly turned to the subject of boats.

'*The Sultan* and *King William* are overwinterin' at the slipway,' said Scotty. 'It's good to see 'em back.' He sighed. 'When I were a nipper, I remember seeing more'n twenty old spritties packed in 'ere waitin' for a fair slant to take 'em up the coast. Them was the days.' Scotty appeared lost in thought. 'Do you remember sailin' with me in *Osprey* four year ago, Edward? A sou-easter fetched us to the mouth of the estuary ... an' bugger me if we didn't get tangled up in the annual barge race. Quite a sight, it were. Brought back memories.'

'Have you always sailed, Scotty?' asked Adam.

'Yeah, like me dad. 'E were at the fishin' all 'is life.' Scotty pointed his stubby finger at an old photograph hanging on the wall adjacent to them. 'You come 'ave a look at this, boy.' Adam got up and stood at Scotty's side beside the picture. 'Me old Uncle Ned took this shot when we brought up at West Mersea to dodge a foul tide. See that little nipper there? That's me. The big fella on the 'elm is me dad. 'Ard as nails, he were. 'E died two year later in the merchant navy during the war.'

Scotty made to turn back but paused and leaned over to Adam. He jerked a thumb towards Claire. 'You look after Miss Claire. We've got a soft spot for 'er and Edward round these parts.'

Adam was taken by surprise. 'Of course. They're ... both...' He searched for an adequate word and gave up. '...good people. Of course I'll look after them ... although I should tell you Scottie, Claire and I are just friends, barely acquaintances really.'

Scotty placed a large hand on Adam's shoulder. 'Bugger me, boy, but you are blind.' Shaking his head, he pushed past Adam and returned to the bar.

***

Next day, Adam got up late and joined Edward for breakfast. Edward ran over the day's itinerary. 'I've got to sort some medical power of attorney business for old George this morning. I think it'll take a while. I'd hoped to drive into the new chandlery at the docks and pick up a stern gland housing for *Sanderling*'s prop shaft. They've just rung to tell me it's arrived but I won't be able to get there. I won't be much use to you this morning, Adam. Sorry.'

Adam put down his mug of coffee. 'Why don't you let me pick up your package from the chandlery? I could take the bike.'

Claire came into the kitchen, hugging a dressing gown to herself. Her long hair was poofed-up and dishevelled and she was still full of sleep. She yawned and reached for the coffee plunger. 'I'll go for you, Edward.'

As sleepy as she was, she still had a glow of life and a naturalness about her that warmed Adam's heart.

Claire rubbed her face. 'I probably won't get there until this afternoon; I'm going up the coast to a couple of galleries. I need to pick up some of my pictures for the show.' She looked up at Adam and her voice became hesitant. 'Want to come?' She blushed. 'It's a pretty ride.'

'I'd love to.'

'Splendid!' Edward clapped his hands together. 'I'll see you when I see you, then. We'll aim for tea at six.'

***

Claire piloted her small station wagon at a leisurely pace along the country roads. Adam was acutely aware of her but sought to disguise it with a determined show of casualness. Surprisingly soon, the lie became a reality. He looked out the window and watched the skeletal outline of elms against a grey, watery sky with deep contentment.

After twenty minutes of undemanding conversation, Claire surprised him with a question. 'Why do you climb?'

Adam was evasive. 'Why do you paint?'

'I asked you first.'

'I climb because I can't paint.'

Claire gave him a look of reproach and waited, making it clear that she expected more.

Adam, still not sure he was ready to analyse his feelings, let alone articulate them, sought refuge in humour. 'Because nature is the best art.'

She didn't rise to the bait. 'Why do people like you go climbing? I've seen pictures of ... people doing it. They come to a beautiful mountain ... and then turn the experience into something terrifying.'

Adam realised she wanted a serious answer. Mentally, he changed gear and chose his words carefully. 'People climb for different reasons. Some to say they've done it—to prove something to themselves. Some climb to escape from the complexities of life; others, to be at one with nature. It can almost be a spiritual experience.' He searched again for the words. 'Guys who feel like that, never really claim to have conquered a peak. They just share it for a while with something deep within them. They are happy just to have experienced it, happy to have understood it—and maybe themselves—a bit more.'

'Are you one of those people?'

'Um ... usually.'

'Usually?'

'I've sometimes used the mountains to hide.'

'How often have you needed to hide?'

'Only during one period of my life.' From the corner of his eye, he watched her lean forward slightly and grip the steering wheel tighter.

'Do you still feel the need to hide?' She remained looking straight ahead.

Adam took a deep breath. 'No.'

Silence followed. Easy small talk gradually filtered back, reaching out. Exploring. Adam felt strength trickle into their relationship like the quiet of an incoming tide. He savoured the experience.

'And where do you go to hide?' he asked.

***

It was Claire's turn to pause. In an instant, she realised her conversation with Adam was a journey, a brand new journey ... and that they had come to a gate. Would she allow the journey to go further?

She heard her reply from a strange distance. 'I hide in my work. I paint. I paint my feelings, my frustrations, my anger and my love. It's my safe place. It never lets me down.'

He nodded. Claire had the impression she wasn't telling him anything he hadn't already guessed.

She opened the gate further. 'Sometimes I let it become a bit addictive and demanding.' Without quite knowing how it happened, she began to share her story, laying bare her hopes, follies and failures. In the safety of Adam's understanding, she found herself laughing at the lunacy of her life. Somehow, doing so began to rob the past of its tyranny.

Claire was soon threading her way through the traffic of a seaside town. She regretted having to break the spell by arriving anywhere. But one question still played on her mind. She wanted to ask it before the spell was broken. 'Why did you need to hide in the mountains?'

Adam was quiet for a long time, and she began to fear she had pushed too far.

'Because my fiancée died in a car I was driving.'

She was stunned into silence.

Outside, the banality of life continued. She pulled up at some traffic lights. 'Adam ... I'm more sorry than words can say. It must have been terrible.'

'It is.'

His choice of words reminded her forcibly that his loss was still raw and ongoing.

'But it's getting better.'

Ahead of them, traffic was coming to a halt. Claire could see the gallery up ahead. She pointed to it. 'Somehow, that's where we need to get to.'

Getting there didn't look likely. The street was crowded with parked cars. Outside the gallery, some workmen had dug up the roadside with a yellow backhoe and placed a large pile of dirt beside some concrete piping waiting to be installed. They had protected the kerbside and work area with bright orange barriers.

Adam surprised her by opening the car door. 'I'll see what I can do. Drive round the block, if necessary.' He got out of the car and strode towards the workmen. They appeared to have stopped work and were having their mid-morning break.

She watched him talk briefly with the men, smiling and pointing to her car as he did. Amazed, she saw the impassive reserve of the workmen turn into grins. The largest of the men swung himself up into the driving seat of the large yellow backhoe and started the engine. With three deft scoops, he moved the pile of dirt two metres forward. Another workman waved to her, indicating she should drive inside the barrier in front of the gallery.

As she parked and switched off the engine, Adam opened her door. He introduced her to the workmen. 'That's TJ in the backhoe, Winky Dink's on the left, Abdulla and Jack.'

'Thanks so much for helping me,' she stammered.

Adam smiled. 'The deal is, I buy them a cake from the bakery next door and you show them your artwork as we take it out to the car, so they can tell you if its crap or not.'

The men grinned broadly.

Wondering how Adam had managed to arrive at this sort of arrangement in such a short time, she smiled her gratitude. 'It's a deal.'

There followed a ritual that became oddly important to Claire. All of her pictures were quite large. She and Adam carried each one out individually and placed it on a concrete pipe for inspection by the men. After an initial bout of ribald quips, the four road workers warmed to their task as art critics.

Claire valued their instinctive responses.

'Cor, look at that colour. Guy Fawkes night on steroids. My missus would like that. She likes colour.'

'Nah, couldn't live with that. It would give me the heebie-jeebies. Hey Abdulla, I can see your nose there. Do you see it?'

'Ya dreaming. Wassat?'

'Wow! I like that. That's good, that is.'

Adam bought a fruit cake from the bakery next door and, at the men's invitation, she joined them in eating it as they sat on the pipes.

Before she left, Claire shook hands with them all. It was an unusually formal gesture, but somehow she knew it was important.

She continued up the coast road towards their next destination. Yesterday's rain had cleared and the leaden sea was calm, looking at peace in the dim winter light.

Claire was thoughtful as she tried to come to terms with what she had learned about Adam. He no longer needed to hide in the mountains. That was good—very good.

'Um, how long do you plan to be staying at the school?'

From the corner of her eye, she saw him glance at her. For a while, he didn't say anything and appeared to be deep in thought. 'I've a one year contract. After that, I'm not sure.'

'No plans to stay?' She tried to keep her tone light.

'No firm plans, although...'

Although what? She wanted to rush him.

He smiled. 'I find that my thinking changes every day.'

Claire wondered if she was a part of those changes. Would she want to be?

She frowned and concentrated on the road ahead. *I'd like to at least explore the possibility,* she admitted,*very much.*

She shot him another furtive glance. Lines of tiredness were clearly etched on his face. Seeing them persuaded her to slow the car down and to make her way up the coast road at a more leisurely pace.

Towards lunchtime, she steered the car into the gravel car park of a charming pub with a traditional thatched roof. The portents were good, she decided as she looked at a sign in the car park: *Please park prettily.*

'Nice place,' Adam said, as they put in their order for steak and ale pie.

'It's part of my therapy program for you, helping you to slow down.'

Adam smiled.

After the meal, they donned their jackets and walked down the main street of the village for a few minutes in order to breathe in some country air.

All too soon, they turned back to the car. As Adam opened the door for her, he said quietly, 'Thanks Claire. I've really appreciated this.'

She smiled. It felt good to hear him say that. *Gee, he looks good in that jacket.* He hadn't bothered to zip it up. He wore it carelessly, not noticing that the top edge had folded itself under, against his chest. It teased her. She wanted to untuck it, to put her hand against that well-muscled chest and feel its warmth. But she didn't.

They arrived at the next gallery.

Claire smiled as its owner, whom she knew only slightly, gushed with excitement over her upcoming London show. 'Just promise me you will keep some of your work with me when you're famous, darling.'

Back in the car, Adam asked, 'Do they all say "darling" in the art world?'

'Only when they want something ... or want to portray an image.' She smiled. 'What do they say in your world? The world of rock climbing?'

'Asshole, usually.' He laughed quietly. 'They're a pretty self-deprecating bunch. Sort of ... deliberately offhand. Although, come to think of it, underneath all their casualness, their judgment can be pretty harsh. So I guess it's no less dishonest in its own way.'

'It's funny, isn't it, how we all pretend. I see it a lot in the art world. There are some who really love their art and are moved by it. But for many, it's just the currency of people seeking to pay for an image or identity. They're really just competing to be admired.'

Adam nodded slowly. 'Sometimes I feel as if I'm a visitor to planet Earth and struggle to fit in anywhere. I certainly don't understand it. My generation seem to be friendly yet competing, social but lonely. Most of us wear ripped jeans that speak of adventures we've never had and are meticulous about our casualness.' He flicked his hand. 'We're a weird lot.'

Long fingers. Strong.

He laughed. 'We define ourselves against everything—but somehow arrive together at a place of conformity.'

What an extraordinary man. He sees a whole lot more than most people realise.

The top of his jacket had straightened itself out.

Damn.

Claire noticed the first stars beginning to prick the early winter twilight as she drove through the town's docklands to the new marina. The chandlery was large, modern and new, a far cry from Stan's chaotic boatshed in Edward's village.

They picked up Edward's parcel and, by unspoken agreement, walked outside to wander along the marina's pontoons to look at the boats.

She was reluctant for the day to end. So much had been said and left unsaid. She was conscious of a new level of significance in her relationship with Adam that she wasn't yet ready to define. But for now, she was content.

Claire watched a white fishing dinghy nose its way into the marina. A strongly-built man with a shaved, bullet-shaped head brought it alongside the pontoon. An old man carrying a toolbox along the pontoon, paused to watch him. Claire heard him say to the man in the boat, 'Eckhart, you're crazy to go fishing in that thing in winter. Where'd you go?'

The big man hauled a plastic bin of fish up onto the pontoon. 'Bawsley Bank.'

'Any luck?'

'Yeah. Worthwhile.'

'I still reckon you're a lunatic fishing out there this time of year.' The old man shook his head and walked off, muttering.

Adam nodded to the man in the boat and looked into the bin of fish. The burly man nodded back to him, and began to ferry his gear to the marina car park.

Together, Claire and Adam strolled along the length of the pontoon. She was glad of his nearness. Around her, halyards tapped against masts, and fenders squeaked with complaint as they rubbed against the pontoon.

Eventually, the evening chill persuaded them to turn back. As they retraced their steps along the pontoon, Claire stopped to look at the newly-arrived fishing dinghy.

Adam raised an eyebrow.

'I don't understand,' she said slowly, 'why anyone fishing at Bawsley Bank would need two fuel tanks for their outboard. They'd only use half of one of those tanks.

Adam tapped his fingers against his jeans. 'I don't know much about boats, but I do know that those fish were not caught today. Their eyes were clouded and their skin was discoloured. They were at least three days old.'

Claire looked at him in surprise. 'What's he up to, I wonder?'

Adam's answer was to put his arm around her and guide her back to the car.

Chapter 20

Philippa Ruth woke on Christmas morning to a feast of delights and new toys showered on her by doting parents and grandparents. However, her favourite toy wasn't a toy at all. It was a glass aquarium with a small turtle.

It had somehow become important to Adam to buy Philippa Ruth a Christmas present. He had browsed in the pet shop thinking about the little girl, who, despite her fibreglass shell, was so full of life. Adam had seen the little turtles, also in their shells, busily scrabbling away, and had bought one straight away.

***

Christmas day with Edward wasn't like any other Adam had experienced. There was no forced gaiety, no disappointments, no over-catering. Christmas was peaceful, entirely genuine and intensely enjoyable.

The day began when they drove over to pick up George from *Sapphire Maid.* Edward had apologised that Adam would need to sit on the hard bench in the back of the Land Rover, explaining that George wasn't good at bending down low to get into ordinary cars. 'He finds the front seat of the Land Rover easiest to get into.'

They drove to the edge of the saltings where Edward got out and walked along the duckboards to collect George.

Claire climbed over the tailgate to join Adam in the back of the Land Rover. 'Sixty years ago,' she explained, '*Sapphire Maid* was a rich man's motor launch. But for the last fifteen years, ever since George has had her, she's been a houseboat.' She sighed. 'She's in a terrible state of repair. I don't know how she keeps afloat.'

Adam peered out the back of the Land Rover. *Sapphire Maid* was parked in a mud berth sixty metres away. She looked little more than a floating hulk. Someone had once made a brave attempt to put some pot plants around the deckhouse, but these now sported nothing but a few dead twigs.

Edward returned, holding the elbow of a wizened old man who shuffled along in carpet slippers. He was wearing a threadbare pullover under a grimy tweed jacket. The old man's face bore the ravages of abuse and his hand movements were shaky. Despite this, there was no denying the pleasure in his sagging red eyes as Claire waved from the back of the Land Rover. George's attitude changed, however, when he saw Adam and he hung his head, cowed by uncertainty.

Adam called out to him. 'G'day, George, thanks for letting me join you for Christmas. I'd got nowhere else to go.' George appeared to think about the comment, then he nodded.

Edward helped him into the front seat.

They drove the short distance to the old stone church in the village. Claire and Edward supported George as he shuffled through the lychgate, up the flagstone path to the church door. The priest stood at the door. He seemed to know George and welcomed him inside, helping to seat him in a pew near the front.

Adam had not been to church very often in his life. When he did, he felt awkward, bewildered and a little bit of a hypocrite for being there. Today, somehow, it was different. There was little sense of ceremony and a tangible sense of community among the people. The time-honoured carols were sung, the small choir managed an anthem and the children showed their toys to each other.

The priest talked with the congregation from the lectern in a warm, unaffected manner. Adam heard again the timeless story of a God who died on a cross to pay the price for the thousand and one creative ways humankind had found to disqualify themselves from God's presence. The priest talked of hope and of an invitation to a divine friendship that was as large as the cosmos, as intimate as a child in a manger and as committed as a man on a cross.

Prayer followed. Adam noticed George pushed away the padded kneeler and chose to kneel on the cold stone floor. He stayed there through the prayers and through the next hymn when everyone else stood to sing.

Edward, standing beside him, didn't bat an eyelid.

When the service was over, Edward helped George rise stiffly to his feet. Together, they made their way out of the church and back to the cottage for Christmas dinner.

Adam noticed the subtle change to the normal Christmas fare. All of the turkey was cut into bite-sized pieces. The vegetables had also been cut up and roasted in small chunks. There were no peas. Everything on the plate was deliciously cooked, yet easily speared by a fork held by a shaky hand. No wine was served but Edward produced a non-alcoholic hot mead, gloriously rich in spices. George had his in a half-filled mug from which he drank with a straw. Carols were played in the background and conversation flowed easily.

After the meal, George was seated in an armchair by the fire. Edward asked him his opinion on whether it was a good thing to reclaim the land on the foreshore south of the village for housing.

Eventually, sleep began to steal into the old man's eyes and Edward volunteered to drive George back home. 'Before you go George, here's a gift for you. Happy Christmas.' Edward gave George a new woollen jumper. Claire followed this up with a pair of sheepskin slippers.

George was overcome with emotion and gratitude. He then surprised everyone by reaching into his jacket pocket and producing a small gift for Claire. Claire unwrapped it to discover a piece of blue glass that had been worn smooth by countless tides. It had been glued to a coat pin and made into a brooch.

'I found the glass on the shingle beach. Stan helped me glue it,' George said. Claire showed it to Adam with tears in her eyes. In a large shaky hand, George had written on the gift tag, 'To my *Sapphire Maid.*'

Claire gave George a hug.

***

That evening, Adam excused himself so he could ring his mother in Sydney. She would be waking to Boxing Day. He was a day late in wishing her a happy Christmas. In truth, he was procrastinating. Although he'd corresponded fairly regularly by email, he'd only managed to speak to her a few times over the phone in person. He was a little unsure how he would be able to field her questions, largely because he wasn't very confident he understood what was happening in his life.

She answered the phone after only a few rings—almost as if she'd been expecting his call.

'Hi Mum, happy Christmas ... I'm fine ... I'm glad you had a great Christmas with Aunty Jane ... Me? I'm having Christmas with Edward, the lovely old guy with the sailing boat ... Mum, I wish I could show you the marshes here and introduce you to Philippa Ruth, and ... yes ... she's here too. I'd love you to meet her. I've just seen a whole lot more of her art. It's fabulous...' Without realising it, words began to tumble out as he described the last few days he'd spent with Claire. He stopped abruptly when he realised how much he'd been talking.

'Sorry Mum ... Oh, um, I'm glad you're glad ... It's great to speak with you. And Mum, thanks for writing to Dr Fairclough. It's been ... hard, but...' He hesitated. '...good,' he finished lamely. 'Love you, Mum. Bye.'

He rummaged in his rucksack for two parcels wrapped in Christmas paper, and made his way down the steep stairs to rejoin Edward and Claire. Both were seated by the fireside.

He cleared his throat. 'Umm ... you both give so much, so I see no reason why you should escape Christmas without a gift.' He handed each of them a parcel.

Claire unwrapped her present first. It was a beautifully framed picture of Edward with his arm hooked around *Sanderling*'s forestay, gazing out to sea.

'It's lovely,' said Claire, obviously moved. 'Thank you.' She reached out to him and squeezed his hand. Her fingers lingered a little more than they needed to before they let go.

'I can't even remember you taking that picture,' said Edward as he opened his own present. He pulled it from the paper to discover it was a picture of Claire holding *Sanderling*'s tiller as the boat heeled to the wind. Claire, with her long blonde hair streaming in the wind, was looking directly at the camera and laughing. Her vitality and joy radiated from the picture. 'This is wonderful, Adam. You have a good eye for a picture.'

Claire took the photo from Edward, 'I ... I knew you took my picture but I didn't think it would look quite like this.'

Adam smiled. He didn't confess that Andrea had, for some inexplicable reason given him a spare photograph of Claire ... or that this other picture was now propped up against the lamp on his bedside table.

***

On the day the boys returned to begin the Lent term, Adam walked over to the boarding house, driven by a niggling concern for Gareth. The fact that he'd not heard anything from him over Christmas was uncharacteristic. Gareth was in his quarters and his door was open. He had his feet up on the desk and was looking at the contents of an envelope with bewilderment. Adam leaned on the door post. 'Gidday

Gareth, old mate. I trust your vacation was largely untroubled by sobriety.'

'Hollingworth. It was excruciating. Come in and shut the door—we need to talk.'

Adam obliged. 'What's bugging you?'

Gareth looked at Adam closely. 'Damn it, Hollingworth. You are bugging me.' Gareth threw down the envelope and card he was holding on the desk and put his head in his hands. Adam said nothing and waited for Gareth to continue.

'I've had a wretched Christmas. Every day, I've been haunted by a picture of two people I like a lot embracing each other.' Gareth slapped the desk in frustration. 'The savage irony being that I had fond hopes—very fond hopes—that the girl in this little tryst ... would one day be my girl.' He trailed off forlornly and put his head in his hands.

Adam waited for a while and then said carefully, 'Gareth, what about Margaret? I thought you ... well, were interested in her?'

'I am, you blighter.'

Adam was bewildered. 'Then who...?'

Gareth swung round to face Adam. 'Adam. Don't play the innocent. It was you. I saw you two behind the groundsman's hut hugging each other.'

Adam began to protest but Gareth held up his hands. 'Before you go on, I want to tell you that I've thought about it a lot. I happen to think you are an excellent fellow, and, as much as it pains me to say it, if Margaret is happier with you than she is with me, then ... then that's okay. All I want is for her to be happy.'

Gareth passed a hand over his face. 'But Adam, damn it! Why didn't you tell me? Not to put too fine a point on it, it jolly well hurts.' He paused for breath before continuing. 'I worked my way through a good number of beers before I came to this point of relative grace. I began by planning your grisly murder and ended just wanting Margaret to be happy. I'd prepared this great speech ... but when I got back from the Christmas break, I found this in my letterbox. It's from Margaret.' He picked up the card and threw it at Adam.

Adam picked it up from the floor and read it. A slow smile crossed his face. Adam stepped over to Gareth and squeezed his shoulder. 'Gareth, you are a daft bugger. Yes, I'd invited Margaret to have a walk with me because I wanted to know why she was behaving so badly towards you. She'd been so out of character.' He sighed. 'It turns out she thought your coming home at three in the morning after our night in London meant you had spent several hours enjoying Andrea's voluptuous delights and had felt more than a little betrayed.'

'She what? Andrea! For goodness sake!'

'Yep. When I told her the truth, she had a cry. I just happened to be the nearest thing to cry on.'

Gareth absorbed this information with obvious difficulty. He furrowed his brow. 'Then you two are not an item?'

'No.'

Gareth's face cleared. 'Wow.'

Adam waved the card. 'This was meant to be her peace offering to you.' He looked at it again and started to laugh. 'Sorry, mate...' He tried to control himself, but burst into laughter again. 'It's priceless.'

Gareth watched, trying to look dignified. Then he too started to smile. After a moment he joined Adam in gales of laughter.

When their mirth subsided, Gareth made his way to a cupboard where he poured two glasses of sherry.

Adam, although not much of a drinker, sipped one dutifully and stretched back in the chair. 'Gareth, if you would permit the bastard who stuffed up your holiday to offer a small word of advice. Go slow with Margaret. She has begun to make herself vulnerable, which was why she was hurt. It will take a while for trust to build. So enjoy the journey and don't have too many expectations too soon. Be comforted by the fact that things are looking good. But you have both hurt each other, and Margaret particularly will need time to heal. Just let her see the real you.'

Gareth raised his glass. 'Adam, you've just given me the best-ever Christmas present.'

'I thought hers was priceless.' Adam picked up the card again and read what Margaret had written: *Happy Christmas.*

Stapled to the card was a fully paid-up voucher for advanced driving lessons.

Chapter 21

Winter deepened its hold and the weather became cold and wet. Adam was unused to the continual march of frontal systems that typified an English winter and began to despair of it ever being dry again. His thoughts turned to his home city, of the eighteen-foot skiffs skidding across its beautiful harbour at impossible speeds in the summer sun.

Still thinking about boats, Adam reflected on his last discussion with Alan Waterman. It seemed likely drugs were coming into the town by boat. Adam shook his head to rid himself of the image of the ex-chorister lying dead on the roof of the abbey. Why was everyone so vulnerable and helpless in the face of such evil?

The clandestine movement of boats on the river brought to mind a fishing boat with old fish and an extra fuel tank. *Perhaps ... but* ... Adam sighed. *If only I could find out.*

Later in the day, Adam made his way to the physics block and the office of Sandy Hardcastle. In truth, Sandy's office was barely more than a large cupboard. He had nonetheless contrived to fill it with an extraordinary amount of books, computers and strange-looking gadgets. He was absentmindedly chewing his almonds, whilst soldering a wire onto an electrical board, when Adam put his head around the corner.

'Adam, old son, what brings you here?'

'Hi, Sandy. If I wanted to track the movements of a boat without its owner knowing, could it be done?'

'You want to bug a boat?'

'I want to know where it goes.'

Sandy inspected Adam over his spectacles. 'Are you on the side of the angels?'

'I think so.'

'Nothing illegal?'

'No.'

Sandy turned back to his work. 'Is what you are considering dangerous?'

'Umm, possibly.'

'And would it have anything to do with bodies on the roof of the abbey?'

'I don't want to get you involved, Sandy.'

Sandy looked up at Adam speculatively. 'Things have got quite a bit more interesting since you arrived.' He leaned back in his chair. 'Let's just answer your question hypothetically. How big is the boat?'

'About fifteen feet. It's a large open fishing dinghy.'

'Hmm, not much room. But, yes, it could be done.' He looked at his watch. 'I've got to go off and teach right now. Why don't you come out to my place on Sunday afternoon? I can show you some gear that might interest you.' He pushed his soldering kit to one side and scribbled directions to his house on a scrap of paper.

***

Adam was required to supervise the boarders on alternate Sunday mornings but had the afternoon free. He was grateful—the sun had made a reluctant appearance and he felt the need to get outside and engage in some serious exercise. The dark wet winter weather had given him a sense of claustrophobia.

He studied Sandy's directions and consulted an ordinance survey map. Sandy lived nine kilometres out of town, in a house built on a headland that pushed its way into the estuary. He decided to run there. Putting Sandy's directions, a map and his mobile phone into his waist-pouch, he changed into his running gear and let himself out of the Edgecomb's front door.

Adam ran along the pavements, past the terraced houses that seemed to be huddling together for warmth. He cut through a park with its stark, bare trees. Instinctively, he identified the elm, ash, beech and the horse chestnut—so prized by the boys for their conkers. Here and there, people huddled in overcoats made their way along the footpaths, sometimes stopping to talk with each other as they banged gloved hands together to keep warm.

Now and again, he could smell the acrid lime smell of smouldering autumn leaves that gardeners were still trying to burn. Only England smelled like this.

Adam ran out of town into the countryside and settled down to a comfortable rhythm, jogging alongside the tight, tangled hedgerows edging the dormant farmland. In the distance, he caught the occasional glimpse of the estuary.

He breasted the final hill and, all too soon, arrived at Sandy's house. It looked to be a converted farmhouse as there were old outhouses built out of flint stones scattered around it. The house commanded a spectacular view over the estuary. A grubby aluminium fishing punt was pulled up on the foreshore.

Adam heard the sound of clinking spanners coming from the garage. He found Sandy inside with his head under the hood of his ancient Citroen 2 CV. Sandy stood up and regarded his visitor with evident disbelief, as Adam shrugged his way into his lightweight thermal jacket. 'Come in and get warm. My wife, Jess, is visiting her sister this weekend, so I'm a bachelor. But I can rustle up some shortbread and put a kettle on.'

After a restorative cup of tea, Sandy broached the subject of Adam's enquiry. 'Now, about this skulduggery of yours: what exactly do you want to do?'

'I want to track a boat to see where it goes and maybe even follow it to see what it's doing.'

'You obviously don't want to be seen to be following them?'

'No.'

'Then you don't want a bug. They only have a range of about five miles and you'd be seen over that distance on the water. I think what you are looking for is a battery-powered GPS tracking device.'

'The trouble is, Sandy, I don't really know when the boat will set off. If batteries are required, they'd probably run down before the boat set off.'

'No problem. I've got one with an internal motion detector. It shuts off the unit if the vehicle, or boat in your case, is vibration-free for five minutes. This allows the unit to operate for long periods of time with little battery power.'

'How big is the tracking device? It's got to be very small, if I have any chance of hiding it.'

'The actual device is only the size of a matchbox.' Sandy smiled. 'But don't let its size fool you. It includes a GPS receiver, mobile phone technology, a motion detector, and an internal rechargeable battery. I'll get it and show you.'

Adam was amazed but remained cautious. He didn't want to be swept along by events that generated a life of their own. He knew he needed to stay in control and be able to walk away from the idea, if necessary.

After a few minutes, Sandy returned and put a small black plastic box in Adam's hand. A USB port poked out from one end. Adam weighed it in his hand, impressed. 'How often does this unit give a fix?'

'It's currently set to update data every two minutes, but I can reprogram it to update more frequently if you wish.' Sandy pointed to the USB port. 'This gives you two options. You can retrieve the tracker from where you've hidden it on the boat, plug it into the USB port in your computer and it will give you an exact track of where it's been and when.'

Adam frowned. 'That might be interesting, but we wouldn't know what it's actually been doing. Ideally, I'd like the option of following it, or at least chasing it down once the boat has stopped, so we could see what it is doing.'

'Ah. Then you want the other option of tracking your boat in real time on your GPS map.' Sandy pointed to the small black box. 'This unit will do it. The data is transmitted to a central control. You can access it from anywhere in the world. All you need is a mobile phone, a password I can give you, and access to the Internet. Have you got a laptop?'

'No. I've been using the school's.'

'I have an old one you can use. You'd also better take a couple of spare battery packs.'

Adam laughed. 'You make it all sound so simple. Is it really that simple?'

'It's simple to use but the technology is far from simple. You're bouncing information from satellites orbiting 25,000 kilometres above you. It is just your good fortune I am contracted to help with a certain amount of developmental work for the

Defence Evaluation and Research Agency at Malvern from time to time.'

Adam shook his head in admiration. 'Sandy, how come you have all this stuff at home?'

Sandy looked slightly sheepish. 'Ah. Well ... My son went off the rails a bit in his late teens. He used my car to get up to some mischief. It stopped when I was able to tell him where he'd been and for how long.'

Adam raised his brow. 'How did he respond to that?'

'He wasn't happy. But he's since straightened himself out and we're good friends. He's got himself married and we're currently working on an interesting little project together. Now, let me show you how the unit works.'

***

Claire spent the weekend with Edward. She'd volunteered to help Edward clean *Sanderling*'s hull and repaint the antifouling.

Together, they puttered down the estuary to a hard patch of shingle at Wiseman's Point, where a munitions loading platform had once been built.

Over a century ago, naval ships had berthed against this dock to resupply with gunpowder. Because of the inherent danger involved, Wiseman's Point was remote, well clear of civilisation. Claire loved the moody bleakness of the place.

Not much of the original loading platform remained but there were a number of large posts still standing. Local boats sometimes tied up alongside these posts, taking advantage of the hard shingle to scrub the weeds off their hulls when the tide went out.

Claire spent the middle of Saturday toiling away with Edward, cleaning *Sanderling*'s hull before the tide rose again. They had both stayed on board overnight. At ten the next morning, as the tide receded, *Sanderling* again lowered herself onto the shingle and leaned against two of the old wooden posts. Both Edward and Claire set to work painting.

As the day wore on, it became apparent they would not have quite enough antifouling to finish the job. Edward climbed into the dinghy, shipped the small outboard engine and started the engine. 'I'll be back in an hour and a half, Claire. I'll bring back some fruit buns for afternoon tea.' He waved farewell and buzzed away up the estuary towards the town.

Claire continued to work on, brushing the red paint over the rough wooden hull. After she'd finished the seaward side of the hull, she ducked between the pylons and began to make progress on the landward side.

She'd barely begun when she heard the sound of an outboard engine making its way towards her. It couldn't be Edward; he hadn't been gone long enough. She peered around *Sanderling*'s great rudder and saw a white fishing dinghy. She recognised the man aboard as the one she and Adam had seen in the town's marina with the fish that had been dead for three days.

The man throttled back the engine and took out some binoculars. He seemed to be paying particular attention to *Sanderling.* Claire drew back behind the shadow of the hull and watched through the narrow joint between the rudder and the stern-post.

A few minutes later, the man motored forward and edged up to a small mooring buoy. It floated only fifty metres from where she stood. He pulled the mooring buoy and some of its rope and chain on board, made himself fast, then took out a fishing rod and began to fish. As he did, he continued to gaze around in a relaxed fashion.

Claire was about to resume her painting when she saw the man put the rod down and fiddle around in the bottom of the boat. She moved to get a better view ... and was horrified to see the man jerk his head up and stare hard in her direction. She stepped back from the rudder. *What should I do?* After half a minute, she retrieved her mobile phone from her jacket and rang Adam.

***

Adam experienced a wave of delight at hearing Claire's voice. It was the first time she had rung him. However, his delight turned to alarm as she explained her situation: 'It's that strange guy with the fish at the marina. He's moored up to a buoy, fishing. I just feel a bit ...

vulnerable. Edward will be back in a bit over an hour. We're hoping to finish painting before the tide comes back in. It's already started to turn.'

A dreadful chill ran down Adam's spine. He regretted saying anything about the man's strange catch of fish to her. 'Claire, continue to paint. It will give you something to do and keep you calm. Does Edward have a mobile phone?

'No, he doesn't. He doesn't like them...' Claire trailed off.

Adam mentally cursed Edward's antiquated ways, rubbed his forehead and forced himself to think logically. 'Claire, text me every five minutes without fail. Just text "OK" if all's well. Do that faithfully until Edward returns. When he's back, ring me to let me know. If you fail to contact me every five minutes, I will come and find you as quickly as I can. Is that clear?'

'Yes.' Claire paused. 'Thank you. I'm probably just being silly.'

Adam wanted to say *I love you.* Instead, he said, 'Enjoy the painting.'

When he disconnected, he pulled the map out of his pouch and asked Sandy to show him where Wiseman's Point was. Sandy put his finger on the map indicating a point on the opposite side of the estuary. Whilst it wasn't far as the crow flies, Adam could see it was a considerable distance by car.

As the minutes ticked by, Adam shared the reasons for his concern. Sandy frowned and stared at him over his half-rimmed spectacles.

Five minutes passed. No text message came.

After eight minutes of waiting, Adam came to a decision. 'I don't suppose you have a boat with some sort of engine.'

'No, the punt's only got oars.' Sandy sighed. 'The regrettable situation is, old boy, I can't even drive you there. My wife has taken the only car that's currently in one piece.'

'Couldn't we borrow a car from a neighbour?'

'Of course. But it will take you about ten minutes to run to the nearest, and about another thirty minutes to drive to Wiseman's Point.'

Adam screwed up his eyes in anguish. 'Too long.' He pinched the top of his nose. 'What about calling the police?'

Sandy tapped his fingers on the chart. 'Even if they thought there was enough reason to investigate, they wouldn't be able to get there any quicker. It's a very remote place.'

Adam banged the table with his fist and turned away in frustration.

Sandy cleared his throat. 'Ah ... All may not be lost. I said I couldn't drive you there—I didn't say I couldn't get you there.' He turned and picked up a key from the mantelpiece. 'Follow me.' He hurried out the back door to one of the old barns outside and unlocked its large wooden door.

Inside, Adam was amazed to see a gyrocopter standing on its small tricycle undercarriage. Sandy waved towards it. 'This is the project I'm building with my son. Except for the main rotor blades, everything's in place and works perfectly.' He pointed to the end of the barn. 'Grab that rope from the hook, put it in the cockpit and help me push it down to the punt.'

Adam was bewildered but did as he was directed.

Together, they pushed the gyrocopter down to the foreshore. Its small chassis moved easily. When they arrived at the top of the muddy shingle, Sandy asked Adam to help him lift the gyrocopter into the punt. It was a heavy and awkward lift. Nonetheless, they managed to position the main wheels near the rear of the boat so that the prop and tail fin protruded out the back.

'Wonderful. It fits.' Sandy rubbed his hands together. 'We need the prop to be unobstructed ... and the tail fin to move freely.' He picked the rope out from the cockpit. 'Can you tie it down with the rope? I'm no good with knots.'

Adam nodded and began roping the gyrocopter firmly to the hitching rails running round the edge of the aluminium punt.

'What we're building is a makeshift swamp boat,' Sandy explained. 'You'll be driven along by the propeller at the back and you can steer it from the cockpit, using the left and right pedals to move the tail fin.' He tapped the fuel tank. 'The fuel tank is full and the engine primed.' He leaned into the cockpit and pointed to a small lever. 'To stop, shut the throttle. To start, move it to this START position. When it's running, just move the throttle forward to go faster and back to stop.' He paused, raising a finger. 'You've got a thirty horsepower two-stroke driving a forty-eight inch prop, so you should have more than enough power. The thing is, I've no idea how fast you'll go, or how manoeuvrable you'll be. In fact, I have no idea whether it will work at all.' He looked at Adam. 'Are you game?'

Adam nodded.

Sandy took a deep breath. 'Get in, then. I'll start you and push you off. It starts with this pull rope, just like a lawn mower.'

Adam squeezed into the tiny fibreglass cockpit and experimented with the rudder pedals. He looked around and saw that they moved the tail fin located behind the propeller.

'You ready?' shouted Sandy.

Adam checked the throttle was in the START position and gave him the thumbs up.

Sandy gave the starting rope a sharp pull. The engine spluttered and died. He pulled it again, and the engine roared into life. With no more ceremony, Sandy pulled the punt into deeper water, turned its bow around and gave it a shove.

Nothing had prepared Adam for the noise. It was deafening. He trapped the map between his knees and edged open the throttle. The boat skidded forwards and sideways. Adam instinctively corrected its direction by stamping on the opposite rudder. Instantly, the boat kicked around the other way and Adam needed to correct himself again. Having got used to the sensitivity of the steering, Adam eased the throttle to full power.

If nothing had prepared him for the noise, he was even less prepared for the speed he was travelling. The makeshift swamp boat skidded over the calm waters like a water ski.

Adam roared out into the estuary, too anxious about Claire to enjoy the exhilarating ride. The noise was horrendous but the speed was spectacular. Adam flattened out the map on his knees, checked his bearings and aimed the boat with his feet towards the thin grey smudge marking the far side of the estuary.

Despite his impressive speed, the grey smudge seemed to stay the same size for an eternity. Fortunately, Adam saw from the map that the navigation would be straightforward. There were only two headlands that might be confused. One had a gaggle of houses on it and the other had nothing other than Claire and *Sanderling.* Easy. *Please God.*

The swamp boat skidded across the water and then, quite suddenly, the details of the far side of the estuary began to resolve themselves. Adam saw the headland with the buildings on the end and kicked the boat a fraction to the left.

A moment later, he saw *Sanderling* in the distance. She was just out from the foreshore of the distant headland. Adam steered straight for her. He could see no signs of anyone.

Sanderling was leaning against some posts. Water had nearly covered the shingle bank she was standing on.

Adam aimed for a high spot on the shingle and cut the throttle. The swamp boat came off the plane and sank drunkenly into its own wake before the following bow wave drove the boat onto the shingle bank with a bang. The boat skidded up the bank and came to a halt. Adam wasted no time. Wriggling out of the cockpit, he started to shout for Claire as he ran towards *Sanderling.*

With an impending sense of dread, he darted round *Sanderling*'s bow and leapt up the ladder roped to her side. In the instant he took to check his footing on the ladder, he saw beyond his foot a wisp of gold. He jumped back down onto the shingle and ducked under *Sanderling*'s rounded hull.

Claire was wedged under the bilge, the water of the rising tide beginning to wash around her, moving her hair.

Adam dropped to his knees and turned Claire's head upwards so it was free of the water. Relieved that her mouth had not yet been fully submerged, he dragged her up the shingle bank and knelt down beside her to check her breathing.

He could feel nothing. Immediately, he put her head back, covered her nose, pressed his mouth against Claire's and began to breathe slowly, one breath every fifteen seconds.

To his intense relief, she gave an involuntary cough. She coughed again, and Adam turned her over as she retched onto the sand. He cleared her mouth with his finger and checked her pulse. It was faint, but regular. He turned her onto her side, to put her into the recovery position. As he did so, he noticed blood coursing from a wound on the back of her head.

Adam checked her over for other wounds, talking to her all the time. 'Claire. It's okay. I'm here. It's Adam. You're going to be all right. I'm just checking you over before putting you into a boat to take you to the doctor. Claire, can you hear me? Can you see me?'

There was no response. She was deathly pale and far too cold. Adam raced up the ladder and came down back with a first aid kit and a quilt from one of *Sanderling*'s bunks. He wrapped her in the quilt and then bandaged her head with a crepe bandage.

Having satisfied himself she was breathing regularly, he picked her up and hugged her. The thought of losing her was unthinkable. He looked at her face, so pale and vulnerable. A crushing anguish gripped his heart and he wanted to scream at the heavens.

Not again. Not again.

He scooped her into his arms and carried her to the swamp boat. There, he laid her carefully between the main wheels of the gyrocopter's undercarriage. After gently covering her head with the quilt, he took out his mobile phone and rang 999.

When his call was answered, Adam rattled off the details.

'My name is Adam Hollingworth. I'm with a woman who is recovering from near drowning and who has a nasty head-wound. She is stable at the moment but is in need of urgent care. Possible hypothermia. She isn't alert or responding to questions. Please have an ambulance to meet me at the slipway of the marina in the town docks as soon as possible. I will be arriving in the next few minutes in a swamp boat.'

Adam checked the receptionist had the details and disconnected the call. He pulled at the ropes tying the gyrocopter to the punt and found they had loosened slightly. This presented a risk he was not prepared to take, so he took time to tighten the trucking-hitch knots. Once satisfied all was in order, he reached into the cockpit, set the throttle to START and pulled the starting cord.

The warm engine immediately roared into life and tried to push the boat up the shingle. Adam turned the boat around, stepped carefully on board and climbed into the cockpit. When he eased open the throttle, he noticed the boat moved more sluggishly than it had before. *Extra weight. Please God. Please God.* He pushed the throttle fully open and, to his intense relief, the boat broke out onto a plane and began to skid across the water.

Adam aimed the boat up the estuary he knew would eventually narrow into the river leading to the town. He found he had to keep his wits about him because, the closer he got to the town, the more he needed to avoid moored boats and mooring buoys.

He roared past a white fishing dinghy puttering back up to town. He recognised the man in it as the one he'd seen at the marina. The man stared as he sped past.

A few minutes later, the town came into view.

Adam skimmed past the dockland wharves towards the marina. As he approached, he eased the throttle back and kicked the rudder bar, forcing the boat to skid sideways and head towards the slipway. The shattering noise of his engine echoed back from the buildings on the foreshore.

He switched off the engine and coasted into the concrete slipway. He could hear nothing for several seconds because of the ringing of his ears. As his ears began to recover from their battering, he began to hear the wailing siren of an ambulance. Moments later, he could see it nosing its way through the marina car park towards him.

As he twisted sideways to push himself out of the cockpit, he saw

Edward standing on a nearby pontoon. He was holding a tin of paint and was staring at the swamp boat, open-mouthed. Adam waved to him.

As Edward started to run, Adam bent down to check on Claire. She was still breathing ... but felt disturbingly cold. He pulled the quilt tightly around her and lifted her into his arms.

Edward met him as he carried Claire up the slipway.

'Edward. Claire's had an accident.' His voice sounded strange in his own ears. 'I think she's okay but she is going to hospital in that ambulance. I'll go with her. Please look after this boat.' He rushed on past, stumbling with Claire in his arms, until he reached the gurney the paramedics had pulled from the back of the ambulance.

Chapter 22

It was midnight before Adam was allowed to go in and sit beside Claire's bed. The hospital had put her into a single room with dim lighting. He'd learned she'd been given a thermal bath, X-rayed, stitched and was now on a drip dispensing antibiotics and fluids.

Wires and tubes were hooked up to intimidating machines that blinked their information into the gloom. Adam had been given permission to sit with her, provided he didn't talk or make any distracting noises. She had not fully regained consciousness and had only once drowsily murmured her name upon the insistent inquiry of the doctor.

Upon their arrival, she had been whisked away into emergency. With nothing else to do, Adam had made his way to the pay phone, consulted the telephone directory and made two phone calls. The first was to the police, suggesting they interview a Mr Eckhart, whose fishing dinghy was usually moored in the town's marina. He was known to be nearby when Miss Claire

Sanderson had come to grief. In fact, Miss Sanderson had rung Mr Hollingworth just prior to her being knocked unconscious to express her feelings of vulnerability at his close proximity in such an isolated location.

The police were interested, took down the facts and told him they'd send an officer to the hospital to take down more details.

His second phone call was to Sandy Hardcastle, explaining that his punt and gyrocopter were currently at the town's marina in the care of Edward Bryson. Adam expressed his heartfelt thanks, saying that Sandy's creative genius had, very probably, saved Claire's life.

Sandy was greatly relieved Claire was safe in hospital. He said he'd borrow a car straight away, hook up his trailer and collect his makeshift swamp boat before it attracted too much attention.

An hour later, a young police officer had been to the hospital to collect further details of the incident. He'd eventually left, leaving Adam to continue his vigil.

The interminable waiting was made slightly more bearable when Edward joined him at eight o'clock. Edward told him Sandy had collected his swamp boat but had been unable to escape the attention of the local media.

A nurse had then come out to report that Claire was stable but was undergoing more tests. Adam and Edward had sat together for another three hours before Adam persuaded Edward to get some sleep, promising he would ring the moment there was any news.

Adam was then allowed to go in and sit with Claire.

He looked at the beautiful, pale face and the golden hair spilling out from her bandages onto the pillow. Demons of despair clawed at his heart. Why was he so dangerous to the women he loved? Why did they always suffer? He rubbed his forehead briefly before returning his gaze to her.

Gradually, the softness of her face began to chase away the demons of anguish, leaving him with a deep, profound longing.

At one o'clock in the morning, he fell asleep.

***

At two o'clock, Claire regained consciousness. Her eyes fluttered open and she gazed around in bewilderment until she discovered Adam. He had drawn his chair close beside her bed and had fallen asleep with his hand in hers.

She looked at him. Questions were beyond her. He was there. That was enough. She relaxed in his care and fell back to sleep.

***

At six o'clock, Adam woke. Claire was still sleeping. He got up quietly and reported to the night staff that he was going. He needed to get cleaned up and be ready to teach the first lesson at school. Adam gave them his number and asked the staff to ring him the moment there was any news.

He walked out of the hospital and began the thirty-minute jog back to number four Prior's Lane.

***

At the end of the day's teaching, Adam was exhausted. As he threw his bag of books onto his bed, the phone rang. It was the hospital telling him Claire had regained consciousness. However, they warned, she was very weak and visitors had been restricted.

Adam's incredible relief battled with his frustration at not being allowed to see her. He caught himself pacing up and down, and made himself lie on his bed. It didn't work. He pummelled the pillow to make it more comfortable and lay down again. Still unable to settle, he sat up, turned the pillow over, hit it again and tried once more. Finally he gave up, sat on the end of the bed and wondered what to do. As he did, it occurred to him Andrea may not have been told Claire was in hospital. He would tell her.

Adam made his way down the stairs, pausing outside the lounge room door in the hope of hearing Philippa Ruth's high-pitched antics. There was silence. She was probably asleep. He opened the front door and made his way down to Highgate and *The Borrowed Wheelbarrow.* Before entering the gallery, he crossed the road and bought two takeaway coffees from the café.

When he arrived upstairs in the gallery, he saw that Andrea was showing a middle-aged couple a painting at the end of the room. Today she was wearing a long black dress with a dangerous neckline. He raised the cardboard cup of coffee so she could see it, received a small nod of appreciation and sat down on a red settee to wait for her.

It took only a few minutes to complete the sale of the picture and farewell her customers. 'How's Claire?' she asked him the moment they left. 'Edward rang this morning and gave me the bare bones. It all sounds unbelievable. Is she going to be okay?'

'She's stable. I'm still unsure of the details.' He shrugged. 'They're doing more tests. The doctors are optimistic.' He could hear the catch in his voice.

'What on earth happened? How did she get hurt? Was it an accident? How did you find her? I want details.'

As best he could, he gave them to her. Andrea listened in stunned silence. After she had digested the facts, she looked him up and down. 'You look dreadful, by the way.'

Adam smiled. 'Thanks.'

She remained thoughtful for a moment. 'Thanks for rescuing our Claire.' Turning away, she burst into tears.

Adam allowed the tears to flow for a few moments before he stepped forward, turned her around and held her in his arms. Eventually she sniffed, stepped away from him and brushed her tears from his jacket lapel. Forcing herself back under control, she gave a bitter laugh. 'I'd love someone to rescue me like that someday.' She turned away to dab at her face with a handkerchief and repair her ravaged face.

That done, she began to tidy up a pile of unframed pictures on the counter. Adam watched in silence. After a few moments, she paused, sighed and dropped her shoulders, as if in defeat. 'In fact, I'd like someone to rescue me right now.'

'What's the matter?'

Andrea waved her arms to indicate the gallery. 'It's this place. I desperately need someone to look after it, even if only for three or four hours a day, so I can sort out the office.' She sighed. 'On top of the usual admin, I'm also Claire's P.A. Her art show in London is only weeks away and there's masses to do.'

'Hmm.' Adam reflected for a while and allowed a long silence before he changed the subject. 'Why did you send me a spare photograph of Claire?'

Andrea gave a wan smile. 'Did you like it?'

'Very much.' Adam waited for Andrea to be more forthcoming.

Andrea compressed her lips. 'Before I answer you, let me ask you: how much do you like Claire?'

The question disturbed Adam a good deal. It forced him to face a reality he had been trying to suppress. 'Umm, very much.'

'Well, you darn well better.' She paused. 'Claire has been different lately. Your name keeps popping into our conversations and she's been looking pretty damn fantastic.' Andrea jabbed Adam in the chest with her finger. 'I think you're the reason. When I confronted Claire about it, we had girl talk—which you may not know the details of.'

Adam smiled.

'Anyway, as a result, I decided to give you the extra picture to give you a hint.' In a gentler tone, she added, 'Claire knows nothing about it, by the way.'

Adam nodded and said nothing. He was conscious of the flaring of hope, a hope that was almost immediately followed by crushing despair. He dropped his head. 'Thanks for the picture ... and the hint.'

His mobile phone rang. 'Adam, Headmaster here. Sorry to disturb you. Are you available to meet with me in my office in half an hour?'

Adam was conscious of being bone weary. He had slept very little in the last forty hours and had endured horrendous emotional demands. 'Of course, Headmaster.'

***

Janice had obviously already gone home as the headmaster answered the door at the top of the gracious Georgian steps himself. He ushered Adam upstairs into his office, waved him into a chair and remained standing. Without saying anything, the headmaster picked up the local evening paper from his desk and handed it to him.

Adam scanned the front page and was shocked to discover a picture of Sandy smiling sheepishly in front of his improvised swamp boat. The banner headline read: *Dramatic rescue.* The article following gave the bare details of what had happened.

'I normally like to know about these things before I learn about them from the press. You've had quite a time of it by all accounts. How are you feeling?'

'Tired.'

The headmaster nodded. 'I will ask the science senior to give you tomorrow off. I want you to rest and regain your energy. But that's not why you're here. The press are hounding me for information and interviews with you. The question is, how do you want to handle it? I can invite them here to talk with you, or we can feed them a press release. They will probably require a photo. We have yours on file if you don't want to face their photographers.'

He held up a cautionary finger. 'Adam, be warned, they are very keen at the moment and wanting to paint you as the local hero.'

Adam rubbed his forehead. 'I'm very sorry, sir. I had no idea this...'

The headmaster ignored him and continued. 'I happen to think the press are probably right. The question is, how do you want to handle it ... and can I help?'

Adam tried to think. 'Um, yes. I certainly don't want to meet the press, so I'd prefer to give them a press release with my photo. It's just that I'm not very familiar with handling the press or writing what they want to know.'

'Sadly, I am, so I'll help. Sit down at that computer and write it out. I'll proofread it. We'll scan in your picture and email the whole lot tonight.

Adam noticed that his file, with his picture on top, was already on the headmaster's desk.

When Adam had finished, the headmaster read it through and asked a few questions. 'Right. I'll edit this and send it off. You go and get some rest.'

***

It was two days before Adam was allowed to visit Claire again. She needed rest, the hospital told him. Was he a relative? No. Was he a boyfriend? This made Adam's heart lurch. 'Um, no.' He was then told to wait a few days until Miss Sanderson was more robust. She was fighting off an infection at the moment and needed complete rest because of her head wound. In the end, it was only Edward's intervention that secured him entry into her ward.

Adam came to her room and watched her from the doorway. She was beautiful. There seemed to be fewer wires and tubes around, but her face, once so pale, was now flushed red. *Probably the infection.*

She had her eyes shut and Adam thought she was sleeping. He crossed over and pulled up the chair beside her, as he had done the first night. Taking her hand in his, he sat down.

Claire smiled weakly and said without opening her eyes, 'Hello, Adam.' She opened her eyes and looked at him. 'I knew it had to be you.'

Adam said nothing for a very long time and simply looked at her. He didn't trust his voice. 'I seem to be responsible for getting you...' He paused, seeking for the right word. '...hurt.'

He felt her hold on his hand tighten. She blinked. 'And I seem to play the part of the ditzy blonde, being pathetic and needing to be rescued.'

Adam scoffed at her self-deprecation. She had never been ditzy or pathetic. She was wonderful, talented, and sensitive. All he could trust himself to say was, 'Hmm.'

They both remained quiet for some time.

Claire lowered her gaze. 'I thought for a moment, the other day, that ... well, that we might...'

Adam felt her stroke the back of his hand with her thumb. It was the tiniest of movements, but the effect was electric. It caused him to start with surprise.

Claire let go of his hand. 'But then I thought it probably wouldn't work. You know ... me with my work, the art show coming up; you ... teaching.'

Adam rubbed his forehead. *Yes, it would work. I'd make it work. I want it to work. Desperately.* But he heard himself say, 'I thought ... just for a moment ... the same. But I don't seem to be very good for you, so maybe it's better if...' He paused. *It's not better. I want to take you in my arms and*

protect you. I want to hear you laugh, run my fingers through your hair and make love to you. I want to marvel at your creativity. I want to be warmed by your extraordinary compassion. I want to delight in everything about you.

'Just friends then,' said Claire.

'Yes, I think that's probably best.' Every instinct in him cried out in protest. *Claire, don't do this to me!*

A lengthy pause followed. 'I'm glad you're getting better,'

'Thanks.' She closed her eyes. 'And thanks for rescuing me, by the way.'

Adam swallowed. 'Rescuing you will always be a ... privilege.' He forced a smile. *That, at least, was true.*

More silence.

Adam cleared his throat, 'Um, they tell me that you can't remember anything about what happened after your phone call to me.'

'No,' she said.

'The police had a talk with the guy in the boat and concluded there was no evidence to suggest foul play.' *But I know there is.* There was simply not enough water to have wedged Claire against *Sanderling*'s keel.

Adam's brooding thoughts were interrupted by a nurse who bundled him out of the room, so she could give Claire a cooling sponge bath.

As he stood up to go, he thought he saw a tear on Claire's cheek. He hoped he hadn't wearied her too much.

***

Eckhart wasn't given to fright, but he admitted to himself he'd received a nasty shock. And if the events of the last twenty-four hours were not enough, what he'd now just discovered caused him to swear savagely under his breath.

He had wanted to do violence, needed to do violence, but his quarry had flown.

He'd chosen to let himself into Gibbo's apartment at three o'clock in the morning—a time when resistance was at its lowest. After pulling a stocking mask over his head, he'd drawn his snub-nosed pistol and mounted the stairs. Gibbo was three days late with his payment of six hundred and fifty pounds. It had been a harrowing week—and he was angry.

The girl at Wiseman's Point hadn't died. He'd chided himself for his carelessness. While it was doubtful she'd been able to see anything from where she stood, he needed to be sure. He did admit to himself, he'd also enjoyed the challenge, and the chance to prove himself yet again ... to be dominant, to be unassailable.

For four days he had lived in real fear the girl had seen something and had told the police from her hospital bed. But nothing had happened and now he was sure he was safe. Nonetheless, he would have to be careful.

It had been a close call. He'd nearly chosen to run and lose all he'd laboured for over the last year. In the end, he'd taken the merchandise he'd pulled up, from under the mooring buoy at Wiseman's Point and dumped it. It was now in a weighted bag beside an oyster withy in a side channel. He'd pick it up later. Reasoning there was no way the woman could have reported anything incriminating, he'd continued up the river and brought his boat into the marina.

It was just as well he'd been careful.

The police had questioned him that night. They had been very polite and courteous. Had he seen anything?

'No.'

'Why would this woman have misgivings about you being near her?'

'Women, they're so neurotic these days. I've no idea. Had she been raped or robbed?'

They'd wondered how this woman could have been knocked out and found under the bilge of a sailing boat.

'She probably hit her head on one of the rotten crossbeams of the old loading platform. Rusted bolts are sticking out everywhere. The tide probably washed her under the boat. Is she all right now? It must have been a bad experience.'

They'd asked if they could look around his boat and his rooms.

Eckhart wanted to tell them to go to hell. 'Of course, go ahead.'

They'd found nothing. He was in the clear, but it worried him that the police now knew of him.

How the hell had the person in that crazy swamp boat found her? It was a mystery.

He didn't like mysteries.

And so he was angry. Someone was going to pay. He'd relished the thought of smashing his fist into that pathetic animal, Gibbo.

But it wasn't going to happen. At least, not tonight.

Gibbo's room was empty. Eckhart could see it had been cleared of anything of value. Drawers were pulled open and empty. Only some soiled linen remained.

He'd done a runner.

Eckhart cursed viciously, holstered his pistol and let himself out the way he'd come.

Chapter 23

Adam found Margaret on the first floor landing outside her dispensary. He leaned against the ornate banisters. 'Margaret, do you have a moment for a chat?'

'Of course. Come into my room.' She led Adam into her quarters and sat him down.

Adam looked around again at the impressive display of photographs on her walls. 'Umm. This is a long shot ... and please know there's no pressure at all.' He swallowed. 'Did you know that Andrea is part-owner of the art gallery down on Highgate, *The Borrowed Wheelbarrow?*'

Margaret nodded. 'Yes, I've been in there. It's nice.'

'Well, aah, the other owner, Claire, is in hospital. She was the one who...'

Margaret gave a small smile. 'Yes, I've read all about it. Extraordinary. You did well, by all accounts.'

'Hmm, well ... the point is, Andrea is very short-handed at the moment and is desperate for someone to take care of customers for a few hours each day, so she can catch up with the paperwork. I know you generally have the afternoons off as you're on duty in the evenings. I was just wondering if you'd like to work in a gallery in the afternoons for a week or so.'

'What makes you think I'd know what to say or do in an art gallery?'

Adam pointed to a large book in her bookcase: *The Golden Age of Art.* 'You're well read, intelligent and have a good eye for art. Just look at your photos. I think you'd manage easily. In fact, I think you might enjoy it.'

Margaret ran her eyes around her small living room, and then returned her gaze to him. 'I have to confess, I'm beginning to feel a bit claustrophobic in here these days.' She paused. 'Do you think I can do it?'

Adam nodded.

Margaret drew in a deep breath. 'Then I'll go down and talk to Andrea tomorrow.'

Adam smiled and got to his feet. 'Watch out, Margaret, that wild side of yours is starting to wake up.'

'If it is, it's your fault!

***

At two o'clock next afternoon, Margaret made her way up the stairs to the gallery. When she pushed through the door, she saw Andrea with a sheaf of papers in her hand, rubbing her forehead.

Margaret felt very self-conscious. 'I heard that you were short-handed at the moment and might appreciate some assistance, even if it is very inexpert help.'

Andrea slapped the sheets of paper on the counter, stepped forward and gave Margaret a hug. She stepped back with a beaming smile. 'Adam?'

Margaret nodded.

Andrea glanced past Margaret with a haunted expression as people could be heard coming up the stairs. Margaret turned to see two couples push through the door and begin making their way round the gallery.

Andrea grabbed Margaret's arm. 'I'm desperate. You're hired.' She reached back and picked up a folder from the counter. 'Here's the file on all the pictures in the gallery. I've got to go to the computer in the back office. I'll come out when you make your first sale and show you how to wrap and record the sale. Off you go.'

Margaret was staggered at the speed things were happening. It was ridiculous. She knew nothing. It was ... exciting. A pleasurable feeling of abandon began to steal over her. It was a feeling she'd not experienced for a very long time. 'If you're sure.' She was hungry for more confidence.

Andrea grinned and took her by the arms. 'Darling, I am so sure, you wouldn't believe it.'

She stepped back, looked at Margaret's hair and pursed her lips. 'Margaret, do you mind if I do something to your hair to make you fit in a bit better in this gallery? This isn't usually a place people come looking for a school matron.'

She felt herself blanch. 'What do you want to do?'

'I'll show you.' With that, Andrea turned her around and unfastened her bun. Red hair cascaded over her shoulders.

'Shake,' ordered Andrea.

Margaret shook.

She felt Andrea comb through some loose strands of her hair with her fingers. 'You look fantastic. Now, go get 'em, Tiger.' With that, Andrea gave her a small push, and turned towards the office door.

With a sense of unreality, Margaret made her way to the nearest set of customers.

***

Margaret placed her tray on the table and sat down next to Gareth in the dining hall.

From the corner of her eye, she saw Gareth lean back and smile. For the briefest of moments, he raised his hand as if to brush back a strand of her hair. She hadn't had time to put it up into a bun as tight as normal. Her afternoon at *The Borrowed Wheelbarrow* had been hectic. But he lowered his hand again.

A pity.

Across the table, Adam looked at her and nodded, almost imperceptibly.

'Hi Margaret.' Gareth put his hand into his jacket pocket, withdrew the voucher for advanced driver tuition and began tapping it up and down on his hand. 'I'm booked in for the next three Saturday afternoons for lessons. They've even got this skid pan.'

Margaret smiled and passed him the bread. 'I'm glad you...' She paused, and tried again. 'Gareth, I'm afraid that I have not behaved ... very well.'

Gareth began to interrupt, 'Margaret, if there has been anything...'

Margaret held up her hand. 'It's nothing that you have done. It's just me ... working something through.'

For a while, they both said nothing. Margaret was feeling her way, allowing herself to adjust to the possibility of a new level of friendship. 'The driving lessons are just my way of protecting you...' *Whoa, too far!* She swallowed. '...from your own crazy driving.'

Gareth looked at her. She could feel him running his eyes over her sensible dress and saw him shake his head slowly.

Margaret coloured. She knew he'd seen a less sensible side to her, and understood her dress didn't define her—at least, it didn't define her completely.

'Thank you,' Gareth said.

She allowed the smallest of smiles to play on the edge of her mouth. 'Don't mention it.' She forestalled any more discussion by biting delicately into a piece of bread.

***

Adam was relieved to see the atmosphere between Margaret and Gareth had improved. Margaret still maintained a lot of reserve but Adam noticed her stealing an occasional covert glance at Gareth.

He sighed. He'd managed to get to the hospital only twice more before Claire was discharged into Edward's care. Both occasions had been frustrating. He loved seeing her. Simply being with her was a heady mixture of delight and longing, but he'd noticed she had retreated to a safe place.

For his part, he found silence the easiest compromise. He had simply sat for hours giving her the gift of his presence—if not the gift of honesty. Only once had his façade nearly dropped. He had made to leave, frustrated at his inability to speak his heart. Claire had reached and grabbed his hand. 'Don't go.'

He'd sat down again, holding her hand.

Claire had leaned back into her pillows and closed her eyes.

She'd remained in hospital for a full week, recovering from hypothermia, concussion and an infection. The doctors were quietly surprised her recovery wasn't more rapid and broached the possibility of post-traumatic depression.

It was no surprise to learn Edward had made provisions for her to stay with him and that a community nurse had been organised to visit her regularly.

Two weeks after Claire's release from hospital, Adam caught up with Margaret in the foyer of the boarding house. 'How are you going?'

'Fine. Did you know that Claire returned to *The Borrowed Wheelbarrow* today?'

'How did she look?'

He saw Margaret eye him speculatively before replying. 'Very weak and pale. I think it's way too early for her to be up and about, but she's determined to help organise the final details of her London art show.'

'So your services at *The Borrowed Wheelbarrow* are no longer required?'

Margaret lowered her head. 'No. They want me to continue. I'd volunteered to go but Andrea just ordered me back to work.' Margaret smiled. 'She even gave me a pay packet.'

'I expect you more than earned it.'

'I'd have done it for nothing,' Margaret said. 'I found it...' She paused.

'Liberating?'

She nodded.

***

Adam followed a young businessman up the stairs of *The Borrowed Wheelbarrow* and pushed through the glass door into the gallery just behind him.

Inside, he saw Andrea behind the front counter, pecking away at a laptop computer. She blew a strand of hair from her face and smiled at the young man. 'Welcome to *The Borrowed Wheelbarrow*. Enjoy looking around. Someone will be with you shortly.'

As the young man nodded and ambled off, Andrea beckoned Adam to join her behind the counter. She got up and dragged another stool from behind her to the counter for Adam to sit on.

'Claire not here?' Adam asked, looking around.

Andrea kissed him on the cheek. 'No. She's working from Edward's today.'

Adam tried to hide his disappointment.

Andrea took Adam by the lapels. 'She's not been her usual...' She looked over his shoulder at the sound of footsteps coming from the back of the gallery. She whispered conspiratorially, 'Shhh,' and patted the stool beside her. 'Sit down and watch this girl in action.'

Slightly bemused, Adam did so.

As he sat down, he saw Margaret introducing herself to the young businessman who had entered the gallery. She listened as he asked what paintings would make the best business investment. He wanted to diversify his portfolio.

'And what sort of art are you interested in buying?' Margaret asked.

'I don't really care. I'm just interested in good business.'

Andrea rolled her eyes. Adam had put his head next to Andrea's to give at least some pretence they were not eavesdropping.

He saw Margaret nod slowly before saying, 'Contemporary art is a very uncertain place to speculate. But the art in this studio is some of the best around. Claire Sanderson is about to have her first exhibition in London, after which, it's expected the value of her art will increase, possibly as much as five hundred per cent.'

'Go, girl,' whispered Andrea.

Margaret gestured around the room. 'Good art will always appreciate in value, but why would you choose to possess something you didn't love? Why not buy art you enjoy?'

Adam smiled as Margaret began to take the man around the gallery, asking what he liked about the pictures he saw.

Andrea looked at Adam with a grin. 'See?'

Adam nodded.

'She still says she's as nervous as hell, so I want you to encourage her.'

'Of course.' Adam glanced at Margaret with the young man at the end of the gallery. 'I think they'll be a while, so I'll slip out, do some shopping, and be back in twenty minutes with coffee.'

True to his word, Adam returned with a cardboard tray holding three takeaway coffees. It was no surprise to him to see Andrea wrapping a painting for the young businessman who, Adam suspected, now had a new appreciation of art.

He held the door open for the young man as he left, then headed towards Andrea and Margaret at the counter. He paused briefly to glance at Margaret's luxuriant red hair, swinging free. 'Much better.' He fingered a wisp of her hair. 'Coffee, anyone?' He placed the tray down.

Andrea nodded her thanks and picked up a cup. She looked up at the back wall of the gallery and began drumming two fingers on her lips.

'What's the matter?' Adam asked.

'Oh,' Andrea said. 'Nothing much. It's just that we're starting to look a bit thin, particularly down the far end of the gallery. We've sold a bit, and a lot of Claire's stuff is being packed ready for London.' She sighed. 'I really need more stock but it takes time to find good stuff.' She smelled her coffee appreciatively and grinned. 'Maybe we should set up a cappuccino machine to take up the space.'

'Why don't you hang Margaret's photographs there?' Adam asked.

'What!' Margaret said.

Andrea raised an enquiring eyebrow at Adam. 'They're good?'

'Outstanding.'

'No!' protested Margaret.

'Framed?' Andrea asked.

'Yes. Ready to hang,' Adam replied.

'Size?'

'About fifty by thirty centimetres, including the frames.'

'You're crazy.' Margaret laughed.

Andrea turned to Margaret. 'Can you bring them tomorrow so I can have a look?'

'Well ... I suppose I can. But they're only amateur. I've only had a little bit of training. You must tell me if they're not up to standard.'

'Darling,' Andrea purred, 'Believe me, I'll tell you. But I'll also tell you if they're good.'

***

Life for Adam continued at the pace determined by the school's rhythm. Fairly soon, he noticed the crocuses begin to appear in the parks, giving the first hint of spring. It was time to sow the spring barley on their farm. He organised for some of the boys to hitch up the seed drill to the old tractor and begin sowing the plots. Other boys were put to work in the winter-sown crops that had already emerged, doing seedling counts, measuring root length and counting the number of leaves.

Adam had insisted all farm work be done out of classroom hours. He wanted to leave the maximum amount of time for field studies and lessons. None of the boys seemed to mind. In fact, they seemed to relish it.

He detected a growing sense of seriousness in the air for the senior boys as they prepared to do their mock exams. These tests were a preparation for the sixth form's final school exams at the end of the Summer term. Mocks were taken seriously, as they were a good indicator of how the boys would perform.

The sense of tension amongst the senior boys was somewhat mitigated, however, by the prospect of the Spring Ball. This, Adam discovered, was an annual event organised by the school rowing club to help raise funds for new boats. The glittering affair was to be held in the Great Hall, which would be festooned with spring flowers for the occasion. A dinner, with excellent wine, would be followed by dancing. Most of the senior boys in the boarding house had volunteered to wait on tables and be ushers.

'It's an occasion of unapologetic schmoozing, ego-stroking and exploitation of emotions left slightly unguarded by alcohol,' Gareth explained. The two of them were in the *Pig and Whistle,* enjoying a half pint of beer together.

Adam wasn't paying a great deal of attention. He was nursing a faint concern Gareth was being so careful and measured in his relationship with Margaret, he wasn't being his authentic self. Adam rubbed his forehead, sighed, and decided to let them sort it out themselves. They would have to learn how, if there was ever going to be a future for them together.

Adam realised Gareth had changed the subject and was now talking about his driving lessons.

'You know that I only agreed to the driving lessons in order to give no offence to Margaret.'

Adam nodded.

Gareth smiled ruefully. 'The humbling truth is I've been greatly helped by them.'

Adam raised an eyebrow.

Gareth took a pull from his beer. 'I'd just completed the second lesson.' He belched and leaned forward. 'Boyo, I tell you, the man was a Nazi. He told me to stop the car and then he blasted me. He said I'd got good reflexes and judgment but the problem was in my head. He said I've subconsciously decided that being a bad driver was part of some sort of crazy image thing—and that he'd no bloody time for it because it could get people killed, and that I'd better not waste any more of his time, unless I decided to change my thinking.' The ignominy of the dressing down obviously still rankled.

Adam leant back on his chair and elected to give no comfort at all. 'I think he is entirely accurate. What did you decide?'

Gareth spluttered. 'It's all very well for you.' He paused. 'Do you really think I've been doing what he says?'

'Yes.'

'That's it! Just "yes?"'

'Yes.'

Gareth looked disconsolately into his beer. 'Well, anyway ... I gave it some thought and I decided, sod it, I'll become the best driver he's ever seen. I sort of told the instructor that I would buck up my ideas.' He shrugged. 'He seemed to take me seriously ... but that didn't stop him bawling at me if I was only a fraction too fast, or too slow, or in the wrong position. I tell you, he was merciless. I'm knackered.' He smiled, a little sheepishly. 'But the funny thing is, boyo, I started to enjoy it in the end. It's a skill, a challenge. I've actually discovered I like driving well.'

Adam patted him on the back. 'The town's insurance brokers will sleep easier tonight.'

***

The half-term break was fast approaching. Adam was again unsure of what to do. Claire continued to haunt his thoughts. He hadn't seen her for some weeks. The budding romance he'd hoped for was now dead in the water, he knew, but he'd at least hoped for a friendship. A good friendship. He came fully alive in her company and missed her care, understanding and friendship hugely. The image of her sprawled unconscious under *Sanderling*'s hull had seared itself on his mind, causing him anguish and giving him nightmares. He'd so nearly lost her.

As he ruminated on these things, he realised he was actually very angry. Claire's near-death trauma was no accident. Eckhart was somehow involved, but there was nothing he could do to prove it. Even if he bugged Eckhart's boat, unless they could see what he was doing, they would learn very little.

It was useless and frustrating.

While he ruminated on the problem, the ghost of an idea began to suggest itself. It was a course of action that might help bring some sort of closure, might give them enough evidence for the police to take an interest in Eckhart.

It was an idea that must necessarily involve Edward. He therefore tried to ignore it. The last thing Adam wanted to do was to put anyone else in danger.

But the idea wouldn't go away.

Finally, Adam relented and drove out to the saltings on Sunday afternoon to have a conversation with Edward.

When he shared his idea with Edward in the front room, he was silent for a long time and simply stared into the fire.

Eventually, he tilted his head back and stretched. 'Have I ever told you the story of the battle of Maldon?'

'No.'

'It took place in the spring of 991 AD on the River Blackwater, not too far from here.'

The burning logs on the fire rattled briefly as they settled down.

Edward continued. 'Earl Byrhtnoth and his thanes led an English force against a Viking army who were trying to extort over three tonnes of gold in payment for them sailing away. In fact, it was the first recorded case of Danegelt ever being paid by the English.'

More silence. Adam felt emboldened to ask, 'Why are you telling me this?'

'Ah, because the gold was only paid after the Vikings defeated Byrhtnoth at the battle of Maldon. The story of the battle is recounted in a fragment of old English poetry. The thing is, the poem records a character flaw of the English leader.'

'And that was?'

'The word used to describe it is *ofermōd,* which literally means "overheart".

It means having a pride that results in excessive, foolish courage.' Edward turned to Adam. 'I tell you this because I want you to know that I see no evidence of you being foolhardy in this venture.'

Edward slapped the arm of his chair with his hand. 'What I do know is that there is an evil which should be rooted out. And if Claire or yourself are still in any sort of danger from this man, Eckhart, then I'm all for doing something which might end it.'

'It could get dangerous.'

'Oh,' he waved dismissively. 'I've been retired too long. I'd welcome a little danger.' He smiled. 'We will, however, be careful to avoid the recklessness of *ofermōd*.'

The fire crackled in the hearth. Adam watched the flames and sighed. 'Of course, it might simply just fizzle out and come to nothing. I ... I just thought it might be worth a try.'

Edward nodded. 'I think it is. Let's put the plan into action this half-term break when we'll have the time to devote to it.' He smiled. 'At the very least, it will mean I get to enjoy your company again for another few days.'

Adam looked around Edward's cottage with affection. 'I'm beginning to feel as if this place is my home.'

'I hope it always will be.'

***

Two days later, Adam organised to be in the town marina with a group of boys collecting samples of seaweed, sponges and shellfish from the pontoons and pylons. A large white fishing dinghy was moored where they were working. By the time they had finished work, a small tracking device had been lodged securely inside the hollow rubbing-strake running around the edge of the boat.

As Adam called the boys to return to the school, he glanced at the boat and knew that he'd just seeded the beginning of a new and possibly dangerous scenario.

Chapter 24

Adam was pleased to be returning to the marshes for the half-term break. He loved watching the countryside beginning to wake from its winter slumbers, to bud again with the fresh green optimism of spring.

He had taken Sandy's GPS tracking computer to Edward's cottage. Every morning at seven, he'd logged on to the computer to be ready to monitor any movements. Fortunately, this didn't require him to keep checking the screen as Sandy had arranged for the computer's alarm to sound when the tracking unit started to move.

Adam hadn't given much for their chances of Eckhart going on one of his fishing trips. However, at eight o'clock in the morning, the computer alarm had rung.

Over breakfast, he watched his quarry head east, down the river and out into the estuary. He and Edward decided not to follow Eckhart, unless he left the local waters and headed further afield. *Sanderling* was moored in the saltings near the mouth of the estuary, well placed to push her way out to sea.

Adam could see from the screen that Eckhart was almost level with where *Sanderling* was moored, eight kilometres to the north of the cottage.

Edward, munching his toast and ginger marmalade, looked over Adam's shoulder. 'Hmm, it looks as if he's heading out to sea. I think it's time we got down to *Sanderling*.'

Thirty minutes later, they set sail.

With a sense of unreality, Adam watched *Sanderling* shoulder her way through the choppy sea, smashing the waves into a sizzle of spray. She was leaning to the wind on a fine reach, totally at ease in her restless, grey, native waters. Here, estuary and ocean fought over the treacherous sandbanks and shallows of the fishing grounds, for which *Sanderling* had been bred.

Wisps of silver hair fluttered from under Edward's woollen cap. He had the curved tiller under his arm and had wedged himself against the windward bulwark at the end of the helmsman's bench. Tucked down, though he was, *Sanderling*'s bare layout meant everyone on deck remained exposed to the elements. The bulwark was only half a metre high, allowing both wind and spray to whip across the deck, untroubled by obstructions.

Adam endeavoured to make himself as small an obstruction as possible. He had nestled himself between the windward bulwark and the low deckhouse. With his anorak pulled well over his head, he clutched Sandy Hardcastle's computer and monitored the movements of the location unit lodged in the rubbing-strake of the fishing dinghy.

Although *Sanderling* was just a kilometre offshore, the details of the shoreline were already obscured by mist. Edward was frowning. 'I'm not sure I like this weather. Visibility is starting to deteriorate.'

Adam gazed back at the coast. 'I thought wind was meant to blow away fog and mist.'

'It usually does but we've got a southeaster. The worst visibility comes from the south-east. It's all that pollution from the Ruhr. We've also got a warm front coming.'

'Is that a problem?'

'Yes. Fog is common ahead of a warm front. We've got one front due to move through early this afternoon but, once it's through, we should have clear visibility and a galloping south-westerly to come home with.'

Adam reflected that the schoolmaster in Edward was alive and well.

'Be thankful for the wind. It stops a mist from being a fog. Now, let's get her hard on the wind. Haul in the jib as tight as she'll go when I luff her up.'

Sanderling heeled over on her new course and fought her way to windward.

The tracking unit reported Eckhart's latest position every two minutes. Adam had been concerned the map shown by his GPS had been made exclusively for use on land. While it showed every street and town on land, it only represented the sea as a continuous expanse of blue. Edward had been quick with a solution. He'd reached down through the hatchway into the storage netting and produced what looked to be a palm pilot. 'You're not the only one with a GPS system. Most boats have their own GPS system to navigate by these days. This little unit is mine. If you give me the latitude and longitude of your quarry, I can simply enter them in here. We'll be able to see exactly where he is on the marine chart.'

Adam hunched down low and continued to look at the computer screen as *Sanderling* pushed through the swell.

Forty minutes later, Adam noticed that the moving dot on his computer was no longer moving. *What did it mean?* He drew a deep breath. 'I think our quarry has stopped. For the last six minutes, it hasn't moved. We're beginning to catch him up.'

Edward looked at the gathering mist and swept his eyes over the sails. 'As long as the wind doesn't back further than the south-east and the visibility doesn't get any worse, we'll continue on. At this rate, we should be up to him within two hours. I'll hook up a tiller line so *Sanderling* can steer herself for a few minutes, and you can show me where your little rabbit is hiding.'

Edward hooked a loop of rope over the tiller, made his way over to Adam and looked at the screen. A pulsating red dot remained stationary on a large patch of blue. Adam pushed a button that showed the latitude and longitude of the tracking device. Edward entered the co-ordinates into his GPS system and looked at the result.

'Hmm. That's not a good spot for boats. He's parked himself in the narrow gullet between North Wickam Sands and The Gunflats. It's treacherous if you don't know what you're doing.' He looked at Adam with a worried frown. 'This fellow must either be very stupid, or a very fine seaman. What's fairly certain is that he won't be expecting company hiding in there, particularly on a misty day when all righteous folk are tucked up in harbour.'

Edward made his way to the mainmast, where he sorted out some halyards, stood back, and lowered the radar reflector down on deck. Unhitching the reflector, he returned to the main hatch and dropped it onto the leeward berth.

Adam gave him a quizzical look.

'Ah. It's just an inkling. He doesn't want to be found ... and neither do we, at least, not until we are upon him. If whoever he is meeting wants to ensure they are alone, they may have radar. No point in making it easy for them. Fishing smacks sit low in the water, without much freeboard. We're difficult to see with radar. With the topmast down and with no radar reflector, we're nearly invisible.'

Adam coughed innocently. 'Presumably, it's not a requirement of Her Majesty's Revenue and Customs for ancient fishing smacks to have radar reflectors tied permanently aloft?'

Edward ignored the allusion to the rich smuggling heritage enjoyed by smacks. 'You don't want solid things banging about up aloft when you are tucked up in your berth. You need to be able to take them down, my boy.'

They sailed on through the leaden wastelands of restless water.

An hour later, it was impossible to detect the direction of the sun in the mist. Adam experienced a sense of total disorientation. His disquiet was in no way dissipated by the occasional glimpse of white water crashing against the fringes of nearby sandbanks. Edward appeared unconcerned and simply glanced occasionally at his GPS.

Adam voiced his unease. 'I can't help but find it disconcerting having no idea which direction we are going. The sun could be anywhere.'

'Ah.' Edward smiled.

Adam groaned. 'Why do I get a premonition that I am about to be taught more of the smackman's dark arts.'

'Because, dear boy, you are woefully ignorant. If you would be so kind as to duck down to the drawer under the chart table and fetch something for me, I'd be grateful. At the back of the drawer, you will find a piece of rock crystal sitting in some protective foam. If you bring it up on deck, I'll show you something.'

Adam climbed down the companionway and opened the drawer. Sure enough, right at the back, a curious piece of opaque stone was nestled in a foam cradle. As he handed the stone to Edward, a gust of wind heeled *Sanderling* over.

'Before we do anything else, we'd better put in a reef and take in the jib.

I want to be comfortably under control in the narrows between the sandbanks.

Adam was again reminded that reefing an old sailing smack was neither a quick nor easy job. The peak and the throat halyards were loosened off and the boat luffed up into wind. The halyard was eased off and the inboard and outboard reefing ropes were hauled in. Finally, he tied up the reefing ties along the length of the boom to tidy up the crumpled sailcloth along the foot of the main. The whole process took fifteen minutes.

When they had finished, Edward tacked *Sanderling* south for thirty minutes before heading due east again. 'We need to get some southerly, particularly as the ebb tide is carrying us north-east.'

Breathing hard from the exertion of hauling in the jib sheet, Adam rejoined Edward at the helm. He stood for a while at the backstay, looking at the dirty grey water sliding past. A particularly dark shadow of mist closed around them like an unwelcome premonition. His feeling of desolation was amplified by an incongruous sound, the haunting toll of a bell in the distance.

'That's the bell on the Gunflat West buoy. It marks the western edge of Gunflat Sands. We're only a kilometre from our quarry.' Edward looked around. 'And just as well, this is no longer mist, but fog. I wouldn't normally choose to sail in these conditions.'

'Do you want to turn back?'

'Yes, but as we are here now, let's take a quick look. Then we'll head for home.' He pointed over the left-hand side. 'He'll be coming up on the port side. I suggest you stay below and get your camera ready at one of the portholes. There's no point in being seen taking pictures. In this fog, you may only see your man for a few seconds.'

Adam clambered down the companionway, retrieved the digital camera from his rucksack and took up position by the forward porthole.

Sanderling's hull creaked and groaned around him as she pitched and rolled. It was like being inside a living thing. The rigging made her hull shudder in the wind gusts, and he could hear a loud whooshing sound every time her bow bit into a wave. As he wedged himself in position, he acknowledged that being heeled over at least afforded him an excellent view of the scene over the gunwale.

It was not a view to inspire great confidence. Fifty metres away, Gunflat Sands was being uncovered by the last of the ebb tide. The waves crashing on the exposed sand bank were intimidating.

***

On deck, Edward viewed the bank of shingle, mud and sand with disquiet. He hated being this close to a lee shore. This was no place to play games. A slight misjudgement on his part, and these waters could easily become a killing ground. Death was no stranger to these sand banks.

He thought of Adam down below. He had overcome much, engaged the demons of the mind and won. Although the ghosts of the past remained, they would, with time, enrich the present rather than sabotage it.

He wondered if Adam and Claire would allow themselves to fall in love. Claire was certainly not yet her normal self, and Edward suspected much of it was due to her struggling with her feelings for Adam. Well, whatever happened, he resolved to do all he could to return Adam to her in one piece. He grimaced and had the uneasy thought that messing about on a lee shore in fog, did not constitute a good start to his resolution.

And then suddenly, there it was. Emerging out of the mist was Eckhart's fishing dinghy, anchored just off the sands.

Eckhart was huddled with his back to the wind, speaking into what Edward supposed was a mobile phone, while tugging something from the boat's buoyancy chamber. Sailing without the noise of an engine, *Sanderling* was almost on top of Eckhart before he noticed their presence. He twisted round, open-mouthed, before reaching forward to push a small red case back into the buoyancy chamber.

Edward affected not to notice and waved casually to Eckhart before turning his attention to the sails.

As they surged past into the gathering mist, Edward's last image was of Eckhart yelling urgently into his phone.

Ahead of them, he heard the unmistakable burble of twin diesel engines throttling back to idle.

Sure enough, a fifty-foot motor launch appeared out of the mist. On its stern deck, a fishing dinghy was in the process of being hoisted out of its cradle by an overhead derrick. A large, blond-haired man was steadying the dinghy in mid-air with one arm, whilst speaking into the phone with the other. He turned with a puzzled frown as *Sanderling* surged towards him.

Edward called to Adam to remain out of sight. He watched with alarm as Adam slithered out of the companionway on his stomach to the windward gunwale. There, he photographed the launch, unseen through the scuppers at deck level. Once abreast of the launch, Adam wiggled his way back to the companionway and disappeared below, out of sight.

When they were safely past the launch, Adam called out in excitement. 'I think we have our answer to what is going on. Did you notice the dinghy on the back of the boat? It's exactly the same as the one Eckhart is in. What we've stumbled upon here is a classic "drop and swap".'

Edward was only half listening. He was assailed by the conviction that the scenarios that might soon be played out were distinctly ominous. As the mist swallowed the launch behind them, Edward stabbed at the starter button of *Sanderling*'s engine and pushed the tiller away. The sails began banging and slatting as he drove *Sanderling* into the eye of the wind across the other side of the channel one and a half miles away.

Adam looked up curiously. 'What's up?'

'I'm going to windward as quickly as I can. They saw us sailing close-hauled and won't expect us to be to windward. Once over the other side, I'll cut the engine. With any luck, they will neither see us nor hear us, if they come looking for us along the track they saw us sailing.'

Six minutes later, North Wickham Sand appeared and Edward bore away, allowing the sails to fill again as he sailed just off the surf line of the sand bar.

He flicked his eye on the echo sounder. Half a fathom. He couldn't risk anything less. After glancing aloft to check the sails, he reached forward and killed the engine. Silence descended again, relieved only by the whoosh and sizzle of the spray.

It was ten minutes before they heard the deep growl of engines, as the launch patrolled through the mist along the northern side of the channel.

Edward waited another three minutes before asking Adam to come up on deck to ease off the staysail, so they could bear away from the wind and cross back over to Gunflat Sands.

He thought furiously. If only he could evade those looking for him until they emerged from the channel, he would be free to fly under full sail into the shipping channel, where the steady stream of marine traffic into the Thames would dissuade anyone from doing anything threatening.

Edward again heard the unwelcome sound of diesel engines, much sooner than he had hoped. This time, the launch was working its way through the mist to the south of them. There could be no doubt it was looking for them.

With a sickening realisation, he knew it would only be a matter of time before they were found.

Rational thought and anxiety tumbled over each other, until the beginnings of a desperate plan swam into his consciousness. He must protect Adam, at all cost. Having made up his mind, he moved forward, reached for the computer beside the deckhouse and tossed it overboard.

Adam's head appeared at the gangway.

'Adam, this is one of those moments where I ask you to trust me and do exactly what I say. These men have shown they are capable of killing, and we just happen to have seen rather more than they would have wished. If they come on board to question us on some pretext or other, I feel very confident I can bluff my way out. I'm just an old man in an old boat. You, however, were the one who rescued Claire at Wiseman's Point and caused Eckhart to be grilled by the police. They will have trouble believing your presence here is pure coincidence.'

'Might I point out that Claire is your niece? They can also make the link between you and her.'

'They can't discover that today. My concern is only that we survive the next few hours. Tomorrow we can go to the police. Whilst it's doubtful they will have enough evidence to gain a conviction based on what we have to report, it may at least disrupt their drug-running for a while.'

Edward looked over his shoulder. 'When the launch comes next time, it will probably be zigzagging up the channel looking for us. We can't expect to escape. They will probably come from behind. Here's what I want you to do. I'm going to go as close to The Gunflats as I dare. There's a wetsuit in the locker under the starboard berth. You change into that and clip on a safety harness. Wrap your mobile phone in a plastic bag. You'll find some in the map case under the bookshelf. Zip the phone down your front. Use it whenever you can to report to the police if things turn bad.'

Adam started to interrupt but Edward waved at him to be silent.

'We'll tie a line to the bottom of the bobstay. That's the chain that runs from the base of the bow up to the end of the bowsprit. We'll then run it aft along the hull's waterline, lead it through the transom scuppers and make it fast. When the launch appears, you climb out of the forward hatch and slip over the side into the water. You'll be hidden by the foresail. Once you are over the side, clip your life-line onto the rope. I'll heave-to when they come, so there should be little forward motion.' He smiled grimly. 'It will be cold and uncomfortable but you should remain unseen.'

Edward looked up at the towering mainsail. 'If you have to leave *Sanderling* for any reason, make for Gunflat Sands. Walk along to the eastern edge and swim out to Gunflat

West buoy. Use the line on your harness to help you climb onto it. It won't be easy. Then phone for the coastguard to pick you up.' He turned back to Adam to ensure he had his full attention. 'Whatever you do, don't stay on Gunflat Sands. The tide will come in and cover it within an hour.'

'No.' Adam shook his head. 'I don't like it. Whatever happens, we do this together.'

Edward reached towards him. 'We are doing this together. Adam, these people kill. They will certainly kill me if they see you with me. So ... I'm asking you. Please.'

Adam searched Edward's eyes. Finally, he nodded and ducked back down the companionway.

***

Adam changed as quickly as he could into the clammy wetsuit. Seeing a diving knife in the locker, he picked it out and strapped it to his leg. He wrapped his phone and digital camera in waterproof bags as instructed and zipped them down his front.

When he came on deck, he discovered Edward had already fed a line through the transom scuppers at the rear of *Sanderling*'s overhang. He'd slipped a tiller line in place, allowing the boat to sail with the helm unattended for a few moments. Adam helped him pass the line outside of the shrouds and on up towards the bow.

Leaning over the bow, Edward pointed to the bobstay chain bolted on to the base of *Sanderling*'s bow. It was difficult to imagine anywhere less handy to tie anything. 'We can't let the line be seen. It has to be there.'

Adam nodded. He climbed out to the bowsprit, swung underneath, and hung on with his hands, while his feet fought for a foothold on the bobstay chain.

Sanderling pitched into the waves in a determined effort to dislodge him. She was still sailing quite fast. Transferring one hand to a bowsprit shroud, Adam reached down and tied a round turn and two half hitches one-handed, around the base of the bobstay.

Two things happened at once. A large wave picked him up and crashed him hard against *Sanderling*'s stem, winding him. Second, he heard the unmistakable throbbing sound of the launch coming up from behind.

Adam found his voice. 'I'm all right. Get back and tighten the line from the other end.' Edward reached down and patted him on the shoulder. A moment later, he was gone.

Adam had seriously underestimated the energy needed to ride the bucking bow of a fishing smack. He fought to keep from being swept away by holding on to the bowsprit with his hands and pushing his feet down onto the chain bobstay. His chest ached with pain from his collision with the bow, but at least *Sanderling* was starting to slow down.

He thought, wryly, that he made a sorry-looking figurehead.

***

With as much of a sense of normalcy as possible, Edward hauled the staysail to windward in order to slow *Sanderling* down and heave to. He walked aft and eased out the mainsail to spill wind. Sketching a friendly wave at the launch creaming through the water behind him, Edward pulled at the line coming through the transom scuppers, keenly aware Adam was at the other end of it. He heaved it tight and made it fast to a cleat. He hoped a casual observer would assume he was tidying up his lines.

Standing in the bow of the launch was a thick-set man: the man Adam said was Eckhart. The launch must have stopped to pick him up from the fishing dinghy. His muscular bulk was riding the pitching of the waves with evident ease.

As the bow of the launch edged up to *Sanderling*'s stern, Eckhart stepped outside the launch's pulpit and hung onto its rails, like a swimmer about to start a backstroke race.

The helmsman of the launch wasted no time on niceties. He simply drove the launch into *Sanderling*'s stern, throttling back at the last moment, so the collision was a bump rather than a crash. At the moment of impact Eckhart leaped down onto *Sanderling*'s deck.

At this stage, Edward felt obliged to protest. Eckhart didn't even bother to answer. Pushing Edward aside, he took a snub-nosed pistol from inside his jacket and descended down the companionway into the cabin.

Edward watched in despair as Eckhart kicked open doors and hatchways. Having established no one else was in the boat, Eckhart ripped open a sail-bag and pulled out an old topsail, spreading it out along the length of the cabin floor. He then prised open a tin of paint thinners he'd found in a cupboard and emptied the contents over the sailcloth, splashing it over the cabin bunks and walls. Finally, he reached into the engine compartment and ripped out the fuel line.

Edward recovered from the shock and galvanised himself into action. He grabbed *Sanderling*'s boathook and jabbed it down the companionway at Eckhart.

Eckhart's reaction was simply to raise his pistol and fire.

The bullet crashed through the deckhouse bulkhead beside Edward's ear. The noise of the report was deafening. Edward fell back against the tiller and slid to the deck.

Eckhart climbed quickly up the companionway, stepped over to Edward and kicked him in the head.

Through his pain, Edward felt his pockets being searched. Eckhart found Edward's hand-held GPS system, dropped it on the deck and crushed it under his heel. He then turned towards the foredeck and the emergency life raft enclosed in its fibreglass case. Three quick shots from his gun rendered it useless.

Waving to the launch, he signalled for a pick up. Eckhart then climbed down the companionway, returning on deck with a tin of paint thinner and a tea towel. He emptied the dregs of the thinner onto the tea towel, lit it with a cigarette lighter and threw the burning towel into the cabin.

There was an immediate "whump" as the paint thinner down below ignited.

Edward shook his head groggily in disbelief. Light from the flames began to dance up the inside walls.

The motor launch surged in from behind, grazing *Sanderling's* stern quarter.

Eckhart picked up the wooden belaying pin from the rigging rack at the base of the mast and stood over Edward. 'You saw too much, old man.' His tone was light, almost conversational. 'In the unlikely event you will be found, I won't put a bullet hole in you.' Eckhart raised the belaying pin and brought it crashing down.

Chapter 25

Adam had never been so anxious in his life—and had rarely felt so cold and exhausted. He had dropped into the water near the bow and was hanging on to the line strung along *Sanderling*'s waterline.

The pistol shots filled him with dread. He had to find a way of getting back on board. With grim determination, he pulled his way back to the bobstay and its murderous pitching. As the bobstay crashed into the water beside his head, he grabbed hold of it and allowed himself to be jerked up as *Sanderling* reared. Strength almost gone, he worked his way up the bobstay chain until he was able to throw his hands around the bowsprit.

He paused to catch his breath, then swung his legs up over the spar. Slowly, he inched his way along the bowsprit to the gunwale. He climbed over and fell onto the deck, exhausted.

But there was no time to recover. He was faced with an appalling spectacle. Flames were licking out of the forward hatchway and had already burned more than half the staysail. The furled jib was also well alight.

He lurched to his feet and slammed the forward hatch shut. As he staggered down alongside the coach house roof, he saw Edward lying on the deck. Smoke was billowing over him from the main hatchway. Holding his breath, Adam reached into the hatchway to locate the shelf beside the entrance where three washboards were stored. Pain seared his hand as flames licked at his fingers. He pulled back his hand, splashed them in a puddle of seawater by the scuppers and plunged his hand back into the opening to grab at a washboard. In three attempts, he had all three washboards. He slotted them into the companionway to block up its entrance, then sealed it shut by sliding the top hatchway into place.

He needed to save *Sanderling* in order to save Edward. Adam ran forward with the deck bucket tied to a length of rope. He tossed it into the sea, drew up some water and threw it over the burning staysail and the smouldering jib. Looking back, he saw smoke streaming from the air vents on the coach house roof. He unsheathed his diver's knife and hacked chunks of sailcloth from the jib and stuffed them into the vents.

He checked again. There was nothing else he could do to starve the fire of oxygen.

He leapt across the deck to attend to Edward, checking his vital signs. *Please, let him be...*

Edward was breathing in shallow gasps and his heartbeat was faint but regular. He hadn't been shot. No bones appeared to be broken, although he was bleeding slightly from a depressed fracture on his head. Adam let out a long slow breath and thanked God for the thick woollen cap Edward wore. It must have helped minimise the blow.

Adam knew that the shock caused by such a blow could still kill; it was therefore important to keep the core of Edward's body warm. He unzipped his wetsuit, removed his t-shirt and used the diver's knife to cut it into a long spiral bandage. Carefully, he wrapped it around Edward's head. He then put Edward's woollen hat back in place. He noticed the decking was still warm—disconcertingly so. He grabbed for his mobile phone and unwrapped it from its waterproof bag.

It was broken and useless—probably destroyed when he had been crushed against the bow.

A temptation to despair flitted across his mind. Adam recognised it as a familiar enemy. He forced himself to breath normally.

The sound of crashing waves alerted him to another danger. Although *Sanderling* had been nodding her way slowly to windward when she was hove to, now that the foresail was half burned, she was gradually being blown onto Gunflat Sands.

Adam threw himself on the tiller and heaved it over. Nothing happened. Without a headsail to back her away from the wind, *Sanderling* was behaving like a weathercock. She refused to turn away from the wind.

Think: for goodness sake, think.

Adam tried to recall Edward's hours of patient teaching. The bald fact was: he needed another headsail. He ran down to the foredeck and grabbed the tattered remains of the jib. Only one eye was left at the head of the sail. Could he use it? Perhaps. Adam attached the jib halyard to it. Then he bunched up some cloth in one corner of the sail, hitched some rope around it and secured it to a cleat on *Sanderling*'s port-hand shoulder. It wasn't very seamanlike but he hoped it would do. Finally, he tied some rope around the remaining corner of the sailcloth and tethered it to the stem-head.

He muttered a prayer as he hauled up the makeshift sail with the halyard. It looked terrible. But, to his intense relief, the wind pushed into it and began to turn *Sanderling*'s bow.

Adam hauled in the main sheet. The giant main rattled and banged before it hardened.

The makeshift sail didn't last long. It blew out from the knots Adam had tied in the bottom corners of the sail and flew into the air like a giant flag. However, it had done its job. The sail had pushed the bow away from the wind so *Sanderling*'s great main could begin to drive her forward. After all the anxiety and tension, the sense of being back in control was almost euphoric.

Having decided to sail, *Sanderling* now came alive. With the wind on her stern quarter, she began to surge back down the channel. The great tan mainsail drove her along at impressive speed. If *Sanderling* was dying, she didn't know it.

Adam sailed fifty metres off the sandbank. However, keeping her under control was exhausting work. Without any foresail, Adam had to continually counter *Sanderling*'s inclination to veer into the wind.

'Ease off the mainsheet a bit.' It was a feeble voice but enough to cause a surge of elation in Adam. Edward was conscious again.

Adam unhitched the mainsheet and eased out the boom. Sure enough, the pressure on the helm eased and *Sanderling* was less inclined to fight him like a hard-mouthed mule.

He shot a glance at Edward. His face was very pale and his eyes were screwed shut in pain.

Slowly, Edward opened his eyes. 'What's happening?'

'Everything down below has been set on fire. I've tried to seal off the cabin to starve the fire of oxygen. I don't know if it's worked. It's at least smouldering.' Adam grimaced. 'We've got no jib, no staysail and we are sailing back the way we came just off Gunflat Sands.'

There was a long silence. '*Sanderling* may yet get us home. With the wind behind us, we don't need foresails.' Edward's feeble voice gained in strength as he spoke. 'The diesel fuel in the tank is isolated by a tap. It's unlikely to explode.'

Any sense of relief Adam may have enjoyed was cruelly cut short.

The ghostly form of the grey motor launch appeared out of the mist eight hundred metres ahead of them. She was anchored by the bow off Gunflat Sands. The boat had swung lazily out into the channel as the tide was beginning to change. Eckhart and the large blond-haired man were on the aft deck tying down a fishing dinghy that had been lifted into place by a hydraulic hoist. The other dinghy was streaming from the launch's stern.

'They'll catch us again.' Adam couldn't keep the despair out of his voice.

Edward grunted and winced with pain. He eased himself into a sitting position and studied the scene. 'No, they won't.'

Adam looked at Edward without understanding.

'Ram them. Bear away slightly and ram them. You must hit them at ninety degrees. Aim for their middle. Disable them.' He smiled grimly.

He can't be serious. We'll all die.

Edward must have seen the alarm in his eyes. '*Sanderling* can take it. She's been built to withstand groundings and the abuses of a hard-working life.'

'Surely we'll lose our mast.'

'I don't think so. The mast is low and well stayed. The rig should give.' Edward looked up. 'We will, however, probably lose the forestay. I'll need to rig up some extra bracing.' Lurching to his feet, he staggered up to the foredeck, retrieved the jib and staysail halyards and made them fast round the gunwale posts on each side of *Sanderling*'s shoulders. Returning to the mainmast, he heaved on the halyards and pulled them tight.

Sanderling thundered towards the launch.

Adam could see two men on it. Both seemed to be frozen into immobility at the sight of the ancient sailing smack looming out of the mist. However, their inaction was short-lived. The blond man walked to the wheelhouse, as Eckhart strode up to the bow to oversee the hauling in of the anchor chain. The calm certainty of Eckhart's gait left Adam with no illusions. It was clear he intended to hunt them down and finish the job.

On her current course, Adam could see that *Sanderling* would pass close to the stern of the launch. He heaved the tiller across.

Sanderling was reluctant to turn. She was trimmed for her current point of sailing. Grudgingly, her blunt bow swung around until her bowsprit pointed like an accusing finger at her enemy. With the wind dead behind her, *Sanderling's* vast mainsail drove her onwards. Water boiled at her bow. *It was a savage irony,* thought Adam, *the hunted is now the hunter.*

Adam saw the mood on the launch change dramatically. The blond man was now looking at *Sanderling* in horror. Eckhart had crouched down and was holding on to the pulpit, bracing himself for the inevitable collision.

Adam also braced himself.

Sanderling used her formidable momentum to dreadful effect. Her bowsprit speared over the launch's side deck into the wheelhouse. The blond man leaped for the door, tripped, and fell across the gangway.

It was a lethal fall. *Sanderling*'s bow reared up as her chain bobstay bit into the launch's coaming and sliced through the side decking. It cut the man in two.

A second later, the bobstay parted company from the bowsprit. *Sanderling*'s heavy stem came ramming in behind it. It crashed into the fibreglass hull, turning the sleek, expensive launch into a shattered wreck.

Although Adam had braced himself, he was thrown forward by the impact of the collision.

With her fury spent, *Sanderling* seemed to subside and began to ease herself out of the cavernous hole in the side of the launch. For a moment, her bowsprit pinned her into position.

With a crack, it snapped off and *Sanderling* started to drift alongside her victim. As she drifted round, *Sanderling*'s mainsail crashed over, as the wind gybed it round violently to the other side. The large sail now pressed against the hull of the sinking launch.

Adam looked around him, appalled at the devastation they'd caused. It seemed surreal—as if he was watching some terrible film. Dirty estuarine water surged into the launch.

Sanderling continued to push the stern of the launch around. Her mainsail dragged along the length of the launch as she scraped backwards along its length. She began to pivot around the back of the launch, trapping the dinghy tethered there against the stern of the launch. The dinghy began to crumple—caught in the vice of a giant nutcracker.

Adam stood above it, watching events unfold like a dream. From his vantage point, he could see dozens of white plastic packets stacked inside the dinghy's shattered buoyancy chamber. He realised their significance immediately and knew he only had one chance to get the evidence needed to make sense of all that had happened.

He jumped onto the sinking dinghy, plucked out a plastic packet from the ruptured buoyancy chamber and threw it on *Sanderling*'s deck. Hooking his arm over *Sanderling*'s gunwale, he hauled himself back on deck. The entire action had taken less than six seconds.

Glancing up, he noticed Eckhart lurching his way aft on the sinking launch, seeking to grab *Sanderling*'s bow as it broke free of the wreckage. He was too late. With her forestay flying free and rigging trailing from her bows like drooping whiskers, *Sanderling* swung away.

Adam saw Eckhart look at him with wild eyes. Desperation and terror were clearly visible on his face. He slipped as he tried to climb back up the deck of the launch. It was futile. The angle of the deck got steeper and steeper, until the launch capsized, belching trapped air as it sank under the water.

Part of Adam's brain told him that, if Eckhart hadn't drowned, he'd die of exposure within thirty minutes.

Sanderling broke free of the sinking wreckage and drifted backwards along the channel, carried along by the first of the flood tide.

Edward got to his feet and bent over to steady himself on the deckhouse roof. Seeing the launch tip over and begin to sink, he cried out, appalled. 'The two men! In these waters, they'll be dead within an hour.'

Adam caught him as he lunged forward. Edward tried to wrestle himself free but Adam pinned his arms to his side. 'Just what do you think you're going to do? We've got no foresails. We can't sail to windward without foresails. We can't reach them.'

Edward stood stiffly for a long while and then collapsed on Adam's shoulder. Adam held him as he wept, humbled at his compassion for those who had so recently tried to kill him. He himself was a great deal less troubled by their demise.

'Edward,' he said gently, 'we're going to die too unless we start to sort ourselves out.'

Edward got himself under control and disentangled himself from Adam. Together, they walked down to the foredeck to inspect the damage to *Sanderling*'s rigging. It was almost entirely limited to the bow. The forestay, bowsprit and all its stays were gone but the jury-rigged halyards were keeping the mast up. Edward looked over the side. 'My main concern is whether or not *Sanderling* has sprung a plank below the water line. But other than that...' He patted the gunwale. '...it looks as if the old girl has come through it remarkably well.'

Together, they hauled in the wreckage of the bowsprit and lashed it down on deck where it could do no further damage to the hull. When that was done, Edward stood up and surveyed the scene. 'Let's get her sailing.'

This proved to be much harder to do than to say. With no foresail, *Sanderling* was reluctant to put her nose around from the wind. 'She's "caught in irons,"' Edward said. 'The only way to turn her off the wind is to back the mainsail against the wind.'

Adam nodded and began to push the boom of the mainsail outboard. However, the power of the wind in the sail was too strong. Even with both his and Edward's backs pushing against the boom, they barely made an impact.

Edward signalled for Adam to stop. 'I'll shackle a line to the end of the boom and pass it outside the shrouds to the cable winch at the bow. We'll crank it out.'

Together, they rigged the line and Edward showed Adam how to work the winch.

Gradually, tension came on the line, forcing the boom to swing outboard. As the mainsail canted outwards, *Sanderling* swung her nose away from the wind.

'Here's the tricky bit,' Edward called. 'You need to cut the line while I haul in the mainsheet. Hopefully that will sail us forward enough for us to get steerage way.'

As the line was cut free, it whipped back like a scything serpent, lashing at

Adam's feet as he scampered back to help haul in the mainsheet. With maddening slowness, the giant main was reeled in until it caught the wind and *Sanderling* began to edge forward. Once she started to move, Edward eased the tiller over.

Gradually *Sanderling* turned downwind. Having felt the energy of the wind, she decided she liked it. Once more she began to surge her way through the water.

Adam experienced a wave of relief as the smack settled down to sailing again. He looked around him. She may be a charred, smouldering wreck down below, but on deck everything looked relatively normal.

His relief was tempered by the look of concern he saw on Edward's face. Adam stepped over to the deckhouse roof and peered through a glass porthole. All he could see was blackness. No flames were visible. That, at least, was positive.

In the distance, the mournful tolling of the Gunflat West buoy could be heard. The buoy itself soon became visible through the mist. Adam voiced a growing concern to Edward.

'Edward, we have no GPS, no phone, no compass, no charts and we can't even see the sun.' He gestured over to the sandbank. 'You tell me that these are treacherous waters with sandbanks everywhere. How on earth are we going to find our way home?'

The wind had picked up slightly and the mist was beginning to disperse. High above them, a tiny patch of blue sky appeared for a few moments. Despite this, the horizon was still obscured and the sun could not be seen.

'Ah well...' Edward offered him a weary smile. 'We might not be so completely benighted as you think.' He pointed over the left. 'The wind is from the south-east. If that were to change, we would get an indication of it in the weather and the passing of the warm front.' He sighed. 'This means that whilst the weather stays the same, we can assume that, if we stay on this point of sailing, we'll be heading for home—roughly. We do, however, need to make a dogleg to avoid some sandbanks north of us.'

Adam was not entirely comforted. 'How can we be sure the wind hasn't shifted and we're not sailing into an area of sandbanks? For that matter, how are we going to know when to turn north to avoid the sandbanks?'

Edward fished in his trouser pocket and took out the strange blue stone Adam had fetched for him, what seemed a lifetime ago.

Edward turned the stone over in his hands. 'Some of the greatest sailors ever to have existed were Vikings. Icelandic sagas tell the story of how they sailed from Bergen to Iceland and Greenland.' He waved ahead of him. 'There is fair evidence that they even made it to Newfoundland and the American continent. And they did this hundreds of years ago without the benefit of any compass.' He looked up at the mist that surrounded them. 'The waters of the North Atlantic are notorious for their poor visibility. The sun is often obscured ... and so they invented navigational aids like this to help them. It is a sunstone.' He held it out for Adam to see. 'I call it my "Viking stone."'

Adam could see the quartz-like crystal had soft purplish highlights.

Edward held the stone aloft. 'This is crystal cordierite and it is found on the coastal beaches of Norway. It's also called iolite—water sapphire—and it has a peculiar property. It changes colour and brightness when rotated in front of polarised light, such as sunlight through clouds.'

He began to rotate the stone slowly. 'A good crystal can tell you the direction of the sun on cloudy days. All you need is a small patch of blue sky somewhere. When you've got one, you turn the crystal until its colour changes from blue to yellow.' Edward continued to rotate the stone until its colour changed abruptly from bluish-purple to yellow. 'There it is!' He smiled in triumph. 'When that happens, you know the stone is pointing towards the sun.'

'Knowing the direction of the sun will simply stop us from sailing to Belgium. It's not going to help us avoid sandbanks.'

'Hmm. We can improve on things a bit with a watch. If you point twelve o'clock on your watch at the sun, bisect the angle between twelve o'clock and the hour hand, it will point due south.'

Edward patted Adam on the shoulder and asked to borrow his knife. He used it to nick his woollen jumper and pull out a long thread of wool. Edward tied the wool to the backstay above Adam's head, so that it streamed towards the belly of the main sail.

Edward pointed to it. 'Do you see that row of reefing points along the mainsail?'

Adam nodded.

'When I tell you, mark which reefing point the cotton is pointing at. Then steer to keep it there.'

Edward lifted the Viking stone up and began to rotate it. In his other hand, he held his watch. As he did this, he leant back against the tiller, pushing it until he was satisfied with the course. 'Now!' he yelled.

Adam looked along the length of fluttering wool. It was pointing at the third reefing point from the front. 'Got it!'

'Sail so the woollen tell-tale stays in that position.'

Adam was careful to ensure his expression did not reflect his thoughts. *We're relying on a scrap of wool and a chunk of crystal? Madness.*

Edward put the Viking stone back in his pocket and patted Adam on the shoulder. 'Woollen tell-tales are all very good but you need to use your senses as well, Adam. Get used to sensing how the wind feels around your neck and ears. It all helps to keep you steering in the right direction.'

Adam gripped the tiller even more tightly and watched the red tell-tale.

'And relax. You'll sail better.'

Adam nodded and divided his attention between looking at the telltale and watching Edward as he made his way along *Sanderling*'s deck to the bow. There he prised loose some wooden splinters from the broken stub of the bowsprit and threw them forward of the boat into the water. As the splinters swept down the side of the vessel, Edward walked along the deck, keeping pace with them while looking at his watch. Once the splinter trailed past the stern, he turned to Adam. 'If I know the length of the boat, and can time how long a piece of wood takes to float past us, I can work out how fast we're going. We call it a Dutchman's log.' Edward took Adam's knife and scored a rough compass rose on *Sanderling*'s deck. 'We know the course we set to get here. We simply need to go back on the reciprocal course, allowing an extra ten degrees to counter the flooding tide. The course we steered to get here was essentially a dog-leg to avoid an area of sandbanks to the north.' He pointed to the right.

'This means we will need to change thirty degrees north in half an hour. It should bring us on to a dead run with the wind behind us. I'll tell you when to change course.' Edward paused and put his hand on Adam's shoulder. 'I've got to warn you that this is a very rough science. In reality, we'll be lucky to keep her within forty degrees of where we want to go.' Edward smiled tiredly. 'But at least we'll be sailing towards home.'

Adam nodded and managed a smile. 'With you around, I never doubted it.'

Only once in the next thirty minutes did Edward tell Adam to change course. The Viking stone showed that the wind had veered towards the south.

Despite their dire situation, Adam found his thoughts turning to Claire. He remonstrated with himself.*I should have risked speaking to her more openly.* He ached for her company ... and for what might be. He smiled ruefully as it dawned on him that he very much wanted to live. At last, he allowed the last dark tendrils of his death wish leave his soul and take to the wind. *I want to live. There's so much I want to live for. Claire, Edward, Mum, the boys at school ... and Philippa Ruth.*

His thoughts were interrupted when Edward instructed Adam to change course again. He was continually snatching sights of the sun whenever a pinch of blue sky showed. Now and then he paced along the deck beside another Dutchman's log.

Adam was amazed at his skill. However, he was also starting to notice a gradual change in *Sanderling*'s handling. She was becoming increasingly sluggish and less inclined to rise to the waves. He called to Edward. 'She's not the same.'

Edward nodded.

Adam had the impression he'd known this for some time but had chosen not say anything. He could feel *Sanderling* getting heavier and heavier. Edward joined him at the tiller. Adam discovered that, while it now took a lot to throw the smack off course, if she once fell off course, it took two of them to haul her back on track. The exertion of being on the helm was taking its toll on Edward. His face was ashen and pinched with pain.

They were sinking—slowly and inexorably. Adam looked around. There was no life raft and no buoyancy vests. Nothing. Everything had been destroyed.

Over the next fifteen minutes, they sailed on ever slower. Even moderate waves now came over the decks. He looked at Edward with alarm.

'She's not done yet. They used to sail these things back from the fishing grounds with their decks awash.'

Another ten minutes passed. Above them, the great tan sail tried to push *Sanderling*'s sodden hull through the water. Although the sail pressed hard, *Sanderling* crept along at only a few knots. Her dignity was deserting her.

The visibility, however, continued to improve. It was now possible to see a few kilometres ahead, and a watery haze gave evidence of the general direction of the sun.

Water gurgled across the decks as *Sanderling* drunkenly rolled her scuppers under the water. Yet, still she sailed.

In the distance, the horizon could now be distinguished. It was possible to see the khaki smudge of the low shoreline.

Adam's spirits lifted. As unlikely as it was, Edward and his Viking stone had managed to navigate a crippled, sodden hulk through a maze of sandbanks, back to the coast. He marvelled at what Edward had achieved. It had been an extraordinary act of seamanship.

However, they were not home yet. Although they were two kilometres offshore, it might have been a million. *Sanderling* was never going to make it.

Looking south, Adam thought he saw something white. He stared through the mist, losing sight of it. Then he saw it again. A dumpy modern sailing boat came into sight. It was rolling uncomfortably as it ran north on a course that would soon bring it on top of them.

Edward lowered his head and breathed deeply before sloshing his way through the water swishing over the deck to *Sanderling*'s bow. For just a moment, he turned to look aloft at *Sanderling*'s great tan sail, still trying to drive them along.

Adam watched as Edward steadied himself at the coaming, and began to raise his arms up over his head and down again, giving the international signal for distress.

Chapter 26

Adam looked at the red-headed rag doll sitting on his bed. Marmalade had been given to him by a very serious Philippa Ruth when she'd seen his bandaged hand. He lifted his hand above his head in an attempt to ease the throbbing. It didn't work. The bandage caught the dying rays of light through the window and made it look as if his hand was still on fire.

He sighed and looked at his watch. It was nearly time for him to visit Margaret again to get his bandage changed.

A kaleidoscope of memories from the last two weeks tumbled and swirled in his mind. It was difficult to remember what happened when. He had memories of rescue helicopters and coast guard launches; of being met by police and ambulance when they finally made it to port. Edward had been whisked away to hospital where he'd remained for five days, suffering from exhaustion and from his head wound. A vacuum extractor had been used to pull out the depressed bone in his skull, and they'd kept him in a drug-induced coma for two days.

Adam had needed attention for some nasty burns on his right hand. Following treatment, he was released with instructions to return each day to have his hand re-dressed. After the first week, he'd been allowed to have his hand re-dressed by Margaret in the boarding house.

He'd given the police the memory card from his digital camera and the bag of heroin retrieved from Eckhart's dinghy. He'd also given a detailed account of all that had happened.

Two days later, the police had reported they'd retrieved Eckhart's body but had not found any remains of the blond-haired man. Enquiries about the owner of the launch had led to an investigation at Ostend in Belgium. The identity of the blond-haired man was soon established and the story of how the drug ring operated had been pieced together.

It was as Adam had suspected. Eckhart would meet the launch from Ostend and exchange dinghies at some pre-arranged spot. He would then take the drugs packed inside the buoyancy chamber and divide them up for his network of distributors, leaving them in places as diverse as toilet cisterns and inside canisters attached to the bottom of mooring buoy chains.

The police were pleased. A major drug ring had been broken. Two people had been arrested in Belgium and three in England. The police were anxious not to tip off others engaged in the drug ring, until they had finished their enquiries and made their arrests, so the loss of *Sanderling* had been reported in the paper as an accident at sea caused by fire—only minor injuries had been sustained by the crew.

Adam recalled his first visit to Edward in hospital. It wasn't good. Claire had been there with her head on Edward's bed. He could see the streaks of tears on her cheek. Both appeared to be sleeping. Adam had quietly turned and left without being seen, tormented with the knowledge his actions had been the cause of so much pain.

Fortunately, the demands of school had not allowed him much time to brood. The senior students' mock exams were upon them and Adam, handicapped by his bandaged hand, needed to keep busy. The spring crops in the school farm were emerging and growing rapidly. Sprays needed to be applied and the seedlings needed to be checked for the presence of fungal diseases.

He looked sourly at his bandaged hand, sighed and began making his way over to the boarding house to have his hand re-dressed. When he arrived, Margaret looked him up and down. 'You've lost your bounce. What's the matter? Too many of us rely on you for you to crash.'

Adam smiled wearily. 'I think you all do very well without me. In fact, I seem to have the unhappy knack of hurting people rather than helping them.' He changed the subject. 'How's your level of bounce?'

Margaret had her back to him and was placing tweezers into a metal dish for sterilisation. 'My level of bounce is increasing all the time. But bounce brings with it its own challenges and frustrations.'

'How so? Is it Gareth?'

Margaret nodded. 'I know I've not exactly encouraged him, but I'm not sure what he thinks of me. I'm not sure you are right about his feelings for me. He's been so ... restrained. There's no evidence of...' She paused. '...anything. There isn't even much evidence of the real Gareth.'

'Hmm...' Adam flexed his hand gingerly. 'Give him time, Margaret. It's just that he's dead scared of losing you. He doesn't want to overplay his hand.'

'He's in no danger of doing that, I can assure you. I wish that he would just be himself.'

'Why not tell him? I'm sure he would be mightily relieved.'

Margaret looked at him doubtfully.

'Seriously. Make it plain to him that it's okay to move to the next level with you.' The irony of what he was saying wasn't lost on him. His own heart was broken and he himself was a mass of confusion, guilt and doubt. He looked at Margaret's hair and unflattering dress. He sighed. 'You scarcely encourage him with what you say or how you present yourself.'

Margaret hung her head. 'I'd hoped he would show me that he cared anyway.' She gripped her hands together. 'I'm not all that sure that he does.'

'Rubbish.'

Margaret turned away.

'Margaret, have you been trying to test Gareth's level of commitment by holding back from him a bit?' Adam sighed. 'Because if you have, you will sabotage any chance of an authentic friendship. You need to find the courage to do things ... in a new way.'

Margaret lifted her chin with a spark of defiance. 'I am, actually, doing something new.'

Adam waited for her to elaborate.

'I've resigned from being Matron of the boarding house. I'll leave at the end of term and move into the flat with Andrea and Claire.' She smiled sheepishly. 'The girl who was sharing it is leaving to get married. Andrea has asked me to run a photographic studio at the back of the gallery, doing portrait shots. I'll do that in the afternoons and do supply nursing in the mornings until the photographic side of things gets up and running. So there!' She put her hands on her hips and looked at Adam. 'Does that surprise you?'

Adam smiled. 'Not really. I suspected that the boarding house wouldn't keep you very long. You need wider horizons.'

He put a bandaged hand on her shoulder. 'But you need to have wider horizons with people, too. Margaret, it's time you came out of hiding. It's time for you to be real.'

***

After the final school lesson of the week, Adam made his way down Highgate. After buying a tray of coffees, he crossed the road to *The Borrowed Wheelbarrow.* Andrea and Margaret were seated in a settee in front of a table, shaped and painted like a giant artist's pallet. Andrea, looking extravagant in another flowing kaftan, beckoned him over.

He placed the coffees on the table. 'How's things?'

Andrea smiled her thanks and reached for a coffee. 'You've only just missed Claire. She popped in for an hour after lunch to collect a few things and sort out some paperwork. She's staying with Edward at the moment to look after him.' Andrea fixed him with a no-nonsense stare. 'Anyway, I'm glad you're here. The three of us have had a girl talk and have come up with a plan to help Gareth get his act into gear, regarding Margaret.'

Margaret dropped her head and blushed.

Andrea prodded Adam's chest. 'It involves some mild subterfuge on your part, so you'd better listen to what's required of you.'

Adam raised his eyebrows. '"Lead on, Captain, my Captain."'

***

The following week, Adam was surprised to receive a phone call from Edward.

'Adam, my boy. How are you?'

Adam was delighted to hear his voice and relieved he sounded so warm and positive towards him. He was momentarily lost for words. 'How are you going, more like? I came to see you in hospital but you were with Claire and I didn't want to intrude.'

'I'm fine. The headaches are much better. There's some soreness, but my energy is slowly returning. However, I'm concerned about you. Claire has told me you've not been finding things easy ... and there has been some tension between the two of you.'

'Um ... I suppose so. No, not really. It's just that I haven't...'

Edward interrupted. 'Why not drive over one evening this week and gladden my heart with some male company? You don't have to talk about Claire unless you want to, but you do have to fill me in with the details of all that has happened.'

'Of course. I'm sorry I've not come earlier.' He struggled with what to say next. 'I've not found it ... easy.'

He got off early the next afternoon and drove his motorbike through the spring countryside to Edward's cottage.

Edward greeted him warmly at the door. Adam could see he looked paler and older but was otherwise much his same old self. They made their way into the kitchen and busied themselves organising biscuits and cheese and glasses of wine. At first, Adam was quiet and reserved. He looked at Edward and was appalled at himself for having put his friend into so much danger.

Edward refilled Adam's glass. 'Claire's right. You are not yourself. What's the matter?'

Adam rubbed his forehead and said nothing for a long time.

Edward waited.

'I've nearly caused the deaths of two people I care about more than any others in the world.' He dropped his head. 'I've put both of them in hospital. I've caused you to lose *Sanderling,* a boat that was...' Adam searched for the right words. '...your life. I nearly killed your niece, for goodness sake! How can you ... not resent that?' He looked up defiantly. 'I would have.'

Edward said nothing for long while. At last he nodded. 'You did not seek to hurt or destroy. You made no moral choice to do evil. You did nothing that was foolish.' He waved his hand. 'It is an arrogance to claim an evil as your own when it isn't. You've done no wrong.' He looked Adam in the eye. 'And let me tell you, even if you had, there would still be forgiveness ... For we all need that.'

Adam looked at him balefully. Edward pressed on. 'As for *Sanderling,* yes, I loved her and will miss her, but my life doesn't depend on her. Everything changes. And, if I'm honest, she was getting too much for me to handle.' He raised his glass in a silent toast. 'She died well. What more can you ask? A true Viking burial.' He sipped his wine. 'I've already had Stan on the phone saying that he's found a nice Scandinavian designed Folk Boat for me. He's decided that, being only twenty-five feet long, it would be ideal for an old man.' He reached for a biscuit. 'The insurance on *Sanderling* will more than pay for it.'

'How does Claire feel about me nearly killing her uncle?'

'She is grateful that you were with me to ensure that I got back.' He paused. 'You did get me back.'

'It was you and your Viking stone that got us back.'

'We did it together ... and I hope we always will. So does Claire, incidentally.' Edward waved his biscuit in the air. 'She is, actually, very grateful to you. I've had her living with me all of last week, so believe me, I know.' He smiled. 'You've been like a boat lost in the mists for a long time, Adam. You have your own Viking Stone, but you need to rotate it to find the sun.'

Adam reflected on this for some time. He wasn't entirely sure what it meant. And he wasn't sure he was willing to ask. 'Thanks.'

'Don't mention it. Now, bring me up to date with what's been happening? Will there be an inquest?'

***

Margaret felt her well-ordered life had been hit by a whirlwind. Nonetheless, she acquiesced happily enough. Not, she reflected ruefully, that she would have much chance to do otherwise, given the determination of both Andrea and Claire.

Both girls marched Margaret down to Highgate to a very upmarket dress shop. 'I love this shop,' said Andrea as she steered Margaret inside.

Claire and Andrea pulled Margaret along behind them as they pointed to different dresses, pulling the occasional one out and holding it against her. Margaret knew she wasn't cooperating fully and was having doubts about the whole madcap scheme, when Claire held out a pair of elegant high-heeled shoes. 'Would he like these?'

Claire's question reminded Margaret what it was her heart hungered for, ached for, and needed—hope ... love ... and a new beginning. It was time to move on from the hell of the past. If she wanted a new life, she must grasp it.

She looked carefully at the rack of shoes in front of her and pointed to a pair of beautiful dark green evening shoes with tiny straps. 'Those are the ones,' she said with conviction, for she knew, now, which dress she would buy.

It was emerald green. It fell off one shoulder to highlight her décolletage in a way that was far from shy. The dress then flowed down to show off her narrow waist and continued to hug her closely, until it fell away into a skirt that swished with a free-flowing elegance. It was stunning and showed off her red hair and ivory skin to perfection. She knew she looked good in it. Delight and apprehension battled for her heart as she turned this way and that in front of the mirror.

Then, for reasons she couldn't explain, she started to sob, reaching over to give both Claire and Andrea a hug.

On the day of the Spring Ball, all three girls met in the late afternoon at the hairdressers.

The hairdresser looked at Margaret's long hair with admiration. 'It's beautiful ... and long overdue for some attention.'

After much debate, a style was chosen that displayed her hair to its full advantage. It was washed, trimmed, conditioned and styled. When the hairdresser had finished, Andrea and Claire stood in front of her and inspected the result. Some of her hair had been gathered at the back of her head but much of it tumbled down behind her in a riot of curls

'Damn fantastic,' said Andrea.

Margaret wrapped herself in Claire's hooded cape and allowed herself to be driven back to her flat in the boarding house.

Once inside, Claire produced a bottle of champagne, while Andrea set to work with her manicure set and make-up box. For the next few hours, Margaret was subjected to their chiding, laughter and bullying.

At the end of it, she stood up shyly and allowed herself to be helped into her dress.

Once her shoes were slipped into place, Margaret stood up straight and flattened the dress down her stomach. Acutely self-conscious, she lowered her head and folded her hands in front of her.

No one spoke for a long time.

Eventually, Andrea gave a low whistle. 'Ladies, we have a beauty queen.'

Claire nodded in approval and looked at her watch. 'It's time.' She picked up the phone and rang the extension number for the Great Hall.

***

Gareth had been recruited to help serve behind the bar at the Spring Ball for the first half of the evening, until he had to leave for boarding house duty at nine. Adam had escaped duties, pleading the fact his hand wasn't quite healed and he had promised to babysit Philippa Ruth for Geoffrey and Dizzy. However, he would do what he could to help Gareth set up the bar.

Gareth was not wildly excited about the evening and was looking morosely at his dinner jacket still on its hanger, hooked around a cupboard door handle.

Adam banged on his door and walked in. 'C'mon Gareth, old son. Get your bib and tucker on—we're needed down at the hall.'

'I'd rather spend the evening here with Margaret, to be honest.' Gareth buttoned his shirt up and tied his bow tie. A few minutes later, they made their way down to the Great Hall.

Once there, he set about organising the bar, while Adam busied himself ferrying boxes of wine from the storage room. Gareth felt his good humour returning. He inspected a label on a wine bottle and grinned at Adam. 'It's a bit like putting a poacher in charge of the pheasants, really.'

Eventually, the first of the worthy denizens of the town began to arrive for the ball. They were met by senior students dressed as waiters, who walked about offering champagne and canapés. Adam's work at the bar was interrupted when one of the students came across to say there was a phone call for him. Adam went over to the office in the foyer to answer it. A few moments later, he returned.

'That's a message from the housemaster. Evidently, the gift for the guest of honour has arrived late and has been delivered to the boarding house. It's quite valuable and the housemaster asked me to collect it. I told him I was expected at the Edgecombs, so he's asked if you could slip back to the boarding house and pick it up.'

Gareth sighed resignedly. 'I suppose so. The bar won't be busy for a few minutes yet. I'll scoot over straight away.' He gave Adam a dismissive wave as he went striding off. 'See you tomorrow, boyo.'

***

Gareth strode up the stairs into the boarding house and headed for the housemaster's quarters. When he got there, he found a notice stuck on the door with his name on it. He turned the paper over and read the message. It said the gift was in the care of Matron, upstairs.

Smiling with anticipation at being able to have at least a few words with Margaret, he bounded upstairs.

He could hear gentle music coming from inside her room. She was having a quiet evening in. He rapped on the door.

'Come in.'

Gareth pushed open the door and walked into the room. He stopped, transfixed to the spot. Margaret was standing perfectly still on the far side of the room, highlighted by the soft light from a table lamp. He had never seen anything so completely, breathtakingly beautiful. He was shocked; awed by the woman who now stood before him. He fought to comprehend, but failed. She was so completely ... transformed.

'Margaret,' he gasped. 'You are magnificent ... beautiful ... incredible. Why? How? My goodness. I ... I've come to pick up the gift for the guest of honour.'

She smiled. 'I am that gift ... and you are the guest of honour.'

Gareth blinked. Understanding began to register. His mouth dropped open in delight. Finally, he could bear it no more. In four strides he crossed the room, enfolded her in his arms and crushed her to himself.

Margaret closed her eyes and tilted her head back slightly as she accepted his love.

After his initial passion subsided, Gareth pulled back and looked at her. He saw the love in her eyes. Relief flooded through him.

Margaret smiled. 'There are two tickets to the Spring Ball on the table. Adam is covering for you on the bar.'

Gareth moved his fingers to her cheeks and down her long neck ... and then pulled her gently to himself. Margaret lifted her face towards his.

Her lips hovered tentatively a hair's breadth from his and then came together softly in the sweet surrender of giving.

After a moment, the passion of love, so long denied him, took over. He felt her hunger and kissed her fiercely, responding to her as she pushed her body into his.

***

Adam looked at the very large bottle of single malt whisky in his dresser and wondered how on earth he was ever going to drink it. It had been placed on the landing in front of the door to his attic apartment. Scribbled across the label in black pen was written, 'Thanks!' followed by Gareth's signature. He decided he would take it down to Dizzy and Geoffrey that evening.

He smiled at his memories of the Spring Ball as he made his way downstairs and walked to the staff common room.

When he arrived, he checked his pigeonhole and headed across to the morning papers. Behind him, the headmaster came into the room and pinned up the results of the mock exams on the noticeboard.

Wally Henshaw shambled over to have a look. With his failing eyesight, he pressed close to the notice board to read how his maths students had performed compared to other subjects. He grunted contentedly and took his glasses off to polish them.

Giles Carlingford squeezed in beside him to have a look. Wally chuckled and returned his glasses to his bulbous nose. 'You'd better look to your laurels, Giles. Young Hollingworth here has more credit grade students than you have.

'Rubbish.' Giles pushed forward to look closer at the results. He digested the information and snorted. 'Preposterous. Hollingworth must have marked them gently.'

Adam was standing at a table by the window, idly flicking through the pages of a newspaper. Stung by Giles' insinuation, he looked up. 'I assure you, Mr Carlingford, there is nothing generous about my marking ... just as there is nothing generous about your comments.'

A chill descended amongst those gathered in the common room.

'And what do you mean by that, Hollingworth?'

Adam turned to him. 'I mean that the only contribution you have made to me and the boys I teach is to show us the size of that arrogant nose you look down at us with.' He put down the paper. 'What exactly, is your problem?'

'I'll tell you my problem...'

'Gentlemen, gentlemen. Enough.' The voice of the headmaster stilled their bickering. He walked between them holding a mug of coffee, smiled at them both and strolled towards the door. 'Adam, have you got a moment?'

Adam trailed after the headmaster, mentally kicking himself for allowing Giles to goad him into an outburst. Together they made their way across the courtyard to the Georgian building housing the headmaster's office.

The headmaster sat down at his desk and motioned for Adam to take the chair opposite.

The signs were not good.

'I didn't believe the grades you had given your students, either.'

Adam blinked and began to rub his forehead.

The headmaster's face was stony and impassive. 'So I asked the head of the science department to look at the biology exam papers and reassess your marks.' He paused. 'His verdict was quite clear. Your marking is rigorous, tough and entirely fair.' The headmaster raised a hand in acknowledgement of the fact. 'I was humbled by what I'd learned ... and delighted. I just wanted to tell you that. You have done well.'

Adam smiled uncertainly. 'Thank you, Headmaster. I ... I'm sorry for my outburst in the staffroom.'

'Ah, that.' The headmaster's eyes had an interesting glint in them. 'And how would you teach history in order to get the sort of results you are getting with biology?'

Adam was caught by surprise. 'I have no idea. I know nothing about history. It's not my area.'

'I'm not talking about history, I'm talking about teaching.'

Adam realised Dr Fairclough was asking a serious question and was expecting a serious answer. He closed his eyes briefly, consulted his instincts, blended them with his experience and waited for something worth saying to emerge.

Adam began slowly, 'Boys need a challenge. They also need to take in information through as many senses as possible. They are visually-driven. Boys learn things best when they can see, feel and smell what they are doing ... and they know there's a good reason for doing it.' With growing confidence, he shared his thoughts. 'They love problem-solving and addressing mysteries, but they need to do this against a dynamic, changing backdrop that continually stimulates them.'

'And what does this mean for teaching history? What do I say to Giles if he comes to see me, complaining I've not given him a school farm?'

'I'd suggest he find one.' Adam said, brutally. 'Edward Bryson hardly watches any television, but his favourite programme is a series about a group of archaeologists who go from site to site around the country doing archaeological digs. They limit themselves to three days at each site—and the results make good viewing.'

The Headmaster nodded slowly. 'Yes, I know the programme.'

Adam leaned forward. 'Edward tells me the abbey and the school precincts sit on an old Roman settlement. He's got some of the old Roman site plans. Just imagine if the television archaeologists were invited to this school. It would spawn months of student research projects. If you couldn't get the television crew, you could at least attract the attention of an archaeology department from a local university.'

Adam leant back again in his chair. 'If possible, I'd involve Edward. He has a little more time now that...' Adam faltered. '...now that *Sanderling*'s gone.'

The headmaster steepled his fingers and sat looking at Adam, saying nothing for half a minute. Adam was beginning to feel unnerved when he finally spoke. 'Thank you, Adam. Very interesting.'

With that, Adam was invited to return to his students.

***

Edward was thinking that ginger marmalade on toast probably did not constitute the most nutritious of evening meals when the phone rang. On picking it up, he discovered it was the headmaster, James Fairclough.

'I've been talking with someone who has given me an interesting idea that I'd appreciate having your opinion on.'

'Umm...' Edward swallowed a piece of toast. 'What's that?'

'Do you think it would be a good thing if we could get the TV archaeology team interested in excavating the Roman site around the abbey and school? It might breathe life into the history department.'

'I think it's a brilliant idea. I can help you make a case for it if you like, using my own research.'

'Thanks, Edward, I confess that I was hoping for your help.'

'You've got it.' Edward paused. 'Whose idea was this?'

'It came from a future headmaster who is about to learn that his position at the school is being made permanent.'

'Good for him. Do I know this chap? Where did you find him?'

'You gave him to me, Edward.'

Edward opened his mouth in surprise.

'And I'm grateful,' the Headmaster continued. 'Have a good night.' The phone went dead.

Chapter 27

Adam had not visited Claire since he had seen her lying across Edward's hospital bed, racked with anxiety. It was a sight that had tormented him and accused him every night since. When his anguish got too much, he would reach for the photo Andrea had given him and study it. The windblown hair, the smile, the life. It broke his heart.

Adam was looking at it now, thinking he should do something to resolve the tension he was feeling. The trouble was, he wasn't at all sure what to do. He did determine, however, that he would travel to London in two days and see her art show. It ran over a week. He would attend the second-to-last day. It was unlikely Claire would be present, but at least he could look at her art and enjoy her presence vicariously through it.

Having gained permission to skip a sports afternoon, Adam caught the one o'clock train to London.

The musky smell of tired old rail carriages accompanied him into the city. A sign on the carriage bulkhead advertised the fact the rail company was committed to excellence and to improving their services. Even the sign looked faded, as if it too had given up hope.

Why am I doing this? Adam didn't know exactly. He just had a desperate ache to connect with Claire in any way possible. The current situation was intolerable. He had nothing to lose.

He reflected on the time he had once climbed with soldiers from the Australian SAS. Spending a week with them in the mountains had been enlightening. They had taught him that, if a situation was bad and you didn't know what was going to happen, then the best tactic was often to go in and make something happen, something you at least had some control over. It moved you from being a passive victim to a position of control. They'd quoted their motto: *Who dares wins.*

Adam didn't feel the least bit in control. Nonetheless, he was doing something that might throw up the possibility of new developments. Anything had to be better than the dreadful frustration he was currently experiencing.

The train deposited him under the cavernous arches of a city station, and he descended via escalator to the underground.

With a whoosh of warm air and a whining hum, the train thundered out of the tunnel and slid to a stop. Its chugging air compressor urged passengers on board before the doors hissed shut behind them.

Adam eventually emerged onto the grimy London pavements and began walking along the busy, lonely street.

Five minutes later, he reached the showrooms. A sandwich board outside advertised *The Claire Sanderson Collection.* He stepped through an imposing doorway into a carpeted foyer that boasted large sculptures and chilly, minimalistic art murals.

Definitely not Claire's work.

He looked helplessly towards the people at the front desk, until he spotted a sign pointing left to *Gallery A: The Claire Sanderson Exhibition.* He made his way along the corridor into a gallery where Claire's work definitely was in evidence.

An official-looking person smiled a professional smile at him, beckoned to a waiter with a tray of drinks and invited him to buy a catalogue. Adam bought one and then wandered self-indulgently amongst Claire's art.

She was present in every one of her moods. He could name them all and picture the expression on her face as she painted each picture; reflective, passionate, playful, questioning—and sometimes simply exploding with life. This was Claire: colour, lots of colour, but not careless colour. There was order and structure that gave each work real depth. Adam had seen a few of Claire's pictures, but to be surrounded by her was overwhelming.

The big room had several bays, and Adam idled his way from one to another, entranced and brimming over with emotion. He was pleased to see many of the labels beside the pictures had a red sticker placed on them, signifying they had been purchased. It was quite obvious Claire's art show was proving to be a success.

There was a tight gaggle of people in the bay at the top of the room. They looked to be media people, as some were carrying expensive-looking cameras. Adam avoided them and made his way across the room into another bay.

He stopped dead in his tracks.

He was there ... on the wall.

Six charcoal pictures with different expressions of anguish and despair were fitted together in a collage. The sketches were linked together with spiralling sweeps of red and black paint. It was a powerful picture.

How on earth had she managed to sketch him? When? He looked around, slightly self-consciously. Relieved he was the only one in the display bay, he stepped forward to inspect the picture more closely.

All the pictures had a small information board beside them that gave the picture number, title and a description of the work. The information board beside this picture only had a title. It said: *His anguish ... and mine.*

Underneath was written: 'NOT FOR SALE.'

Adam stared at it for a long time.

Tears started to fill his eyes as the state of Claire's heart became apparent to him. It wasn't just his anguish—it was hers as well. He mattered to her. She loved him.

At last, he knew it. In fact, he admitted, he'd always known it ... but only now did he allow himself to believe it.

He tilted his head back and closed his eyes in relief. He could go to her and say the things he had so desperately wanted to for months. He wanted to leap and yell for joy, but he restrained the impulse and turned to leave. He'd seen enough.

He started to walk down the centre of the gallery hall to the door. But as he did so, a loud voice called out from behind. 'Adam Hollingworth, don't you dare walk out of my life!'

He spun round.

Claire was walking towards him from the knot of media personnel at the end of the hall. When he saw her, she stopped still and stood there with her hands clenched by her sides. She was dressed in an elegant black cocktail dress, over which she had thrown a vibrant blue pashmina.

Adam swallowed. She was beautiful, but pale—and very angry. He was dimly aware that the journalists and photographers were starting to take an interest in what was unfolding.

'I have no intention of walking out of your life.' He straightened himself up. 'In fact, I plan to spend the rest of my life with you.'

The significance of his comment took a moment to register. Her frown turned to puzzlement and then melted away.

An excited buzz came from the press as they moved in closer.

Claire put a hand to her chest. 'Oh,' she said, weakly.

Adam walked slowly back up the hall to where she stood. He reached out and took her by the hands. Claire gave a little choking sob and then buried herself into his chest. He wrapped his arm around her as she wept her delight.

'And what do you have to say about that, Claire Sanderson?' He stroked her hair.

It took a while before she was capable of saying anything. She sobbed ... and laughed ... and then sobbed again.

Eventually, she sniffed her tears away and got herself under control. She held him at arm's length. 'I will.'

A buzz went around the crowd: 'Has he proposed?'

'Is this real or is it performance art?'

'He's just asked her to marry him, Sidney. Did you hear that?'

'Oooh, it's lovely.'

A younger child tugged at her mother's arm. 'Mum, Mum, did she just get married?'

One of the members of the press walked over to Adam. 'And who are you, sir?'

Not taking his eyes off Claire, he said, 'My name is Adam Hollingworth. I am Claire Sanderson's fiancé.'

***

Edward stood with Adam and Claire at the end of the headland on a blustery spring day, looking over the choppy estuary. Sunlight slanted between the scurrying clouds. The three of them had walked along the sea wall, well rugged up against the chilly breeze.

Edward watched the few hardy yachtsmen who were out on the water. Their boats were heeled well over as they dashed through the sea. He looked at the scene with deep contentment.

After a few minutes, he put his hand in his coat pocket and brought out the Viking stone. He weighed it in his hands for a few moments. Its deep blue heart seemed to whisper a message. He turned it slowly in his hands. Very briefly, it turned to gold.

'Ahh.' He understood. It was time for the Viking stone to sail another sea. He drew a deep breath and handed it out to Adam. 'It's yours.'

Adam, with Claire hanging onto his arm, looked at him questioningly.

Edward smiled. 'So you can always find your way home.'

Also from Nick Hawkes

The Celtic Stone

Chris Norman's dreams of being a commercial pilot are shattered when he crashes his light plane in central Australia and is badly wounded. His life hangs in the balance—a balance that is swayed by the intervention of an Aboriginal bushman bent on his own murderous mission. The bushman leaves Chris with a mysterious and incongruous legacy, a Celtic cross made of stone.

Partly blinded and in deep grief at no longer being able to fly, Chris finds his way to the inhospitable Hebridean islands off the west coast of Scotland where he seeks to unravel the secrets of the Celtic stone.

A blind Hebridean woman, shunned by many in ther local community, becomes Chris' reluctant ally—along with a seven-year-old boy who is as wild as the storm-tossed seas surrounding the islands. Two other allies in the form of a gamekeeper with his own dark secret, and an alcoholic writer with a love of sailing, introduce Chris to the culture of the islands.

It soon becomes apparent that the violence of the island's history has carried on into the present. Chris must recover from his grief, discover his identity ... and avoid being murdered.

www.rhizapress.com.au